Praise for Manda Collins's delectable Regency novels

DUKE WITH BENEFITS

"A delight to see a classic Regency hero so smitten with a truly unusual heroine. Driven by multiple passionate scenes and the hunt for a murderer, it's a swift and intense read. A bluestocking Regency romance of unusual intensity." —*Kirkus Reviews*

"Intense romance." —*Publisher's Weekly*

READY SET ROGUE

"Displaying a deft hand at characterization, a superb ability to craft an engaging plot spiced with intrigue and danger, and a remarkable flair for graceful writing richly imbued with a deliciously crisp wit, Collins launches the Studies in Scandal series on a high note." —*Booklist* (Starred review)

"*Ready Set Rogue* has an assortment of bold, brilliant female characters and showcases the strength and resourcefulness of women." —*Fresh Fiction*

"This story is classic Manda Collins, her writing is witty, smart and is full of surprises. This series is going to be a keeper to read again and again." —*The Reading Wench*

Also By Manda Collins

Duke

with

Benefits

MANDA COLLINS

St. Martin's Paperbacks

30823 1891 R

This is a work of fiction. All of the characters, organizations, and events portrayed in this novel are either products of the author's imagination or are used fictitiously.

DUKE WITH BENEFITS

Copyright © 2017 by Manda Collins.

All rights reserved.

For information address St. Martin's Press, 175 Fifth Avenue, New York, NY 10010.

ISBN: 978-1-250-10988-0

Our books may be purchased in bulk for promotional, educational, or business use. Please contact your local bookseller or the Macmillan Corporate and Premium Sales Department at 1-800-221-7945, ext. 5442, or by e-mail at MacmillanSpecialMarkets@macmillan.com.

Printed in the United States of America

St. Martin's Paperbacks edition / July 2017

St. Martin's Paperbacks are published by St. Martin's Press, 175 Fifth Avenue, New York, NY 10010.

10 9 8 7 6 5 4 3 2 1

To Vince, Kate and Adair. Your little family, born from love, is the essence of everything I'm writing about. (Without the murder, obviously.) Love you guys so much and I'm proud to say we're family.

Acknowledgments

As with every one of my books with St. Martin's Press, I'm so grateful for the guidance and support of my team there: Holly Ingraham, Jennie Cosway, Marissa Sangiacomo, Meghan Harrington, Jordan Hanley, and I'm sure dozens of other people who work tirelessly behind the scenes.

Thanks also to my lovely and talented agent, Holly Root, who is top 'o the trees as my Regency heroes would say, and is cheerleader, guide, friend and bulldog all rolled into one tiny charming package.

My fur companions—Charlie, Toast, Stephen Catbert, and Tiny—have kept me company through the writing and editing of this book and are wonderful at reminding me that though I'm a published author now, I'm still required to man the feed bag on a regular basis. Thanks for keeping me humble, you guys.

And finally, to my friend, the inestimable Lindsey Faber, who has saved my bacon more times than I can say. And without whom this book would not have emerged from the creative fires intact. You, madam, are awesome.

Prologue

You will soon embark on a quest for something very valuable,
but along the way you will risk losing your greatest love.
MADAME ALBINIA'S FORTUNE FOR LADY DAPHNE FORSYTH

Lady Daphne Forsyth's boots crunched over the gravel of the drive leading up to the entrance of Beauchamp House as she walked behind the group of men carrying her wounded friend.

Someone had shot Miss Ivy Wareham.

It would have been impossible to believe if she hadn't seen it with her own eyes, but even now the sight of a clenched-jawed Lord Kerr, Ivy's betrothed, walking beside her makeshift litter told her it was all too real. As did the drawn faces of the others who had gone with them today.

It had all begun when the party from Beauchamp House had set out to visit Madame Albinia in the gypsy encampment near Little Seaford.

At first Daphne had assumed Ivy, who along with Daphne and the misses Sophia and Gemma Hastings had inherited Beauchamp House from Lady Celeste Beauchamp, had wished to visit the fortune teller for all the usual reasons. To hear some silly predictions about her future or the like. But as the four ladies, accompanied by Lady Celeste's nephews, the Marquess of Kerr and the Duke of Maitland, had walked to the edge of the village, Ivy had confided that her reasons for the visit were far more serious.

Lady Celeste had been poisoned to death, and the vehicle for the poison had been the tisane recipe supplied by Madame Albinia to Lady Celeste's maid.

That her benefactress had been deliberately poisoned was a shock, and it had been the main topic of conversation as they made their way along the path to the village.

All four ladies had been the unexpected heiresses of the late Lady Celeste Beauchamp, who as a scholar herself wished to see her home and extensive library collection go into the hands of those who would make best use of it. The bequest had come as a shock. None of them had met before their arrival at Beauchamp House, and each had dedicated themselves to different scholarly endeavors. But somehow in the time since they'd arrived, they'd managed to become friends.

Daphne had enjoyed the fresh air and the company despite the revelation about Lady Celeste's death. And if she were honest, she'd also enjoyed the chance to converse with the Duke of Maitland away from the watchful gaze of his sister, who took her job as chaperone quite seriously now that Ivy had been compromised by Lord Kerr.

That is, until on their journey back some unknown person had actually shot at them and wounded Ivy.

As luck would have it, their return had been spotted by young Jeremy Fanning, the son of their chaperone,

Lady Serena. At the sight of the injured Ivy, the boy's eyes widened and he clung to his mother's skirts. "Mama, what happened?"

"Ivy had a bit of a mishap, old fellow," said the Duke of Maitland before Lady Serena could respond. Stepping forward to lift the small boy into his arms, he continued, "But she'll be right as rain in no time. Won't she, Mama?" This last he addressed to his sister who threw him a grateful glance before rubbing the little boy's back.

"Of course she will, Uncle Dalton," she said brightly. "Jem, will you stay with your uncle and the other ladies while Quill and I see to Miss Ivy?"

The boy, whose watchful blue-gray eyes were very like his uncle's, nodded. "Can we play hide-and-seek, Uncle Dalton?"

"Of course, we can, lad. Ladies, will you join us?"

"I don't suppose there's much else we can do at the moment," Sophia said with a worried glance toward upstairs, where Ivy had been taken.

"And I do love a good game of hide-and-seek," Gemma said, her cheery tone echoing Lady Serena's of a moment earlier. "Though if you don't mind, Jem, could we ladies have a cup of tea before we get started? I think perhaps we can convince cook to send up some tarts as well."

The mention of treats did the trick with the child, and they all retired to the drawing room for tea and something stronger for those who needed it.

Now some time later, Jem had gone off to hide, while the others set off in separate directions to look for him.

As she turned the corner, lost in her thoughts, Daphne caught her breath as she slammed into a hard male chest.

"Caught you," said Maitland with a grin as he grasped her by the elbows. But as soon as he saw her face, his smile faded.

"What is it, my dear?" he asked, still holding her arms.

Unwilling to admit her residual upset, Daphne shook her head. "It's nothing. And may I remind you, I'm not the one you're meant to be seeking."

When he didn't let her go, she continued, "Let me go, Duke. I am quite well. And don't need anyone to fuss over me."

He let go of her but didn't step away. He was close enough that she could smell the scent of his shaving lotion and see the glint of lamplight on the blond stubble of his beard.

"Why do I get the feeling you're pretending to be more sanguine about this than you actually are?" His perceptive gaze was narrow, as if he was trying to see into her thoughts.

Not for the first time, Daphne was grateful for the fact that mind-reading had never been perfected. She had a difficult-enough time dealing with the fallout from her spoken words. If her thoughts were subject to the same sort of scrutiny, she'd find herself in a difficult spot indeed.

Since the moment he arrived at Beauchamp House, the handsome duke had drawn Daphne's interest. Not only because he was a fine specimen of masculine beauty—though he was certainly that with his broad shoulders, tall build, and twinkling blue eyes—but also because of something intangible. It had been there from the moment she'd spied him across the drawing room. Some spark of attraction between them that was unlike anything she'd ever felt before.

And that afternoon, she'd almost asked him about it. Daphne was nothing if not plain spoken and to her mind, the most sensible thing to do about the attraction between them was to talk about it and decide if they wished to pursue it.

Of course, her own ideas about what was and was not an appropriate topic of conversation had never been entirely in keeping with what the rest of polite society decreed. Since her arrival at Beauchamp House, Ivy, Sophia, and Gemma had taught her a great deal about what she should and should not say aloud.

Her mother had died when she was only four years old, and the series of nurses and governesses who had been hired by her father had only lasted a short while before they each gave up in defeat. Only the male tutor— an expert in mathematics—had managed to stay for any length of time. And that was perhaps because he saw her not as a young lady, but as a mathematical genius. A mind to be molded rather than a prize to be auctioned off in the marriage mart.

And so, her lessons in gentility had been abandoned in favor of higher maths. Which left her with the ability to solve complex equations more quickly than most Oxbridge fellows and almost no sense of how to speak without setting up the backs of those around her.

The walk to the gypsy encampment had seemed like the perfect opportunity to lay her case before the Duke of Maitland. They might be relatively private without fear of being overheard, and there was no danger he'd mistake her words for a marriage proposal, which was the furthest thing from her mind. But despite her determination to speak, Daphne had found that, once the opportunity presented itself, she was reluctant to broach the subject, her usual sangfroid replaced with a rare shyness. So she'd kept to less-volatile topics and had enjoyed herself immensely on the walk.

Now, however, she was surprised by just how easily Maitland could see past her mask of calm. "I might still be a bit overset," she admitted. "But I will recover."

Looking down to where his hands still grasped her arms, she repeated, "You may let me go."

He let go of her but didn't step back. "Perhaps I haven't regained my balance yet, Lady Daphne."

But that was nonsense.

"Of course you didn't lose your balance. A man of your size is hardly going to be knocked over by me, tall though I am for a lady."

Moving to her side, Maitland slid her arm into his. "You are of course correct." She could hear the smile in his voice, and she was relieved he hadn't been annoyed by her correction. Sometimes conversation was a trial for Daphne, who wished people would simply say what they meant instead of using metaphors and the like. Turns of phrase made life very frustrating for her.

"Shall we continue down this hall to look for Jem?"

After the events of the day, she was glad to have the company. And perhaps now that they were truly alone she'd be able to speak to him frankly.

"That's what I was doing before I ran into you," she said allowing him to lead her past the bust of Mary Wollstonecraft that marked the passage leading to Lady Celeste's private rooms. "But I shall enjoy the company. Especially after what happened to Ivy."

"It was distressing, wasn't it?" he asked, as he moved to open the door to a small sitting room. "Jem?" he called out.

From behind him, Daphne could see that the room was dark and there was no fire in the hearth. None of the heiresses had been willing to take over the mistress of the house's rooms. Daphne hadn't had the courage to enter them, so strong was the feeling that Lady Celeste had only gone out for a walk and would return at any minute.

But Maitland, who had run tame in Beauchamp House from childhood, had no such diffidence. He lit the lamp nearest the door and moved to light the other two as well. Soon the cozy room was bright and the shadows that had made it seem gloomy were vanquished.

Daphne could see now that it was a charming space, with butter yellow walls, a pair of comfortable chintz chairs before the fire, and when she stepped closer to look, she saw a basket of mending beside the farthest chair. Something about the needle still plunged into the chemise Celeste had been repairing was more poignant than any of the testaments she'd heard thus far from the people who'd known her.

"This was her inner sanctum," she said, and it wasn't a question. She knew, as she moved to look at the shelf of books beside the window, that though the library had been the place where Celeste had placed the books and artwork that would be valued by the world at large, the items here, in this room, were those that meant something to her personally.

"It was," Maitland said as he moved to stand beside her as she scanned the shelves. "I can remember when I was a boy she would give me adventure novels from these shelves and tell me never to forget that reading was first and foremost for pleasure."

And indeed, most of the shelves here were the sorts of things that engendered criticism from a certain element of society for whom words were meant only for edification. There were the familiar bindings of Minerva Press, and many other four-volume sets of popular novels as well as what were likely Celeste's personal copies of Wollstonecraft, Mary Shelley, and other greats.

"I do wish I'd have been able to meet her," Daphne said, reaching out to touch the gilded spine of what looked to be a private journal. "I wonder if she'd have found fault with my blunt talk." It was something she hadn't meant to reveal—certainly not to the man who made her body tingle whenever he was within arm's reach, as he was now. But there was something about being here in this room that put her off guard.

"She'd have loved you," Maitland said, his voice much closer than she'd expected.

Swallowing, she dared a look up at his face and saw that his blue eyes were dark with an emotion she couldn't name.

"She would have found your forthrightness refreshing," he continued, reaching out to touch his thumb to her cheek. It was a light caress. A whisper of skin over skin. "And so do I."

The words hung in the air between them as Daphne tried to process what was happening.

"Do you?" she asked, turning so that she was facing him now, too. "I'm not too rude? Too blunt?"

To her surprise, she found she wanted to know. For some reason, it mattered—mattered desperately—what he thought of her. Whether he was truly not bothered by her tendency to put everyone to the blush.

"No," he said, his golden head lowering to hers. And just before he pressed his lips against hers, he whispered, "I like it."

Daphne had been kissed before, but never like this. And never by someone she'd felt such an overwhelming degree of attraction for.

She felt her heart leap up in her chest at the gentle pressure of his mouth, and instincts had her slipping her arms around his neck and pulling him down to her. In answer, he groaned and slipped his hands around her waist.

It was heady, this moment that was at once surrender and vanquishment. And when he pulled her more closely to him and his kiss grew more heated, his mouth opening over hers, she gave herself up to the sensations engulfing her.

But almost as soon as it had begun, he was pulling away from her, and putting a foot of distance between them.

Trying to make her brain work against the flood of emotion that threatened to overwhelm her, she asked in a breathless voice, "Did I do something wrong?" It had seemed as if he was enjoying himself very much. And goodness knows she'd had no objections to the feel of his strong body pressed against hers.

Taking in a gulp of breath, Maitland thrust a hand into his golden curls, already disarrayed from her hands. "No, you were perfect. It's just that I can't . . . that is to say, it wouldn't be appropriate . . ."

Ah, this she understood. "Of course, you are worried about the proprieties. It makes sense for a man in your position. But I can assure you that I won't insist you marry me or any such nonsense. It is perhaps unusual for unmarried young ladies of the *ton* to take lovers, but hardly unheard of. And I think the attraction between us is unusual enough that it shouldn't be ignored."

But far from agreeing with her as she'd hoped—indeed expected—the duke looked shocked.

The one thing she'd never considered, in all her imaginings of this conversation, was that the object of her desire would have his sense of propriety wounded.

"Lady Daphne," he said, his deep voice almost hushed, as if he feared they'd be overheard, "I don't know what sort of man you think I am, but I am not in the habit of deflowering virgins. And I certainly would not do so without doing my duty and paying the consequences for my actions."

Daphne frowned. "But I just told you that there will be no need to do so. I don't intend to marry. And I certainly don't wish to trap you into a marriage simply because we acted on what is a perfectly natural attraction between us. What harm can there be in the two of us indulging in our desires? There's no one who can be hurt by it as you have no wife. And besides that, I have given you my word I won't trap you. I don't see the problem."

His handsome features twisted in disbelief. "I thought

I liked your plain speaking, my dear," he said, shaking his head, "but I fear I may have been too quick to say so. For there is so much to object to in your little speech that I don't know where to begin to dispute it."

Daphne blinked. She hadn't thought is possible that such a short acquaintance would make her vulnerable to being hurt by anything he said. But by taking back his assurance that he enjoyed her plain speaking— something that was as intrinsic to her as her mathematical abilities—he had hurt her more than she'd ever imagined he could. She hadn't realized how much she'd come to value his opinion. And she'd certainly never imagined he had the power to wound her in this way.

Not wanting to prolong the discussion, she took a deep breath, and with one last quick glance at his lovely face, she straightened her spine.

"I apologize for offending you, your grace. Please think no more of it."

Brushing past him, she hurried from the room, wanting to sprint, but refusing to make a cake of herself any more than she already had.

Behind her, she could hear him hurrying after her. "Daphne, wait. You didn't offend me, it's just that . . ."

But before he could catch up to her, Jem came hurtling around the corner.

"Uncle Dalton!" the boy cried as he threw himself into the duke's arms. "I hided and Miss Sophia found me!"

Daphne could feel Maitland's gaze on her, but she dared not look at him fully. Her cheeks burned with embarrassment at her miscalculation.

"Where are Miss Sophia and Miss Gemma, Jem?"

she asked the little boy, hoping that the distraction of her friends' conversation would help her forget what had just transpired.

"They're back in the drawing room," Jem said from where he sat perched in his uncle's strong arms. "They were looking for you. And Uncle Dalton, too."

"We were looking for you, sport," said Maitland in a cheerful tone. Clearly he hadn't been as upset by their disagreement as she had been.

"Excellent," Daphne said, adopting the same upbeat tone. "I'll just go find them then."

"I still would like to speak with you further, Lady Daphne," she heard the duke say from behind her.

But that was a conversation she would avoid with every last fiber of her being, Daphne thought as she hurried down the stairs toward the drawing room.

As she reached the landing, the words of Madame Albinia came back to her. *You will soon embark on a quest for something very valuable, but along the way you will risk losing your greatest love.*

She stopped mid-stride.

No, it was too ridiculous to consider, she chided herself. While technically, she had been searching for something valuable, i.e., Jem, a game of hide-and-seek was hardly what one would call a *quest*. And though she was attracted to the Duke of Maitland—correction, while she *had been* attracted to the Duke of Maitland, she would hardly call him her greatest love. Her mind was simply falling into the trap that thousands before her had succumbed to, twisting the vague words of a fortune-teller into a self-fulfilling prophecy that had no basis in reality.

Just as her assumption that the duke would simply agree to a liaison with her had no basis in reality.

She had made the mistake before, and it had left her with more than simple wounded pride, as this afternoon's encounter had done.

With this hard-won determination in her mind, she went off in search of the other ladies.

Chapter 1

THREE MONTHS LATER

Lady Daphne Forsyth would rather listen to a thousand lectures on decorum from her chaperone than listen to another word from the Marchioness of Kerr about her husband's thoughtfulness. Or his loyalty. Or his humor.

Or any of a myriad of qualities about which the former Miss Ivy Wareham—once a quite sensible classics scholar, capable of conversation on any number of interesting subjects—now extolled morning, noon, and night to anyone who would listen.

At this point, even young Jeremy Fanning, the six-year-old son of the aforementioned chaperone would be a more intriguing conversationalist.

She kept her own counsel, however, as she, Ivy, the Hastings sisters, the Marquess of Kerr, and the Duke of Maitland walked along the cliffside path running from Beauchamp House inland toward the village of Little Seaford.

It had been several months now since she'd received the news that the celebrated bluestocking leader, Lady Celeste Beauchamp had left her beautifully appointed manor house—complete with one of the most impressive libraries in the country—to a quartet of young ladies with their own artistic and academic *bona fides,* the mathematics prodigy, Lady Daphne, among them.

The letter from Lady Celeste, forwarded by her solicitor, had been effusive in its praise, but that hadn't been what convinced Daphne to pack her bags and travel from London to Beauchamp House. If praise was all she wished for she could sit down for a hand of cards in any drawing room or gaming hell in Mayfair—though admittedly the praise would be peppered with envy and anger over lost fortunes. No, it had been the promise in the carefully worded letter that the library at Beauchamp House contained more than first editions and scholarly tomes.

> You will find Romance and enough intrigue to Riddle even the most unschooled of ladies with envy among the Treasure of my collections.

Any other reader would have supposed Lady Celeste merely had an odd habit of capitalizing random words in her writing—it was common enough among the ladies of the *ton,* who were hardly the most educated of creatures. But to Daphne, who was able to see beyond the set order of letters to the pattern beneath, her benefactress's words had been a message intended just for her. Without needing a pencil, her mind rearranged the letters of Romance into Cameron. And the rest of the clue was hidden in plain sight.

Cameron Riddle Treasure

It had been the promise that the library at Beauchamp House contained the famous Cameron Riddle, which legend said would lead the one able to decode it to a treasure hidden away by the leader of Clan Cameron in the days of the last Jacobite rebellion, that led Daphne to travel south to take her place among the four Beauchamp Heiresses. That and the hope that she could separate herself at last from her father's clutches and would never have to play cards for money again.

But in the time since she came to the coast, she'd found no trace of the promised puzzle, and she'd searched nearly half the contents of the admittedly impressive book room's collection. She'd told the rest of the household that she wished to familiarize herself with the collections before she began any in-depth research on the maths books, but the other ladies knew she found other subjects tedious at best and she'd begun to catch them exchanging amused glances when she started her methodical searches each morning.

Of course, their amusement might have been because many of these sessions included the "assistance" of the Duke of Maitland, who was inexplicably still on an extended stay at Beauchamp House. He claimed it was to spend time with his sister, their chaperone Lady Serena Fanning, and her son Jeremy. But Daphne was no fool.

She saw the way he looked at her from beneath his criminally long eyelashes.

"A penny for them," said the object of her thoughts as they reached the signpost that marked the outskirts of the village.

This was what came of woolgathering, Daphne thought wryly, unable to stop herself from giving her companion a sidelong glance as the rest of their party walked along ahead of them.

With his sun-burnished hair, tall athletic frame, and dimpled grin, Dalton Beauchamp, the Duke of Maitland, was certainly no hardship to look at. And yet, after a few weeks of enjoyable flirtation just after he arrived, he'd begun treating her more like a sister than a potential lover. She'd made the mistake—only once, mind you—of suggesting that they conduct an affair, such as she'd seen were commonplace among the London *ton*, and he'd acted like a scandalized maiden. Given his reputation as a bit of a rogue in London, she had been disappointed at his response. She had hoped he would be less conventional, but his rebuff had been plain. If he was holding out for marriage, however, he wouldn't get it from her. She would never, after being used as a means of gathering income by her father for so many years, willingly enter the institution that would give another man control over her. She found Maitland attractive, and so far as she could tell, he found her intriguing as well. Why did they need to bring marriage into the equation at all?

Since he insisted on remaining in residence at Beauchamp House, she was forced to interact with him. And if she was honest, she enjoyed some of his nonsense.

He was no scholar, but he was amusing and kind. And he hadn't chosen to shun her, as she knew many men in his situation would have done.

"If you must know," she said, knowing her confidence was safe with Maitland, "I was debating whether a gag or a muzzle would be a more appropriate means of silencing Ivy on the subject of her husband's every waking thought."

This startled a bark of laughter from the duke, who quickly turned it into a cough when the others turned to see what had caused it.

"Carry on," he said with a wave at them. "Nothing to see here."

"I know it is churlish of me," Daphne admitted once they were relatively private again, "but even a paragon among men would not measure up to Ivy's praise. Certainly not the Marquess of Kerr."

"Still haven't forgiven him for the way he arrived on the scene calling for the lot of you to be tossed out on your collective ear, eh?"

Maitland hadn't been there for Kerr's first meeting with the heiresses, but he'd no doubt heard about the ugly encounter from his sister.

"It's not just that," Daphne said, though admittedly it was a large portion of it. She'd learned to judge people based on first impressions from an early age, and with a few exceptions she'd come to find that more often than not they held true. "It's Ivy. She's turned into just the sort of besotted fool I learned to avoid like the plague in London. You can hardly get two words of sense from her these days without the other three being about her darling husband or some other nonsensical tale. A line from

Catullus the other day sent her into peals of laughter and all she would say was that it reminded her of something Kerr had said. I want my sensible friend back."

Even as she spoke, Daphne knew she was exaggerating the degree to which Ivy had changed since her marriage. But even if there was a bit of envy in her assessment of the pair, she'd hardly admit as much to Maitland. He'd never let her hear the end of it.

When he remained silent, she looked up to see that he was biting his lip.

"What?" she demanded. Really, it was as if everyone in the house had gone mad.

Looking rueful, Maitland said with a grin, "It's just that Catullus is known for being a bit . . ." He paused, clearly searching for the right word. "Ribald," he finally settled on.

Which meant that Kerr had likely said whatever had so amused Ivy in bed.

Daphne felt her cheeks redden. This was what came of neglecting one's classical education in favor of a diet of only maths.

She wasn't accustomed to embarrassment over such things. She'd been privy to conversations unfit for most adult ears before she reached her thirteenth birthday, and could swear in three languages thanks to the card rooms of the *ton*. She'd long ago schooled herself to ignore such things as just another coded language. One that she herself had no desire to partake in.

That had been before she lay eyes on the superior physical specimen who walked beside her now.

Of course, he'd rejected her one and only attempt at seduction almost before the words were out of her mouth. Which was just as well, Daphne thought wryly, since she'd not long afterward discovered that Maitland wasn't quite the most bookish of men.

The idea that Ivy was now sharing libertine jokes, and more, with her new husband, though? That gave Daphne a pang of loneliness she'd not experienced since she'd first met the three ladies with whom she'd share Beauchamp House for at least the next year.

It was perhaps silly of her, but in the other bluestockings she'd thought she'd found kindred spirits. They might not understand much of her conversation about the finer points of trigonometry, but they understood what it was to be the best in a field dominated by men. And Ivy, it would seem, had traded in her bluestocking hat for a matron's cap.

"If it's any consolation," Maitland said, breaking into her thoughts once more, "Kerr is just as besotted. Serena and I have taken to adding a penny to a jar every time he extols one of Ivy's virtues. We've not counted yet, but I suspect there's at least ten pounds in it by now."

"But he was never a man of sense. He's like you in that reg—" Daphne stopped because she'd learned from her friends that speaking her mind as truthfully as she would like sometimes led to hurt feelings. And she had no wish to insult Maitland. Tardy though her judgment was.

If the duke was insulted, however, he didn't show it.

"Oh, I'm well aware of the gulf that exists between you ladies and the rest of us," he said with a staying gesture. "At least when it comes to intellect. We're not simpletons, mind you, but neither are we great minds. My old nanny told me that you've got to know your good points. I'm a likable fellow. I can sweet talk a spooked horse like nobody's business. And I'm not too awful to look at. But you and the other bluestockings can think rings around us."

At his tone of understanding, Daphne heaved a sigh of relief. "Yes, that's it precisely. I'm so glad you understand, Maitland, because I wouldn't like to think I'd said something hurtful. The others have taught me, I think, finally, that my plain-speaking sometimes makes others unhappy."

What was he thinking? she wondered, as the duke gave her a long look. She'd always had trouble guessing what feelings lay behind a person's words. When she said something, it was exactly what she meant.

But before she could ask for his thoughts, she heard the others greeting a pair of gentlemen as they entered the village.

"No harm done," was all Maitland said as they caught up with the others.

The two newcomers were dressed in what Daphne assumed was the current country fashion. She had little use for such things, but she'd grown accustomed to seeing Maitland and Kerr and the gentlemen of the neighborhood at large dressed in boots and breeches and more casual neck cloths than were required in town. The taller of the two men looked up as she and the duke approached, and Daphne felt a constriction in her chest.

"Lady Daphne Forsyth, as I live and breathe! Is it really you?"

Through narrowed eyes, Dalton examined the man who greeted Daphne, only just resisting the urge to remove his quizzing glass and subject the fellow to his most ducal glare. He might have a reputation for being affable to a fault, but even Merry Maitland had his limits. And, he thought wryly as Daphne greeted the newcomer with a cry of recognition, it seemed that seeing another man look at Daphne like an oasis in the desert was his.

Daphne, on the other hand, did not seem quite so pleased. "Mr. Sommersby," she said, her expression unreadable as she stopped in her tracks.

Maitland would be the first to admit she wasn't the most effusive of women, but something about her reaction to this fellow put him on alert. Perhaps it was the way she didn't advance to take his outstretched hand. Or maybe it was the slight pallor that overtook her when she recognized him.

Daphne wasn't overly emotional, it was true, but neither was she devoid of emotion.

Maitland knew very well that she felt some things strongly. One only had to hear her wax rhapsodic on one of her mathematical bits to know she was capable of great joy. It was just that she wasn't demonstrative with people. Perhaps because she had difficulty gauging what response they would have to her unpolished conversation. He had only been in her company for a short while before he recognized that she deeply regretted the fact that much of her plain-speaking led to hurt feelings, but she knew of no way to curb her errant tongue.

She was feeling some strong emotion now, however. If only he could read her well enough to know what it was.

"Why on earth are you in Little Seaford?" Daphne

asked Sommersby, her eyes narrow with suspicion. "The last letter I had from your father said that you were in Egypt." It was almost an accusation. As if he'd broken some oath by leaving the land of the Pharaohs for England.

At the mention of Egypt, however, Maitland bit back a groan. Of course, this fellow had just returned from Egypt. He looked exactly the type. Right down to the tanned skin and slightly rumpled coat.

"Mr. Sommersby and Mr. Foster were just telling us why they're in the area, Lady Daphne," said Lord Kerr. He had a possessive arm around his wife's waist.

Maitland's cousin was no fool. He saw that these fellows were not to be trusted just as well as he did.

"They're on the hunt for lost treasure, if you can believe it," the marquess continued before quirking a brow in Maitland's direction.

Treasure hunters? Really? his cousin seemed to ask.

Maitland gave a slight shrug. It was as likely a scheme as any, he supposed. He might also have guessed that the two men were riverboat gamblers, if they'd happened to be in the Louisiana territory of the Americas. They just had that look about them.

Up to no good.

"You always were one to dream of riches and treasure, Nigel," Daphne said tartly. "Your father would be attempting to teach us both some new mathematical principal and you would be attempting to read a penny dreadful about some lost jewel or the like under the table."

"And I always got caught," Sommersby said with a laugh. "Because you always told my father."

"So this is the son of your tutor, Lady Daphne?" asked Ivy with a raised brow.

"Indeed," Daphne said with nod. She seemed less than pleased at meeting him here. At first Maitland had thought she was just surprised, but there was something else at play here.

Something darker.

But that was likely his imagination, he chided himself. He had no reason to think badly of a man he'd only just met.

Still, when Sommersby said, "We grew up together, you might say. Though not as brother and sister," he saw Daphne's spine stiffen. There was definitely something about the fellow she didn't like.

If Daphne didn't trust him, then neither did Maitland.

She didn't say as much however, instead turning the conversation to Sommersby's reason for being here. "What lost treasure are you searching for hereabouts?" Her tone implied that there could not possibly be treasure or anything like it within five hundred miles of Little Seaford.

Foster, who up until now had been silent, chose that moment to speak up. "We've actually heard a rumor that the lost Cameron Cipher is in a library collection in the vicinity."

Some niggle of memory from his childhood fired in Maitland's mind, but he could not recall any specifics. But the cipher was better known to Daphne if her sharp intake of breath was any indication.

Her next words only confirmed his assumption. "That is impossible. There is no Cameron Cipher. It is just a myth."

Poor Daphne. She didn't have a dissembling bone in her body. And it was evident that whatever she thought about the Cameron Cipher, it wasn't that there was no validity to Foster's claim. Rather the opposite. Though she was trying in her way to convince him otherwise.

"You weren't so skeptical when we first heard the legend, Daphne," said Sommersby with a grin. "You were the first one to get out the map and trace the likely route Cameron took on the way to Dover with the chest of gold in tow."

Before Daphne could retort, Miss Sophia Hastings broke in. "But what is this Cameron Cipher? I must confess I've never heard of it. I am woefully ignorant about such things."

"I'm sure that's not true, Miss Sophia," Foster assured her. "The Cameron Cipher is a coded message that holds the secret of where the leader of clan Cameron hid the Jacobite gold meant for the Pretender in 'forty-five. He was on the way to France to deliver the gold when his party was set upon by the English army, and he took safety somewhere along the coast. He hid the gold nearby and trusted the coded message telling where it was hidden with someone hereabouts. Or, as the alternate theory goes, hid it somewhere nearby where it was subsequently found, but proved too difficult to decrypt. A letter was found among the papers of Cameron's wife that said it was somewhere safe, but it was no more specific than that. And thus, a legend was born."

"That's right," Maitland spoke up as the memories flooded back to him. "Don't you remember we used to search for it in the caves when we were boys, Kerr?" He and his cousin had spent countless summers hunting for the cipher without success. "I haven't thought about it in years."

"Nor I," the marquess said with a grin. "Those were fun days."

"Why wasn't I included in these searches?" Serena asked crossly. "I should have enjoyed treasure hunting."

"Because you were a girl, Serena," Kerr said with a roll of his eyes. "It was just us lads."

"I want to hunt for treasure," young Jem piped up from beside his mother. "Will you take me, cousins?"

But Daphne it seemed, was still determined to dissuade the men from their quest. Over the sound of Quill assuring Jem that they would indeed go search the caves for treasure soon, she spoke up. "I am sorry you both came all this way for nothing. But it is highly improbable that the cipher exists in any of the libraries hereabouts."

"I had heard that the library at Beauchamp House is quite impressive," Sommersby said with what to Maitland's eye looked like calculation. "You wouldn't care to allow us to examine it, would you, Kerr? Just for our own amusement if nothing else. You are no doubt right about the cipher not being there."

"You'll need to ask all four of these ladies," Lord Kerr said amiably. "My wife, Lady Daphne, and the Misses Hastings inherited Beauchamp House from our aunt. But you likely know that already."

"Indeed, I do," Sommersby said with a grin, making no attempt to hide the fact that he'd just dissembled. "It was the talk of town for weeks. The four bluestocking heiresses of Beauchamp House. Congratulations to all of you."

"I'm afraid it will be quite impossible for us to allow you to search the library," Daphne said before any of the others could speak up. "We are all quite busy with our respective studies. I'm sure you understand."

A hard expression flitted across Sommersby's face before he masked it with one of affability. "We understand perfectly, of course. Perhaps one evening after you've finished your studies for the day, then?"

Something about this fellow was putting Maitland's back up. And it wasn't his ingratiating manner with Daphne. At least, that wasn't all of it. Aloud he said, "Perhaps you both can come by tomorrow evening for dinner, gentlemen? I, for one, would enjoy hearing about your travels. And I know Kerr will wish to question you about them."

At his words, Daphne gave him a glare. But the duke wanted to know more about Sommersby, which he would prefer to do when the man was on familiar territory. Besides, he was curious about the man's relationship with Daphne. And he could hardly seek him out at the local inn and demand to know what he'd done to make her distrust him so.

Of course, he could just ask Daphne outright, but they weren't exactly on the easiest of terms at the moment. He thought back to that moment in his aunt's bedchamber with a pang of regret. He couldn't have handled it worse if he'd tried.

"Capital," said Sommersby, his triumphant grin, showing he was unaware of the direction of Maitland's thoughts. "We'll see you all tomorrow then."

And after making their farewells, the two continued on their journey to the beach.

"Why were you so rude to him, Daphne?" Sophia asked with a frown as they began walking again. "He seemed quite friendly. And I should think you of all people would be intrigued by this Cameron Cipher. You're just the person to unravel its code, I'd think."

Daphne looked as if she would simply refuse to respond for a moment, but finally she said with a sigh, "Because I do not wish him to find the Cameron Cipher."

"That much was obvious, I think," Gemma said wryly.

"But why, Daphne?" Ivy asked, her expression concerned but not angrily so.

Maitland watched as Daphne blinked several times. *Were those tears?* His own chest constricted at the very idea.

"Because it's *mine*," she whispered. "Lady Celeste promised the Cameron Cipher to me."

Chapter 2

Daphne felt the ribbon of her hat brush against her cheek in the wind as she listened to the others' silence following her announcement.

All were silent but Jem, that is.

"What a Cam'rn Sife, Mama?" he whispered loudly from where he skipped along the path to Little Seaford beside Lady Serena.

"Hush, Jem," she said in an undertone. "Why don't you see how fast you can run to that dandelion up ahead?"

With a squeak of delight, the boy lifted his legs and ran ahead of them.

"When were you going to tell us this?" Ivy asked, once the child was out of earshot. "We've been here for three months, and this is the first I've heard of this cipher."

"Is that what you've been searching for in the library every day?" Sophia asked, her head tilted in exasperation. "You told us you were especially interested in the mathematics volumes, but I knew you had been through the art books, too."

"Well, I don't blame you a bit," Gemma said firmly. "I know very well how difficult it is to maintain your credibility in the sciences as a woman. If it got out you were treasure hunting, your academic reputation could be ruined. Unless, of course you were keeping this quiet because you didn't wish to share your gold with us, in which case, I am quite put out."

But it was obvious from Gemma's grin that she was nothing of the sort.

"Perhaps you would like for Maitland and me to leave you ladies to discuss this on your own," said Ivy's husband with a speaking look at Maitland. The duke, Daphne was relieved to see, looked only concerned for her, which she couldn't quite fathom after how she'd been treating him.

"No," she said with a wave of her hand, not meeting any of their gazes—not that she was particularly fond of eye contact at the best of times. "You should stay, since Ivy will tell you whatever I say anyway. And then you'll tell Maitland, who'll tell his sister."

Since none of the named gossips denied the accusation, she took that for their agreement with her assessment.

"Perhaps we should wait until we reach town and can safely sit down to a nice cup of tea in a private dining room at the inn?" she asked. It was illogical, she knew, but she feared Sommersby might somehow overhear them out here in the open.

"If that's what you wish," Maitland said, taking her arm in his and leading her past the others and toward the village, which they could now see as their party approached.

A more subdued group, they made the short trek into the village and had little trouble procuring a dining room at the Pig & Whistle. Serena, aware that what Daphne would say was perhaps not something Jem should overhear, made an excuse and took him back to Beauchamp House.

Once they were seated around a large table, full teacups before the ladies, pints of beer for the gentlemen, and two plates of sandwiches and an assortment of cheese and fruit for all of them, Daphne began her story.

"There isn't all that much to tell," she said staring into her teacup. "Like the three of you, I received a letter informing me that I'd inherited a quarter of Lady Celeste's estate, and telling me that per the terms of the will I needed to remove to Beauchamp House at once and remain there for a year or I'd forfeit my share."

The other ladies nodded. This was information they'd exchanged before.

"But I also received a letter from Lady Celeste herself, which I didn't tell you about."

The fact that only the gentlemen expressed surprise at this news told Daphne that they had also received personal letters from their benefactor.

"What did it say?" Maitland asked. He'd refrained from peppering her with questions on the way to the inn, as would have been his usual wont. But now that they were enclosed and away from prying eyes and ears, he seemed more relaxed. At least his posture seemed so to Daphne. She wasn't very good at reading his expressions.

Quickly, she told them about the line of the letter that was pertinent to the discussion at hand. They didn't need to know the other parts of the letter, where Lady Celeste talked about how lonely she had guessed Daphne must be, and hoped that she could find friends among the other bluestockings at Beauchamp House. That was personal. And for once, Daphne stopped herself from blurting out exactly what she was thinking. "So," she concluded, "I knew she was telling me that the Cameron Cipher was somewhere at Beauchamp House. And since she mentioned the library several times in the letter, I guessed that it was probably hidden there. It's taken me longer than I thought it would however, because I keep getting distracted by the other treasures there."

"All those summers of searching for the blasted thing and it was in the library all along," Kerr said with a shake of his dark head. "Aunt must have known what we were up to but she never said a thing."

"She would hardly have put the things into the hands of a couple of grubby schoolboys," Maitland said with a shrug. "And it was the chase that was fun. I sincerely doubt either of us would have been able to decipher a code like that. Try though we would have done."

"It's possible that she didn't find it herself until later on," Ivy said reasonably as she peeled an orange. "Or perhaps she acquired it from someone else and then secreted it in the library herself."

"She did spend a great deal of time in the library," Kerr said thoughtfully. "I always thought she was reading or writing letters or whatnot. But since I had an active boy's loathing for staying indoors, I never joined her there if I could help it."

"Nor did I," the duke agreed. "She might have been trying to solve the puzzle herself for all we know. Though I suppose she wouldn't have told Daphne about it if she had done so."

Daphne gave a nod of thanks to Gemma, who had just poured her another cup of tea. "She gave no indication one way or the other in her letter. Though my guess is that she was unable to unravel the cipher because if she had done so, she would likely have told someone about it. She knew as well as anyone how much of a coup being the woman who solved one of the greatest puzzles in a generation would be. Woman being the operative word. As someone who valued women's contributions to scholarship and the arts, she'd have found a way to use the accomplishment as a means to further the cause."

"That is my thinking as well," Sophia said, her dark brown hair showing chestnut highlights in the light from the window. "I knew who Lady Celeste Beauchamp was long before I received my own notification that I was one of her heirs. And it was always in reference to some way she was celebrating the accomplishments of other women. Perhaps I misinterpreted her actions, but despite her own modesty, I think she'd have felt duty bound to report her feat if it meant shining a light on just what sort of things women were capable of."

"So, she chose to leave it to the one person she knew would be able to solve it," Ivy said with a nod in Daphne's direction. "The winner of the *Ladies Gazette* editor's prize."

Two years ago, the editor of a prominent ladies' magazine had printed a series of ciphers in its pages, promising a free year's subscription to the person who could solve them. Though not a reader of the publication, Daphne had been unable to resist the opportunity to use her ciphering skills to unravel the puzzles. She'd always been fascinated by codes and secret messages and had studied some of the more famous ones with her tutor. She'd quickly dispatched her solutions to the editor and had won the contest handily. According to her letter, Lady Celeste had taken note. And so she had chosen Daphne to inherit the Cameron Cipher.

"So." Kerr sat his now empty pint glass on the table. "If we're agreed she didn't solve the thing herself, why didn't she just tell Daphne in her letter where to find it so that *she* could decipher it? Why go to the trouble of hiding it again?"

"I think I know," Daphne said, grateful that none of them seemed angry with her for keeping her own counsel on the matter up to now.

Because there was something else Daphne was keeping from her friends. There had been another note waiting for her once she reached Beauchamp House. And its contents she would keep to herself. Not only because its contents were somewhat personal. But also because they pertained to another member of their party.

In full, the second note had read:

> *My dear Lady Daphne,*
> *I cannot tell you how pleased I am to welcome you to Beauchamp House. I have long admired your*

intellect, and mathematical genius, as well as your facility with solving equations of other sorts, like the ciphering contest in THE LADIES GAZETTE. What joy it gave me to see an intelligent young woman do that which scores of men could not, by solving their nonsensical coded phrases. I knew I had to include you amongst my Bluestockings in that moment. And I hope you will sharpen your ciphering skills for a much more difficult task now that you're here.

You will find Romance—and enough intrigue—to Riddle with envy even the most unschooled of ladies among the Treasure of my collections. And as you peruse them, I hope that you will accept the assistance of my dear nephew, Maitland.

His father, my sister's husband, was a devilish creature and I am happy to say that not one drop of the scandal attached to his father's reputation has splashed onto dear Dalton. His happy disposition might make you question his intellect, my dear, but do not be fooled. He is quite as clever in his way as any man. (Though not, of course, as clever as you—but who among us is, dear Daphne?)

I hope you will do your benefactress the favor of allowing him to provide any assistance you might need as you begin to plumb the depths of mystery to be found within the many wonderful shelves of my library.

You see, I think as much as adventure, you need a friend. I've seen too many brilliant minds brought low by the more emotional toll of loneliness. And if nothing else, I think dear Dalton's sunny humor can give you a bit of light.

I have every faith that you are the special one I've

DUKE WITH BENEFITS   37

hoped for. And I know you will dazzle the world when
your quest is complete.

Yours in intellect,
Lady Celeste Beauchamp

Now, feeling a pang of conscience over her deception,
she tried to explain the contents of the note without actually disclosing its existence. "I believe all that Lady
Celeste wished was to make an adventure of it. A sort
of real-life puzzle, as it were, to lead me to the cipher.
She told me as much in her letter."

That the lady had also wished for her to let the Duke
of Maitland be her assistant in the matter was something
that they didn't need to know. Besides, after *her* indecent proposal, and his perfectly respectable one, she
considered that she'd done a creditable job of attempting to let Merry Maitland ease her loneliness. Perhaps
they were even friends now. Whatever the case, it was
not a matter for the ears of the whole of Beauchamp
House.

"There is a certain logic to it," Gemma said with a
nod. "A puzzle that leads to a puzzle."

"And Aunt Celeste was fond of mazes, riddles, and
all sorts of games," Maitland said with a grin. He turned
to Daphne. "You rather remind me of her in that way."

"I can see that," Kerr said with a tip of his head to
his cousin.

"Then why are we waiting?" Gemma demanded with
excitement in her eyes. "We need to get back to the
house at once and start looking for this cipher!" It was
ironic how quickly she'd turned from skeptic to true

believer, Daphne thought with an sigh. Which was quickly followed by another as she thought about the consequences of having their entire household pawing through what she'd come to think of as her own territory.

But, there was no time to waste. Sommersby was here now, and he was going to find a way into the Beauchamp House library whether she liked it or not.

The walk back to the house seemed to pass more quickly than the one into the village.

Maitland had watched Daphne as she carried on a lively conversation with the other ladies, an unruly blond curl bouncing against the sensitive skin of her neck. He'd never really considered the back of a woman's head to be particularly enticing before, but he supposed there was a first time for everything.

To his relief, Kerr left him to his own thoughts and when they filed into the front entrance of Beauchamp House, he managed to separate Daphne from the others without being seen.

She must have recognized the need for discretion, because she made no protest as he led her by the arm into the small antechamber his aunt had used as a waiting room for unwanted guests.

With its dull gray walls and mismatched furniture, it was hardly the appropriate setting for a proposal of marriage, but with the arrival of Sommersby that afternoon Maitland had realized that he couldn't abide the notion of Daphne going to the other man because he'd been too principled to bow to her wishes.

"What did you wish to speak to me about?" she asked, her lovely face tight with impatience. "I should like to have another look at Lady Celeste's letter before dinner. Especially now that Sommersby has arrived to search for the cipher."

Her thoughts were a million miles away, and Maitland was suddenly determined to bring her back here to this room. With him.

Pulling her against him, he lowered his lips to hers in a soft, seductive kiss, full of all the pent-up desire he'd been fighting against since their first encounter weeks ago.

She was surprised, but it took only the barest moment for Daphne to catch him up. And when she opened her mouth to his, and slipped her arms around his neck, he hummed with satisfaction. Whatever might have passed between them, whoever might have arrived to distract her, the spark between them was still there.

Coming up for air, he leaned his forehead against hers, and looked down into her half-lidded eyes. "Marry me, Daphne. So that we can explore what's between us."

When she didn't reply at once, he realized his mistake.

Shaking her head, she pulled away from him, and reluctantly, Maitland let her go.

"I won't marry you simply so that we can lie together, Maitland," she said with exasperation. "It's too high a price. If I were already married, or a widow, you wouldn't even feel obliged to offer at all. Why can you not afford me the same courtesy as you would a willing widow?"

At her words, he huffed out a startled laugh. "You do realize that you're probably the only unmarried lady in the country who doesn't wish to become the next Duchess of Maitland?" He thrust a hand through his hair, disheveled from her hands. "I vow, Daphne, you are the most frustrating lady it has ever been my misfortune to meet."

"If it's such a misfortune," she retorted dryly, "then I wonder at your wanting to spend the rest of your life with me."

"You would try the patience of a saint, madam, and make no mistake about it," he said with a sigh. "And no, that is not a contradiction of my wish to wed you. It is rather a statement of fact."

He stepped close to her again, looking down into her defiant green eyes. "Another statement of fact is that there is unfinished business between us, and I will not insult either your or my honor by attempting to bed you without an understanding between us. You might wish to be treated like a different sort of woman, but the truth is that you are not. And a gentlemen would not, could not, forget that."

"Then I fear you will be doomed to disappointment," Daphne responded with a shrug. "Which is a shame. For I think we'd get on well together."

How she could be so hot in his arms one minute and cool as a cucumber the next, he couldn't know. But he couldn't deny it added to his desire for her. Even now his fingers itched to pull her against him and persuade her to change her mind.

He wondered suddenly if others were tempted by her in the same way. And was beset with a rare fit of jealousy. "I won't stand by and let this Sommersby chap take advantage of your friendship, either," he warned her.

But rather than the irritation he'd expected, he saw instead a shadow pass over her eyes. He realized at once that he'd mistaken her feelings for the other man. Whatever was between her and her former tutor's son, it wasn't the sweet tale of young love's dream he'd conjured in his imagination. If he wasn't mistaken, it had been fear he'd seen in her eyes.

"What is it, my dear?" he asked, noting that the hands he pulled into his own were trembling. "Daphne, what has that blackguard done?"

But she took a deep breath and pulled away. "Nothing," she said with a hollow laugh. "We simply knew each other in our youth. That's all. And I do not wish him to find the Cameron Cipher before I do."

But Maitland couldn't let her get away so easily. "Simple acquaintance does not explain the way you paled when you set eyes on him. Nor the way you trembled just now."

She looked as if she would speak for a moment, then stiffened her spine and gave a slight shake. "Do not be absurd, Duke," she said with a sunny smile. "I fear you are letting my rejection go to your head. But please do not repeat your proposal again, for I do not know how many times I can tell you I have no wish to wed."

"You will have to do so one day," he warned her. "I doubt your father will simply allow you to do whatever you wish."

Daphne's lips curled into a genuine smile. "You'd be surprised, Duke. Very, very surprised."

He watched her, trying to guess what she was thinking. Finally, he shook his head. "I'm going to wear you down, you know. I can be very persuasive."

"I'm sure you can be," she replied with a catlike smile. "And so can I."

Lifting his chin, he said, "Then may the best man, or woman, win."

With a nod, she accepted his challenge. And without a backward glance, she sailed with head held high from the room.

Watching the sway of her hips as she went, Maitland knew he had his work cut out for him.

And more than ever he wanted to know what had passed between Sommersby and Daphne. Because judging from her response to the man, it hadn't been anything good.

After dinner that evening, the ladies—clearly eager to discuss matters they did not wish to share with male ears—headed upstairs to bed, while Kerr and Maitland retired to the room they still thought of as Aunt Celeste's study, though she'd been gone for months now.

"What did you make of him?" the duke asked his cousin as he settled his large frame into one of the oversize chairs his aunt had purchased expressly for her nephews. "I didn't believe his story a bit."

Kerr, who had been pouring them both generous snifters of brandy, looked up, his brow furrowed. "Who?"

If Daphne was frustrated with her friend Ivy's recent lapse into absent-mindedness, then Maitland was equally put out with Kerr, who spent most of his time away from his wife gazing off into space with a vague smile on his face. "That Sommersby fellow, of course. He looked at Daphne like she was a prize calf at the cattle show."

His cousin nearly dropped the glass in his extended hand. "You'd better not let her hear you describe her thus. Or any of the ladies, actually. They would flay you alive."

"You know what I mean," Maitland said pettishly as he took the brandy. "That chap is up to something, make no mistake about it. And he has designs upon Lady Daphne as sure as the sun rises in the west."

"It rises in the east," Kerr corrected absently, "but I suppose I agree about your point. He did seem a bit . . . calculating."

"East, west? What does it matter when there is a wolf on the doorstep?" Maitland had never been particularly interested in such things. But he was interested in Daphne, who had clearly not been pleased to hear of her old friend's reasons for being here. Whether the man wanted her for romantic reasons, or strictly because he knew her agile mind would far more easily unravel the Cameron Cipher once it was found, Maitland was unsure. Hell, it might be both.

"You really are enjoying the animal metaphors this evening, aren't you?" Kerr quirked a brow at him. "Though the wolf one does seem apt."

"Well, this is one wolf who will not catch his prey." Maitland would allow the fellow near Daphne again over his dead body.

"You can hardly bar the door to him when he arrives for dinner tomorrow," Kerr said reasonably, crossing one booted foot over his knee. "Aside from the fact that the house doesn't belong to you, you really have no claim on Daphne aside from friendship." He narrowed his eyes at his cousin. "Unless of course, you've changed your mind recently and allowed her to have her wicked way with you. You haven't, have you?"

"Of course, I haven't." Maitland scowled. "Not that it's any of your business. But, no, my mind is made up on the subject. I will not besmirch her honor. Even if she is willing to let me do so."

"You're a stronger man than I am," Kerr said, shaking his head. "If Ivy had approached me with such an invitation . . ."

"She'd have to have done so before you even met in order to beat you to the mark, cuz."

It was no secret that Kerr had compromised his now wife only a few days after their arrival at Beauchamp House.

"I think you've proven your inability to control your baser urges around your wife, else you'd not now be married." Maitland gave his cousin a speaking look. "Though I will admit to a certain amount of envy at your situation. It's certainly no easy feat to get through every day around her knowing that she'd be mine for the taking if I only agreed to her terms. But I am not in the habit of seducing innocents. And bold though Daphne might be, she is no wanton. I won't bed her without at least the promise of marriage. It's as simple as that."

"I'm not saying it's not noble of you," the other man said. "It's just that not many men would be able to resist temptation like that."

"Not many men were raised by my father," Maitland said, his mouth tight. "I will not repeat his sins, no matter how strong the urge. He was a rake and a scoundrel and is likely somewhere in hell beside himself with laughter over my priggishness. But I will not relent. I saw what havoc his dishonor did to not only my mother, but also to the women who were unlucky enough to fall prey to his charms."

Kerr nodded solemnly. "I know, old fellow. I shouldn't have teased you on the matter."

Maitland only nodded in response.

"It was rather a shock to hear Sommersby mention the Cameron Cipher," Kerr said, changing the subject. "I haven't thought of it since we were boys. And I certainly had no idea that Aunt Celeste knew anything about it other than the legend."

"I begin to think there was a great deal that Aunt Celeste knew but didn't share with us," Maitland said wryly. "The identity of her heirs, the secrets of her youth, and now the fact that she knew the location of the infamous Cameron Cipher. I wonder if we knew her at all."

"It's no secret that she disliked mysteries," Kerr said with a shrug. "And it would appear that she's left two at least as part of her legacy to the four heiresses. I wonder what the Misses Hastings are keeping back from us."

"For now, let's concentrate on the Cameron Cipher," Maitland said, more concerned with Daphne than the Misses Hastings, fond though he had grown of them. "Daphne has been searching the library for it since her arrival, it would seem. And has thus far had no luck finding it. Which, given her intellectual abilities leads me to believe that it isn't there."

"Or it's somewhere she hasn't looked yet," Kerr retorted. "It's one of the largest libraries in England. One lady searching for three months is hardly going to find it quickly. No matter how brilliant she is."

"You have a point, I suppose," Maitland said with nod. "What I want to know is how Sommersby learned that it was hidden in Beauchamp House. Or that there was a connection at all."

"Someone must have told," Kerr said reasonably. "Perhaps we can learn from him at dinner tomorrow. Aunt certainly had innumerable friends and acquaintances. She might have hinted at the cipher's presence at Beauchamp House to any one of them."

"She clearly chose Daphne as one of her heirs because of it," Maitland said. "I wonder if she feels any discomfort over that. That she was picked because of her ciphering abilities."

"I can't imagine Lady Daphne is the sort to dwell too much on such things. She seemed eager enough to find the thing. It's Sommersby's arrival on the scene that's set the cat among the pigeons. For all that they're old friends, she didn't seem particularly happy to see him."

Maitland thought back to her response earlier when he'd brought up Sommersby's name. There was definitely something from the past between them. And on Daphne's side at least, it was an uncomfortable memory. If he judged Sommersby aright, he thought Sommersby had some sort of an in with Daphne. There had been no mistaking the proprietary way the man's eyes had roamed over her.

He'd proposed tonight because he thought perhaps Daphne would turn to her old friend in the face of his own rejection of her advances, but the way her hands had trembled at the mention of the man told him she'd sooner proposition a snake.

He looked down to see his hand clenched tight around the brandy glass. When he glanced up, he saw Kerr was watching him knowingly.

"I don't think there's anything particular between them, you know," his cousin said. "If there were, Sommersby would have looked far more smug than he did. He was trying to win back her trust, I think. Ingratiating himself with her."

"Perhaps," Maitland said, not wanting to speak of his suspicions regarding the newcomer just yet—at least not with any specificity. "Regardless, I will continue to keep an eye on him. Until he proves otherwise, I don't trust the man."

"What did you make of his friend? Foster?"

"Most of my attention was on Sommersby," Maitland admitted. "But Foster seemed a nice enough chap. He didn't strike me as anything but what he seemed. Certainly not like Sommersby did. There's just something about the fellow I cannot like."

"Foster didn't look familiar to you at all?" Kerr asked, his eyes troubled. "I could have sworn I knew him from somewhere, but I cannot think of where for the life of me."

Maitland thought back to the scene on the path to Little Seaford. Sommersby, he could recall with exact detail. His companion, however, was less clear. He had an impression of reddish hair and a medium build. But he'd not lied when he said he wasn't focused on the fellow. Kerr was usually good at recognizing faces, however, so he didn't dismiss the other man's words.

"Perhaps you saw him somewhere in town? Or at university?"

"Maybe," his cousin replied. "Doubtless it will come to me as soon as I stop trying to remember."

"If you'd stop mooning over that wife of yours, you'd probably remember quickly enough," Maitland said, setting down his now empty brandy glass and stretching. "You were a rather clever fellow before Ivy came into your life."

"I was a rather *lonely* fellow before Ivy came into my life," Kerr corrected him with a wink. "And you cannot blame me for being a besotted fool when I have such a prize."

Despite his jest, Maitland could see that his cousin was happier than he'd ever been. It was as if Kerr had become lighter somehow. As if the cares of the world had lifted from his shoulders and been replaced with a mantle of joy. Or something. He was no poet. He only knew his cousin was a different man since he'd married Ivy. And the duke couldn't help but be a wee bit envious.

Aloud he said, "I won't agree too heartily, because I do not wish to be called out."

"Now, who's the clever fellow?" Kerr asked with a wink.

And on that note, the cousins made their way upstairs. Kerr to his own room where he would likely share every syllable of their conversation with his wife, and Maitland to his bachelor bedchamber, where he would lie awake for some time mulling over the events of the afternoon.

Chapter 3

"Why didn't you tell us you were searching for the Cameron Cipher?" Sophia demanded once the ladies were safely ensconced in the sitting room they shared upstairs near their bedchambers. "We could have helped!"

"I knew you weren't simply cataloging the books," Gemma said with a scowl.

Ivy only looked at Daphne with disappointment.

Daphne could tell that the other ladies were hurt by her deception, but she could not regret her decision to keep her own counsel on the matter of the cipher. Not only had Lady Celeste chosen to share the presence of the puzzle in Beauchamp House with Daphne alone, but some sense of inner caution had warned her that once the others knew, the secret would not be secret for long. News like this had a way of getting out. And given the number of people who had traipsed in and out the house following that business with Ivy's search for Lady Celeste's killer, Daphne knew she had made the right choice.

"You know now," Daphne said aloud. "And that is what matters, is it not?"

Sophia opened her mouth to object but closed it again.

"What matters is that we find it before your Mr. Sommersby does," Ivy said briskly. "For he seems quite determined. And unless I mistake the matter, he will arrive on our doorstep first thing tomorrow morning rather than waiting until the dinner hour."

"He did have the look of a man on a mission," Gemma agreed. "I was rather surprised he didn't invite himself along with us on our trip into Little Seaford. He certainly wanted to spend more time with you, Daphne."

"Yes, he did." Sophia's shrewd gaze rested on Daphne's, as if assessing her response. "If I know men, and I believe we'll all agree I do, then he wants more than just the Cameron Cipher from you, Daphne."

Daphne felt her cheeks heat. She had, once upon a time, thought Nigel Sommersby the most handsome gentleman of her acquaintance. And for a fleeting moment that afternoon, her old feelings had come to life again, like the reanimated being in Mary Shelley's novel *Frankenstein*, which she and Nigel had devoured in the schoolroom.

But, like the monster, her feelings were not something that could be allowed to flourish. There had been a moment, years ago, when she thought perhaps . . . but those fanciful notions had been snuffed out almost as soon as they'd come to life.

"Do not be absurd, Sophia," she said aloud. "He's desperate to find the Cameron Cipher since he was a youth.

If he has any thought that it could be in the vicinity, he will stop at nothing to retrieve it."

"Those are rather strong words," Gemma said with a frown. "Are you saying he has no thought for the law? Or that he would physically harm someone to get to it?"

Daphne swallowed. It was possible that Sommersby was not at twenty-eight the same man he'd been at eighteen. But there had been a glint in his eye that afternoon that told her he was still capable of the sort of ruthlessness he'd demonstrated to her all those years ago. Back then she'd been unable to protect herself, but now, she knew better than to let herself be caught alone with him. Still, it would not do to let her friends think he was harmless either.

"I am saying that if you can help it, do not allow him to maneuver you into a corner," Daphne said, looking down at her hands, knowing that if she showed her friends her eyes they'd read her true feelings in them. "Do not allow him to charm you with his words or to physically cow you. He is not a nice man, for all that he appears so."

The other ladies were silent for so long that Daphne wondered if they'd even heard her.

Finally, Sophia asked softly, "Daphne, did Mr. Sommersby hurt you? Perhaps press you to do something you did not wish to do?"

But Sophia's words brought back the memory of that night in her bedchamber at her father's house, and it was all Daphne could do to breath, much less stop herself from trembling.

Though she did not as a general rule encourage other

people to touch her, Ivy's hand on her arm gave her comfort.

"I c . . . c . . . can't t . . . t . . . talk ab . . . b . . ."

"Shh, it's all right," Ivy soothed. And she tried to calm herself as she listened to Sophia and Gemma kneel before her on the floor, just touching the skirts of her gown lightly. "You needn't talk about it if you don't wish."

In some faraway part of her mind, Daphne was mortified at appearing thusly in front of her friends. She was not given to outbursts of emotion. Nor was she one to wear her cares on her sleeve. What must the other ladies think of her?

She only thanked the heavens that she hadn't behaved like this earlier when she'd first seen Sommersby. For a brief moment, she'd even felt her old affection return. The mind was deceptive that way, allowing you to feel two opposing things about the same person at the same time. Fortunately, that old affection was soon pushed aside by fear and loathing.

"I will have a word with Quill," Ivy said to her. "He will not let this cretin within a stone's throw of Beauchamp House. If I ask it, he and Maitland will usher him out of the county."

At the mention of Maitland, however, Daphne's head snapped up. "No," she said in a strangled voice. "Under no circumstances is anyone to tell Maitland about this. You must all promise me."

The idea of the Duke of Maitland knowing even a hint of what had been the most shameful moment in her life was anathema to her. She could bear many things in this life, but a look of pity from him was not one of them. Or worse, disgust. For she was not entirely blameless in the matter. And most men would lay the blame not where it belonged, on the man who did the debauching, but instead upon the woman. She knew Maitland was not most men, but she didn't wish to risk the odds.

"We promise," Gemma said, placing a hand on her arm. "No one will tell him. But that does not mean that he and Lord Kerr shouldn't see to it that Sommersby is ushered out of the area. We needn't tell them the reason. Just that he makes you uncomfortable."

"Or we could say that you do not wish him to get near to the Cameron Cipher," Sophia said practically. "That is also true, is it not? And there will be no need to raise either gentleman's suspicions about anything else."

By now, Daphne had stopped trembling, and she was able to breathe easily. She had not been this overset by memories of Sommersby's assault on her—because that is what it had been, even if he hadn't been able to get all of what he wanted from her—in a long time. Not since she'd learned from his father that he was bound for Egypt. And now that she had regained her composure, she refused to allow him to upset her for a minute more.

Even so, she craved the calm that only putting things in order could give her. She hadn't been completely deceitful about organizing the library. While she'd been searching, she'd also been rearranging things in what she thought of as the proper order. None of the other ladies had complained thus far, so she supposed they agreed with her arrangement.

She'd thought removing herself from her father's house, where she was subject to his insistence that she use her skills at the card tables for his own financial gain, would be such a relief that she would be able to overcome her sometimes uncontrollable urge to tidy. But despite her fondness for her new friends, there was quite a bit of anxiety associated with her new surroundings. And now that Sommersby had arrived on the scene, she was even more fraught with nerves.

Aloud, she said, "I suppose that will work. Though I wish it were not necessary to tell them anything at all."

Unable to stand one more minute of scrutiny from the other three, she stood abruptly, and said, "I need to go to the library now." And supposing they would want some more explanation, she added, "To think." Surely thinking was something one was allowed to do alone. And if anyone should understand such a need, it would be these particular ladies, who also prized contemplation as a worthy pastime.

And without waiting for a response, she fled.

After an hour or so of tossing and turning, Dalton threw back the counterpane and pulled on a pair of breeches, a shirt, and a pair of slippers. If anyone was scandalized by the sight of him wandering the house in shirtsleeves, then they would simply have to endure it. He was in a bit of a mood, and surely a trip to the library for something to occupy his mind and perhaps lull him to sleep was not so objectionable. It wasn't as if he were going about in the altogether.

A scowl on his face as he contemplated his earlier conversation with his cousin, the duke stalked down the corridors of Beauchamp House until he came to the library door, which was ajar. And there was light shining from within.

Well, whoever it was would just have to excuse his state of undress. Because he wasn't going back upstairs.

But when he stepped inside, he could see no one amongst the mahogany tables and floor-to-ceiling walls of books, although several of the lamps throughout the room were lit. And he could see that several books on the far side of the room had been removed from their shelf and were stacked haphazardly on a nearby table. And to his surprise, the French doors leading out to a balcony overlooking the gardens were wide open.

Something was wrong.

With a low curse, he hurried over to the open balcony doors, but a quick scan of the parapet showed that no one was there.

"What are you doing here?"

Startled, he turned and saw Daphne glaring at him from inside the book room.

"I asked what are you doing here?" she repeated. "And why are you on the balcony? Surely you can find some other place to enjoy the evening air."

He was on the brink of telling her that he didn't answer to her, when the sound of a pistol firing sent him into motion borne of instinct. Careless of her temper, he threw himself at her, bringing them both crashing flat onto the thick Aubusson carpet.

They lay there breathless for a moment and listened for another report, but after some moments of quiet, it was clear whoever it was had finished his assault.

Gradually, Maitland became aware of the fact that the body underneath his was distinctly female and that

Daphne's soft curves fit with aching perfection against his own hardness. Moving back a little, he scanned her face, noting a hint of pink in her cheeks as she stared at his mouth.

"Are you all right?" he asked, his voice hoarse to his own ears. "I didn't hurt you, did I?"

"N . . . no," she said, her breath soft against his cheek. He waited for her to continue, but the usually talkative Daphne was unusually quiet.

"We'd best wait for a minute or so more," he said, knowing the decision was justified, but feeling like a cad all the same as he felt her breasts rise and fall with each breath. "Just to make sure there are no more shots."

"He shot at us," Daphne whispered. As if whoever it was could hear them from his coward's hiding place out there in the dark. "Why would he do that?"

"I don't know," he said, closing his eyes against the scent of the lemon verbena she must use to wash her hair. Then what she'd just said sank in. "What do you mean 'he'?" Maitland demanded. "Do you know who this is? Is it that Sommersby fellow? Why would he shoot at you?"

At the mention of Sommersby, she stiffened and pushed against his chest. She was no match for his superior strength, but he pushed away from her all the same. He sensed the panic in the gesture as she scrambled away from him, scuttling backward across the floor like the crabs down on the beach below.

"Why would you say that?" she demanded rising swiftly to a standing position. "What makes you think he'd have reason to shoot at me?"

Taking his time as he got to his feet, Maitland thought back to their encounter with Sommersby that afternoon. At the time, he'd thought Daphne was merely annoyed with the other man because of his interest in the Cameron Cipher. But this response now was something else. Something darker.

He shut the French doors firmly and pulled the curtains so that they couldn't be seen from outside.

Turning, he surveyed her. Taking in her clenched hands and downcast eyes.

"Daphne," he said softly, "are you frightened of this man?"

Though her answer was clear in her expression, she said, "No, of course not. He's an old friend. That's all."

"Is he?"

The question seemed to give her pause. He could see worry, and something else in her face. Fear?

He was assailed with a sudden, intense urge to find Sommersby and beat him into a bloody pulp.

"We were friends once," she said stiffly. "And now he is here. He wants the cipher."

While that might be true, Maitland thought, it didn't mean Sommersby was only here for the cipher.

He would have liked to question her further about her relationship with the treasure hunter, but he could see that she was eager to leave the subject.

"Is he willing to kill someone to get to it first?"

"I don't know," she said in a hoarse voice. "I don't know what he's capable of."

With a strangled sound, she hurried over to where the stack of books had been removed from the shelves and began sorting through them. Then, as if just realizing what she looked at, she said, "Why were you looking at Scottish histories?"

There was a frown in her eyes, and she was clearly unsettled by the idea.

"I wasn't," he said, wondering why it mattered. "Those books were off the shelf when I came in here this evening. And all the lights were lit. I thought one of you ladies had done it."

Turning, Daphne scanned the shelf behind her, where one shelf was empty of its contents, like the gap in Jem's smile where he'd lost his two front milk teeth.

She slid her hand over the underside of the shelf above, then down over the inside of the box created by the four sides. "Will you bring that lamp, please?"

Wordlessly, Maitland took up the flickering light and carried it over to where she stood staring into the dark space of the empty shelf. "Hold it just there," she requested, tilting her head to the side, as she looked at something on the inside of the left-hand border of the shelf. He complied, and she squinted as if she wasn't quite sure what she was seeing. Then with a nod, she stood up straight and said. "Step back, please."

He obeyed, and watched as she pressed against the side of the shelf where she'd been looking and gasped in amazement as the entire shelf, from floor to ceiling, swung inward silently, revealing a chamber beyond.

"I'll be damned," he said with a shake of his head.

Then, recalling just how they'd been alerted to the presence of this hidden room, he said, "Let me go in first. Whoever was here earlier might have set some kind of trap in there."

Though she looked as if she'd like to argue, Daphne nodded, and stepped back so that Maitland could pick up the lamp and slide into the narrow doorway.

Almost as soon as he stepped inside, he was hit with a foul smell. And a quick glance at the floor told him it's source.

"Daphne," he said calmly. "Go get Kerr and Ivy."

"What? Why?" she asked, coming up to stand behind him and trying unsuccessfully to see around him. "What are you hiding from me? And what is that awful smell?"

And before he could stop her, she'd wiggled around him and stopped in her tracks beside him with a gasp.

"Oh!"

Quickly, Maitland pressed her face into his shoulder so she would not see any more of the horror on the floor.

It was Mr. Nigel Sommersby. A small trunk lay on the floor beside him, open, and empty. And he was quite, quite dead.

Chapter 4

"And you say this Sommersby fellow was looking for the Cameron Cipher?" Squire Northman, the local magistrate asked, his bushy brows conveying his opinion of those who engaged in such frivolous behavior.

After the initial excitement had died down, Maitland had instructed the two sturdiest footmen to remove Sommersby's body to the icehouse for the night. Mindful of the empty box they'd found with the man's body, he himself had searched the body for any sign of the Cameron Cipher, or any other clue to who might have done him in. But he'd found only a set of what looked to be lock picks. No purse or papers of any kind. He'd returned to the house exhausted, and the household had decided to get what rest they could before the coming day.

Kerr had summoned Mr. Northman before breakfast and now the four heiresses, and the Beauchamp cousins—with the exception of young Jeremy—were all assembled in the library answering the man's questions, while his private secretary scribbled down their every word in a book with a lead pencil.

"That is what he told us when we met him on the way into town yesterday," Kerr agreed with a nod. "He and his friend, a Mr. Ian Foster, were staying at the Pig & Whistle in Little Seaford, I believe."

Northman nodded, and said to his secretary. "Write that bit down. We'll need to talk to this fellow Foster at once."

"I sent one of the footmen to inform Mr. Foster first thing this morning," Maitland said, "but he was told that the fellow had traveled on his own to visit friends in Pevensey for a few days. The innkeeper didn't know their name, so he will get the bad news when he returns I'm afraid."

Daphne, who had enjoyed the first restful sleep she'd had in years last night, felt a pang of guilt over the relief she felt at Sommersby's death, given how upset his friend Foster would be when he learned of it. Not to mention how his father, her mentor, would take the news. It wasn't that she'd wished the man dead. She might have wanted him to never set foot in the same vicinity as her ever again. But she hadn't wanted him to die a horrible death.

And his death had been horrible. That she'd been able to see from the quick glance she'd managed before Maitland pushed her face into his shoulder.

Nigel's expression had been one of pure agony, and his hand had been clasped uselessly around the dagger protruding from his chest.

"How did he get in?" Northman asked, scanning all

of them, as if he could extract the information with the power of his gaze alone.

"As I said earlier," Maitland said, with barely repressed exasperation, "the doors leading out onto the balcony were open when I entered the library. As Kerr and I know from when we were boys, it's quite easy to climb the yew tree near the balcony and gain access that way."

"And you're sure you didn't find the fellow there in the hidden room, your grace?" Northman's brows were intent now. "You didn't perhaps struggle with him over the knife and accidentally kill the man? It would be well within your rights, your grace. After all, this Sommersby was an intruder. You were protecting your family." He paused, giving a speaking glance at Daphne and the Hastings sisters. "And your friends."

"That would be quite impossible, Mr. Northman," said Daphne, unable to stop herself from leaping to Maitland's defense. "Because as we have told you once before, I was the one who found the latch for the secret doorway, and the duke and I were together when he discovered Mr. Sommersby's body. It would be quite impossible for him to have stabbed the man to death without my witnessing it."

"But Lady Daphne," the squire said slowly, "you might have reason to lie. To protect his grace. Especially if he was protecting you."

Daphne, however, had had quite enough. "If anyone had reason to wish Mr. Sommersby dead it was me. And yet, neither I, nor the duke, was responsible for the man's death. We found him in the very way which we have already described to you more than once. I am sorry if you were not gifted with a great deal of intellect, but even you can understand that we do not wish to respond to the same question repeatedly while you do nothing to search for the person who shot at Maitland and me last night, and very likely murdered Mr. Sommersby."

Northman's mouth opened and closed a couple of times, like a newly caught fish.

Daphne felt herself flanked on either side by Maitland and Kerr.

"I think that's enough for today, Northman," said Lord Kerr in a tone that brooked no argument. "As you can see, the ladies are quite overset by the events of last evening and are in need of rest."

Though he looked as if he would like to argue, Northman rose, his secretary popping up to his feet beside him like a jack-in-the-box. "I'm not finished with my questions," the magistrate said ponderously. "And I will wish to speak with Lady Daphne in particular. She knew him from before, I believe you said. Perhaps this had nothing at all to do with this Cameron Cipher."

Daphne opened her mouth to speak but was silenced by a not-so-subtle squeeze on the arm from Maitland, who then stepped over to usher Northman bodily from the room.

Once they were gone, Daphne sank onto the nearest chair.

"What were you thinking, Daphne?" Ivy chided from where she'd gone to stand beside Kerr. "You cannot antagonize the magistrate like that. He could have decided to throw you into the nearest gaol."

"I said nothing that wasn't true," Daphne said,

puzzled. "He must know that he's not as clever as any of us. That is why he kept asking the same questions again and again. And it is highly unlikely that he would have had me put in gaol. He has no proof that I killed Sommersby. And even so, I am the daughter of an earl. He could probably be bought off with a promise from my father to stand him membership in one of his clubs."

"She's likely right about the latter," Kerr said with a grimace. "Northman is a dreadful toadeater."

She was spared from reply by the reappearance of Maitland, who stalked over to her and glared. "What did you mean that you had a reason for wishing Sommersby dead? Because I know very well you weren't speaking about the cipher. There's something else between you that you aren't telling us. What is it?"

"You needn't be such an ogre about it, Maitland," said Lady Serena, coming to stand beside Daphne, much to her relief. "Anyone can see that she's overset by what happened last evening. And aside from that, I believe she was standing up for you when she dressed down the squire. Who is a boor, without question. He was quite rude to keep us for so long."

"You'll forgive me for not stepping back, sister," the duke said. Daphne could feel the heat of his gaze on her as he continued to speak. "But, last night I found a dead body in a house I've run tame in since I was a child. The body of a man who has some connection to Lady Daphne. Something more than just their mutual quest for a cipher telling the location of lost Jacobite gold. She said it herself when she was defending me to Northman. I am merely asking her to elaborate."

He was angry. Daphne could see that. But she wasn't sure why. He hadn't known Sommersby before yesterday, so it couldn't be grief. And there was really no other reason for him to be upset.

Surely he wasn't jealous? The very idea made her heart beat faster.

"You do not need to say anything you do not wish to, Daphne," said Sophia stepping up to stand on the other side of her. Daphne swallowed, feeling perilously close to tears. "I think she's had quite enough interrogation for today, your grace."

"Come on, man," Kerr said, stepping up to clasp Maitland by the shoulder. "Leave it be for now."

Daphne peeked up at him from beneath her lashes and saw that though his jaw was set, his eyes were troubled. She was able to recognize that, at least. For the barest second, her gaze locked with his, and she felt a jolt of emotion surge through her. Breathless, she quickly looked away.

With a sigh, Maitland said, "Fine. But this isn't over, Daphne. You will tell me whatever it is that gave you reason to want him dead. Because if you had a reason, then it's likely someone else had the same one. And that's why he's dead."

A chill ran down Daphne's spine at the thought. Could Sommersby have forced himself on some other young lady? Had he perhaps been killed by an angry father or a vengeful brother?

She had thought it was simply someone else who wanted the cipher. There had been no sign of it in the hidden room, so they'd thought the killer had taken it with him. But what if it had had nothing to do with the cipher at all?

What if Sommersby had been killed by someone just like her?

Deciding she couldn't remain indoors for a moment more lest she say something she'd regret, Daphne muttered her excuses to the other ladies and slipped out the back door and followed the well-worn path to the stone stairs leading down to the little beach below.

She breathed deeply, taking in the salt-tinged air, and let the wind whip through her hair, disarranging the tidy chignon her maid had worked so hard on that morning. The sea was rough this morning, churning up wave after wave before surging forward to break on the pebbled shoreline, which was in keeping with her tumultuous emotions.

Daphne was not generally the sort of lady who flew into fits of emotion at the least little thing. But in the past two days she'd found herself grappling with such dark feelings as she'd not endured since Nigel Sommersby's betrayal years ago. She'd long ago learned not to trust her father. And though she felt great affection for the elder Mr. Sommersby, indeed considered him something of a father figure, she had never been made to question his loyalty to her. Not in the way her father and Nigel Sommersby had done.

It occurred to her now, as she perched on a large stone there where she could watch the sea, that it was not until she'd come to Beauchamp House that she was able to know what real trust was. She may have been skeptical of the other ladies and their immediate offer of friendship at first, but in the months since they'd arrived here, and perhaps thanks to the events leading up to Ivy's marriage to Lord Kerr, she had come to realize that though their acquaintance might be short their offers of friendship were genuine. She would trust Ivy, Sophia, and Gemma with her life if need be. And though she was not as close to Lady Serena or Lord Kerr, she sensed in them a genuine decency that she hadn't often encountered in her relations with the *ton*.

The Duke of Maitland? Well, her feelings regarding him were more complicated. The one time in her life she'd had the courage to ask for what she wanted, he'd rejected her. And that still stung. She'd thought perhaps that taking someone like him—someone she liked and chose for herself—to bed would exorcise the demons of her encounter with Sommersby all those years ago. She would have given her virginity, of course, but she had thought the price worth it if she could replace the memory of Nigel Sommersby's degrading advances with more pleasant ones. Because despite the fact that he would never be able to compete with her intellectually, Maitland was a decent man. And he would never—she knew this instinctively about him—take from her that which she did not want to give.

Unbidden, her mind recalled the feel of his taut, muscular body covering hers on the library floor. Despite her genuine fear at being shot at, her heightened senses had seemed to revel in the weight of him. In the warmth and masculine scent of his skin. Even as she listened for another shot, some part of her had yearned for him to bend his head just the tiniest bit forward and take her mouth with his. She closed her eyes at the memory, remembering that sense of urgency as the brisk wind whirled around her.

"The tide is coming in."

As if she'd conjured him from memory, Maitland's voice broke into her thoughts, making her jump.

He squinted against the brightness of the weak sun on the sea, and she could not guess what he might be thinking. Not that she ever could. Reading faces was far more difficult for her than reading equations.

Uninvited, he dropped down onto the beach beside her rock, and stared out at the churning water for a moment. She was keenly aware of him there next to her. Especially given where her thoughts had just been.

"Quill and I used to spend nearly every summer day at this spot," he said easily. "Playing at pirates and sailors. Whatever make-believe game that might whisk us away for a while. Away from responsibilities and the demands of our parents. Away from worries."

She tried to imagine him as a boy, and had little trouble conjuring a tow-headed child, a little tall for his age, with fine almost girlish features. Funny how such a pretty man might yet be the picture of masculine strength.

"It's a good place for thinking, too," he continued, never turning to look at her. "I have an idea of what you might be thinking about."

She felt her cheeks heat at his words. She doubted very much he would guess the direction of her thoughts. At least, she hoped he could not.

"I apologize for being so hard on you earlier," he said. This time he did turn to look at her. His blue eyes were bright with some emotion she could not name. She allowed herself to sneak a look at them before she looked away, her heart pounding at the connection, almost as if they'd touched hands rather than gazes. "It's just that I . . ." He paused, as if searching for the right word.

"I don't like the idea of a connection between you and him," he admitted, looking away from her again. "And my imagination is quite adept at conjuring reasons why you might wish him dead. None of them particularly palatable."

She wasn't sure what he meant by that—one didn't eat reasons, after all.

"Why should that bother you?" she asked instead, focusing on the part of his confession she did comprehend. "That we knew one another before, Sommersby and me?" She did not speak of what he might imagine her reasons for wanting to kill her former friend. That was too tender a subject.

At her question, Maitland stared at her for a moment and then burst out laughing. "You really are the most fascinating lady," he said softly.

Her stomach gave a flip at his words. It wasn't so much what he said—she knew she was not fascinating, unless one were considering her mathematical and ciphering abilities—but how he said it.

Like an endearment.

Still, the memory of Sommersby's death lingered. And she suddenly felt the need to tell him just why she had reason to stab her oldest friend, innocent of the crime though she might be.

"He tried to force me," she said in a low voice. So low she could barely hear herself over the wind.

But Maitland had heard her. She could sense it in how utterly still his normally active countenance grew. In how his hand, which had been in the process of thrusting itself through his windblown hair, halted there atop his head as if he were a debutante striking an attitude: Arrested Gentleman.

Then, everything woke up again. The wind continued to blow, and Maitland dropped his hand to rest, fist clenched, on his muscular thigh.

He muttered a very foul word, one that Daphne had only ever heard stable hands utter. And that only when they thought she was out of earshot.

"When?" he asked, his voice vibrating with some emotion she could not name.

"It was years ago," she said, feeling strangely relieved to have told him. No, she corrected. Not strange at all, because this was just how she'd felt when she told the other ladies the night before. "Long before I came here. Before he embarked upon his travels."

"I daresay that is *why* he embarked upon his travels," Maitland said in a growl. He seemed to be taking this far more badly than she could have imagined. It had happened to her, after all. Not to him.

But, he had a point. *Had* Sommersby left England because of what had happened between them? She remembered shouting that night, after her maid had saved her by arriving unexpectedly to stoke her fire for the night, sending Sommersby rushing out of her room. It had never occurred to her that the girl would have told someone. Daphne certainly hadn't. And yet, Sommersby had been gone the next morning.

"Perhaps," she admitted. "He was gone the next morning, so it's a possibility."

"You told your father, of course?" Maitland asked, though it didn't sound like a question.

"Certainly not," Daphne said, aghast at the idea. "He would have ordered Nigel's father to leave, too. And I was at a critical stage in my studies. Besides, the son was gone the next morning. There was no need to tell Papa."

She didn't say that her father would likely have placed the blame upon her instead of on Nigel Sommersby. Oh, he would have told both Sommersbys to leave immediately, since he'd been looking for a reason to be rid of the tutor and his son for years. But once they were gone he'd have found a way to use the incident as a means to force Daphne into doing his bidding. He had always done so. Used her own weaknesses against her. To get his own way at her expense.

Maitland cursed again.

"He never came back," Daphne assured him, thinking that his anger was because he perhaps thought it was an ongoing problem. "I hadn't seen him again until yesterday on the path to Little Seaford."

"And he did not . . . succeed in forcing you?" the duke asked, his fists still clenched where they rested on his thighs. "I believe your words were that he 'tried to force you'?"

"No, he only touched me a bit," she said, though she knew that made it sound much less traumatic than it had been. She swallowed, remembering his hot breath on her face, his hand rucking up her skirts. She must have made some noise, because Maitland turned to her and placed a comforting hand on her arm. Only that, his hand. But it did what he'd no doubt intended.

Though she was not generally a demonstrative person, she felt compelled to place her hand over his. Seeking comfort from the feel of his warm skin beneath her fingertips.

"So, you see," she said, calmer now, "I did have reason to want him dead. Or at the very least to harm him. But you know I did not. We were together when we found him. As you told the magistrate."

He was quiet for a minute. So long that Daphne wondered if he'd fallen asleep, though a peek told her his eyes were open.

"The devil of it is, Daphne," he finally said stroking his thumb rhythmically over her arm, "I might know you didn't do it, and the others at Beauchamp House might believe us both, but there is no guarantee Northman will do so. You admitted to him that you had reason to want the blackguard to die, and he was found in your residence. In Northman's position, I might find myself considering you a suspect."

"But you aren't in Northman's position," Daphne said, frowning. "And you don't consider me a suspect."

"That is right," he agreed. "Which means we need to find out who actually murdered Sommersby. Because if we do not, Northman might just decide to prosecute you for it."

Chapter 5

The next morning, Maitland was still thinking about his conversation with Daphne as he made his way downstairs for breakfast.

He wasn't quite sure what to do with what she had told him about Nigel Sommersby's attack on her. What could be done, after all? The man was dead, and it wasn't as if Maitland had any claim on Daphne beyond that of friendship. The knowledge had put her awkward proposition not long after they met into some sort of perspective, however. And he wished he'd known about her past before he'd rejected her with so little finesse. One thing was clear, however. They had to learn who had actually killed Sommersby. Not only because of Northman's suspicions about Daphne, but also because despite what he'd said earlier that day in the heat of the moment, it was all too likely that whoever had killed the man had done so because of the Cameron Cipher.

There were simply too many elements that pointed

in that direction. First that Sommersby and Foster were in the area expressly to search for the cipher. Secondly, that the man had mentioned, and then been found murdered in, the library at Beauchamp House, where Daphne had been told by Lady Celeste the Cameron Cipher was hidden. It was too much of a coincidence that the man would be killed while in the midst of searching for the thing.

Was it also coincidence that had Foster away on the night of Sommersby's murder visiting friends whose existence no one could verify? The innkeeper had seemed to think Foster would return, but what if he'd simply disguised his flight by inventing the story of a quick journey? He'd just stepped onto the first-floor landing, when Serena came hurrying toward him, her familiar countenance flushed with anxiety.

"What is it?" he asked his sister, knowing she didn't upset easily. Especially not after the hard life she'd lived with her now mercifully dead husband. "Is Northman back?"

A gasp sounded behind him, and he turned to see Daphne, looking pale. "Is he here to arrest me?" Clearly she was more worried about the magistrate's suspicions than she'd earlier let on.

"No, no," Serena assured her with a strained smile. "I'm afraid it's a different visitor, though. And I am not sure whether it will be a happy one for you."

Maitland's brows drew together. It was likely Sommersby's father. Though how he could have gotten here so quickly was a mystery. Still, when family was involved, speed was possible.

"Who is it?" Daphne asked, frowning.

Serena bit her lip. "I'm afraid it's your father, dear. And he does not appear to be in the best of tempers."

This didn't lighten the other lady's expression. If anything, she looked even more troubled.

"What can he be doing here? I expressly told him that I was not to be disturbed during my time here at Beauchamp House." She rushed forward, leaving the siblings to trail after her as she headed for the drawing room. "If he has need of funds then he will simply have to win it at the tables himself."

Maitland exchanged a look with his sister as they followed the somewhat windblown Daphne. Surely she hadn't meant that *she* had won money for her father in the past. Though God knew she was a gifted card player. She showed no particular fondness for whist as a general rule, but it had only taken a few hands with her to know she possessed exceptional skill there. Likely because of her extraordinary memory.

It might have been more discreet for him to leave her to speak to her father alone, but Maitland found himself pushing past Serena, who seemed reluctant to go back into the drawing room where Daphne and her father were closeted.

"There you are, my dear," said the Earl of Forsyth with a beaming smile that didn't quite reach his eyes.

Maitland saw at once that Daphne favored him. Her green eyes were the same shade as his, though there were lines of dissipation bracketing the earl's. And though his expertly cropped blond hair was shot through with silver, what remained of its original color was the same shade as hers. But whereas Daphne's gaze was focused off to the left of whomever she conversed with, like a bird hovering just over a branch, Forsyth's speared one with cold calculation. As he did to Daphne now.

"You are looking well, Daphne," the earl continued, stepping forward to embrace his daughter, who looked as uncomfortable with the contact as Maitland had ever seen her. "The sea air agrees with you. As I knew it would."

"The sea is very beautiful," Daphne replied woodenly. "Why are you here, Father?"

"Is that any way to greet your Papa?" the earl chided, stepping back from her and wandering farther into the room, standing to stare out at the gardens below through the window. "I've traveled all the way from London to see you. And this lovely estate. I must admit that when I first learned of your inheritance, I thought it was all some sort of trick. But you would have your own way and leave the loving bosom of your family no matter what I said. Now that I'm here, though, and see it in person, I must admit that it's a lovely spot. And your chaperone, Lady Serena, is quite beautiful, isn't she? A widow, I take it?"

His jaw clenched at the man's mention of Serena, and Maitland thought perhaps it was time to announce himself. Daphne seemed not to realize he'd followed her in, and the earl was too busy waxing rhapsodic over the beauties of Beauchamp House.

"I don't believe we've met, Forsyth," he said forcefully, stepping up to stand side by side with Daphne. He gave a slight bow, perhaps not quite as deep as was warranted, but not caring. "The Duke of Maitland. I am a friend of your daughter's, you might say."

What he meant by that last, he could not say, but the man made every bit of protective instinct within him go on the alert. He was her father, but all the same Maitland knew that Daphne was no safer with him than she would have been with Sommersby if he still lived.

At the sound of the duke's voice, Lord Forsyth turned with almost comical haste from the window and stared. For the barest flicker, he looked angry. Well, if he were upset at the knowledge that his daughter was not without friends, then he would simply have to swallow it. Because Maitland was damned if he'd leave her alone with the fellow.

"Duke," Lord Forsyth said with a tilt of his head, "I am pleased to make your acquaintance. I was a friend of your father's, and had little notion I'd be meeting you here. He was a good man, your father."

His father had been nothing of the sort, but Maitland was hardly going to discuss it with Forsyth.

"I am here visiting my sister, Lady Serena," Maitland said coolly, letting the other man know in tone rather than words that he had not appreciated the older man's speculative words about her earlier. "And of course my cousin, Kerr. He only recently married another of the heiresses here, and resides here with her."

Forsyth's eyes narrowed at the implication that Daphne was well protected should her father wish to cause trouble. At least that was the message Maitland was endeavoring to send. And by the looks of it, Forsyth read him loud and clear.

"Capital, capital," the earl said with false cheer. "A merry party you must all make here. I had no idea you were in such fine company here, Daphne. No notion at all."

"Because we have not spoken since I left," Daphne

said, looking from her father to Maitland then back again, as if wondering what went on between them. "And now, father, I really must ask you to leave. I have a great deal of work to do and . . ."

"Don't be absurd, Daphne," her father said with a shake of his head. "I only just arrived. And there is something very important I must speak to you about." He turned to Maitland with a raised brow. "I'm sure you'll excuse us, Duke. I'm afraid what I need to tell my daughter is private family business."

Maitland was opening his mouth to tell the man he would leave Daphne alone with him when hell froze over, when Daphne did it for him.

"Maitland stays," she said, reaching out to grasp him by the arm. It was as much of a cry for help as he'd ever thought he'd see from her. Wordlessly, he slipped her arm into his, as if they were about to promenade round the room. He covered her hand with his, keenly aware of the thread of tension in her.

Once more, the earl's eyes narrowed, and he turned an assessing gaze on Maitland, perhaps realizing for the first time the threat coming at him from that direction.

His jaw clenched, Forsyth said grimly, "Very well. If you wish your *friend* to witness our dirty linen, so be it."

As if needing to be in motion in order to speak, the earl began to pace the area between the window and the fireplace. "You know, Daphne, you left me without any obvious means of recouping what I lost from years of paying that tutor of yours, old man Sommersby."

"You agreed to pay him," Daphne said tightly. "After I threatened to expose . . ."

Hastily, Forsyth continued, "And I am currently in

need of funds. As such, I must insist you return to London with me for the time being and meet a particular gentleman who has expressed interest in marrying you. Though his birth is not as high as yours, he's quite wealthy and will make you a good husband, I trust. He's assured me he has no concern about your odd ways, if you're as beautiful as your portrait."

Before Maitland could burst out with the string of invectives the other man's pronouncement inspired in him, Daphne said, "I cannot marry this person. I've never even met him. You promised me that I would not have to marry someone for money as long as I won enough at the tables. I did so. You promised me, father."

"I never actually promised, Daphne." Forsyth said with a shake of his head. "If you chose to interpret it as such, that is not my fault. Now, go pack your things."

Daphne's hand on Maitland's arm gripped him tightly. And before he even knew what he was doing, he said, "I'm afraid that's impossible, Forsyth. Daphne is staying here."

"I don't know who you think you are, Maitland," said the earl through clenched teeth, "but I am her father, and I am well within my rights to take her back to London. Now, kindly take your hands off of her and let her go pack."

"It might once have been your right, Forsyth," Maitland said coldly, "but Lady Daphne is my betrothed now and as such, she will remain here. With me."

"Maitland, what are you . . . ?" Daphne could barely articulate the question she was so flummoxed. Why on earth would he say such a thing?

"Hush, dearest," he said in a chiding tone, while his hand that covered hers squeezed in some sort of signal. "I know we did not wish to make our betrothal public yet, but you must admit that your father has a right to know. Especially in light of his reasons for coming here."

Which gave Daphne pause. She might be of age, but he was still her father, and could if he so chose remove her from Beauchamp House and force her to marry this fellow he had waiting in London. It had happened twice before, that he'd tried to force her into matrimony with some wealthy man with no more sense than hair. She'd thought that by leaving him with the small fortune she'd managed to win at the tables before she left to the coast, she would be safe from his importuning for a while. But clearly, she'd underestimated the amount of time it would take him to blow through twenty thousand pounds.

Glancing at her father's face now, she saw that he was calculating how he might squeeze as much or more money from Maitland than he'd have gotten from the prospective suitor in London. His next words told her she was right.

"What a charming surprise," said the Earl of Forsyth rushing forward to kiss her on the cheek and pound Maitland on the shoulder.

"I should have guessed it as soon as you entered the room together," he continued, beaming at them. "It was as plain as the nose on your face."

Daphne couldn't help reaching up to touch her nose. She'd always rather liked it. But, there was no accounting for taste.

"So," Maitland was saying, "you can understand why I should not wish her to go back to London with you. Aside from the fact that she truly does have work to do here, I shouldn't want her to catch someone else's eye while she's in town. You understand, of course."

Except that her work would need to be put aside for the time being because she needed to find out who had killed Sommersby, Daphne thought. Which reminded her, she'd not told her father about that.

"Of course, my boy, of course," Forsyth said jovially. "And I suppose you wish to be married just as soon as the banns are read? She's not getting any younger, is she, eh?"

"I'm only one and twenty, Father," Daphne said defensively. "Besides which, I can marry at any age. What's that to say to anything?"

"And I would marry you at any age, my dear," Maitland said in a soothing tone. "Perhaps you can leave me alone with your father for a bit so that we can discuss the business details. Marriage settlements and the like."

"But we aren't act—"

To her shock, Maitland stopped her words with a quick kiss. In a low voice, he whispered, "Stop talking. Trust me."

Too startled to gainsay him, she nodded, and with one last glance at her father, she hurried from the room, shutting the door firmly behind her.

Once they were alone, Maitland turned back to Lord Forsyth. "Let us speak plainly, Forsyth."

"By all means," said the earl, indicating with a flourish of his hand that Maitland could have a seat if he wished. A gesture the duke found amusing considering the man had only just entered the room for the first time a little over half an hour ago. "I cannot say I understand what reason you might have to want my daughter, considering she has only the small marriage portion left to her by her mother's side of the family, but I daresay you wish to keep Beauchamp House in the family."

Could the man really have no notion of just how beautiful and intriguing his own daughter was? Maitland had thought the man was more clever than that. Clearly he was wrong.

As if reading his thoughts, the older man waved a hand in the air. "Oh, I know she's lovely enough. But she's got no conversation to speak of. Unless one wishes to discuss maths all the day long. Or worse, to be told to one's face the innumerable ways you fall short. It's a high price to pay for a bit of skirt, which I should know since her mother was just the same way, though she brought me enough of a dowry that I was able to overlook her strange ways."

Disgusted at the man's callousness, Maitland bit back a sharp retort. "Let's just get down to business shall we? How much to make you leave for London on the next mail coach?"

"How eager you are to get me away from her," Forsyth murmured, his eyes searching. "One would almost think you didn't wish to know your future bride's family. What if I have a wish to remain here for a little while? To meet my daughter's new friends? Or would that put a crimp in your plans, Duke? Are you enjoying the benefit of her favors before the banns are called? If that's the case, then I shall expect to be compensated."

"Thus making you your daughter's panderer," Maitland spat out. "I thought it was impossible for you to fall in my estimation but I see now I was mistaken. Though I suppose I should not be surprised given how little you did to protect her from Sommersby."

At the mention of Sommersby, Forsyth's anger turned to puzzlement. "What has the old tutor to do with anything? She had no need of protection from him. If anything, it was the other way round. I thought she'd exhaust him with how she demanded more and more lessons from him."

"Not the elder Mr. Sommersby," Maitland said with a shake of his head. "The younger. Nigel Sommersby."

Forsyth rolled his eyes. "There was nothing to protect her from there either. He was a weakling. Barely strong enough to lift his boots. If you're telling me he posed some sort of threat to her, you're sadly mistaken. He was enamored of the chit, of course. But he left when she was fifteen. There was nothing between them."

"Then you will perhaps be interested to know he was found murdered in this house night before last," Maitland said coldly. He wasn't sure why he wished to see the earl's response to the news that Sommersby the younger was dead. Perhaps it was the fact that Daphne's father had shown up unexpectedly on their doorstep so soon after Sommersby's death. Or maybe it was because he wished to be the one to tell him that the fellow had attempted to rape her and he'd done nothing to stop it. Or avenge it.

That, however, was Daphne's secret to divulge, much as he'd like to cram the news down her father's throat.

Forsyth's response to the news of Sommersby's murder, however, was all that Maitland could have wished.

"Nigel Sommersby?" the older man sputtered. "Dead?" Gaping, he looked as if he would collapse, but in a show of determination, he soon recovered his composure.

"What was he doing here of all places?" he continued, his face a mask of mild interest. "And what sort of protection are you offering my daughter if you would allow a man to be murdered beneath the very same roof where she sleeps? I cannot like it, Duke. I cannot like it at all."

It was somewhat reassuring to see Forsyth react like a father—even as tepid as his indignation was. Of course, he ruined the effect with his next words. "Perhaps I should remain here for the time being. Just to ensure her safety, you understand?"

Or to use as an excuse to extort more money from his supposed future son-in-law, Maitland thought wryly. He had to give it to the earl, he was up to every rig.

"I do not think that will be necessary," he assured Forsyth. "I simply thought you might wish to know, given that the man once resided in your London residence. I also thought you might know how we might contact the elder Mr. Sommersby. He will wish to know at once what's happened."

Daphne might know the fellow's direction, but Maitland would spare her the necessity of contacting him if he could.

"It isn't as if I spend time with these men, for heaven's sake," Forsyth protested. "We barely spoke. The tutor was there to perform a service. And his son was of no consequence to me. As for the whereabouts of the elder Sommersby, I have no idea. Once he left the house without notice, I never heard from him again."

"Without notice?" Maitland was startled despite himself.

Forsyth shrugged. "It was of no matter. Between you and me, I was glad he was gone so I no longer had to pay him."

Which didn't surprise Maitland in the slightest.

"It was Daphne who was overset by it. And I can't say I blame the gel," Forsyth continued, "for she spent nearly all her time with the man for years. Excepting of course those occasional evenings out when I encouraged her to accompany me. She was far too good at the tables to leave at home, you understand?"

Maitland would have liked to speak a few home truths to Daphne's father about that, but he knew it was no use. Men like Forsyth were unrepentant. Maitland knew that well enough from dealing with his own father.

He ignored the question and asked one of his own. "The man simply packed his bags and left without telling anyone where he'd gone?"

"That's the long and short of it," Forsyth agreed. "I don't know if my daughter's strange ways got to him or if he found a better position or what. But he left, and there was no way to know where he'd gone."

Daphne hadn't mentioned any of this. Perhaps she knew more about the tutor's disappearance than her father did. He would ask at the next opportunity.

"Is she upset by it, the death of Nigel Sommersby?" Forsyth asked, looking troubled for the first time since Maitland had met him. At this rate, Maitland didn't know if the man was coming or going. "I don't think she was fond of him in the same way he was fond of her, if you get my meaning, but they were friends, I suppose. It can't have been easy to know he died here while pursuing her."

"Pursuing her?" Maitland echoed.

"That has to be why the fellow was here, after all." Forsyth shrugged. "He must have got wind of Daphne's inheritance somehow and come to ingratiate himself with her."

Just as *you* have done, Maitland thought, scowling.

Able to stand no more of the earl's scheming, he clapped the other man on the back. "Let's discuss the marriage settlements now. Of course, I will be more than happy to give you something to tide you over until the marriage."

Chapter 6

"Maitland just announced our betrothal to my father," Daphne announced baldly as soon as she stepped into the library, where the other three heiresses were busy searching every nook and cranny for the Cameron Cipher. "And I let him!"

Ivy spoke first, leaping from her kneeling position before the volumes of Greek poetry—perhaps she wasn't looking for the cipher after all?—and hurrying to take Daphne's hands in hers. "My dear, this is wonderful news! If you only knew how much we've all been hoping this would happen."

"He's been smitten with you from the moment he first laid eyes on you," Sophia agreed, her skirts whispering over the carpet as she moved to join them.

"He's no fool," Gemma agreed. "Any man with sense would wish to stake his claim before some other chap entered the picture. I'm only surprised it took him this long."

They must have lost their minds, Daphne thought

shaking her head. "I do not know what you have been conjuring amongst yourselves," she said hastily, "but this was most assuredly *not* something I was anticipating. And Maitland certainly did not speak to me about the matter before he told my father."

She suddenly felt weak in the knees and collapsed into a nearby overstuffed chair. "Papa was attempting to whisk me back to London, you see. And though I thought he'd given up the notion of selling me off to the highest bidder, it would seem that my surmise was premature. He has some plump-pocketed cit eagerly awaiting my arrival so that he can marry me with my father's blessing."

All the pleasure in the other ladies' expressions turned to horror. "Oh, Daphne," Ivy said. "I suspected your relationship with your father was not a good one, but I had no idea that he was this awful."

"It is worse than awful," Daphne said with a sigh. "Things were different when my mother was alive. At least what I can remember of her. She was clever like me. And was always encouraging me to learn more. I think Papa would have paid me more attention if I'd been a boy. As it was, he didn't notice me until long after Mama had died. But from the moment he realized my skill with numbers and memory might be used to his own advantage, he's used me as his very own prize horse, only instead of races, he's had me playing whist in drawing rooms all over the *ton*."

"But he must have had some care for your education," Ivy said with a frown. "After all, he hired your tutor, Mr. Sommersby, did he not?"

Daphne wished that were true. That her father had

been supportive of her activities of the mind, as Ivy's had been. And no doubt Sophia's and Gemma's had done. "I blackmailed him into hiring on Mr. Sommersby," she said wearily. "I told him that if he did not hire me a competent tutor from whom I might learn the level of mathematics suited to my superior intellect, that I would expose his schemes to the *ton*. The only thing Father values more than a night at the tables is his social standing. Despite the fact that he owed money to almost every peer in the realm, he was still received in all the best houses, and did not relish being exposed as the sort of man who would use his own daughter for profit."

"And he did as you demanded?" Sophia asked, clearly impressed with Daphne's maneuver.

"He did," Daphne said with a nod. "And he did not insist that I accompany him to card parties so frequently after that. It is one thing for a father to trade upon his daughter's virtue in exchange for marriage settlements, but it's quite another to openly be known to take her winnings at cards. So long as there was the pretense that he was using his own funds, his friends overlooked the irregularity of it. But a public accusation? Well, that would have offended his cronies' delicate sensibilities."

"And I suppose when you left for Beauchamp House your father was left without a ready means of earning money?" Ivy asked.

None of the ladies seemed to question the fact that despite his earldom Lord Forsyth was frequently pockets to let. It was not uncommon among peers of the realm for all of their funds to be tied up in their country estates. Thus, they lived on credit and were frequently cash poor. Lord Forsyth, Daphne knew, was more in need of blunt than most since he spent whatever he received from the estate at the gaming tables.

"Yes," Daphne said. "Though I left him with tens of thousands of pounds, thinking it would last him the year, he's run through it only three months in."

"So when he announced he wanted you back in London, Maitland told him you were already betrothed?" Sophia asked, "I must say, that's quite the most romantic thing I've ever heard. He's your knight in shining armor."

"But I didn't need a knight," Daphne protested. "I've dealt with my father's ridiculous demands for years now. And I might have done so again, if only Maitland hadn't stepped in. Now that Papa thinks he's got his hooks into a wealthy duke, he'll never give up. I daresay when Maitland and I attempt to dissolve this farce of a betrothal, Papa will sue him for breach of contract. He is just that sort of man!"

Daphne fought the urge to push away from where her friends were crowded around her and move to the other side of the room, where she might rearrange the shelves devoted to novels. (They were at present arranged alphabetically by author, but she thought perhaps they might work better organized first by publisher, then by author, then by title. Just pondering the possibilities made her feel calmer.)

"Maitland won't give a damn about that," said Lord Kerr who had slipped in a few moments earlier. "He obviously thought you needed his protection and so offered it. He has armies of solicitors. Enough to stall your father's breach of contract suit in the courts for decades. Though hopefully it will not come to that."

"I don't see how it cannot," Daphne argued, all the calm she'd gained from her organizational thoughts evaporating with Lord Kerr's observation. She did not wish Maitland to be forced to fight her father in court. If he'd simply stayed out of it, none of this would be an issue. "We cannot remain betrothed. I do not wish to marry. Especially since as soon as I reach my majority I will be able to escape my father's influence forever."

"But Maitland is hardly cut from the same cloth as your father," Ivy soothed. And when Daphne started to argue, she held up a hand. "I know, I know. Marriage can be just as much of a prison as any gaol. But perhaps we needn't solve all of these problems today? After all, it's been a busy few days. What with finding Mr. Nigel Sommersby in the secret room, then your being questioned none-too-gently by Squire Northman, and now your father's arrival. Any of these things alone would be enough to send the most sensible lady into a decline."

"Are you saying I am not strong enough to deal with all of this?" Daphne asked, not knowing whether to be insulted or relieved to be let off the hook.

"I most certainly am not," Ivy said, patting her on the arm. "But I am saying that we can perhaps deal with these issues one at a time. And I mean 'we'—you are not alone anymore, Daphne. You have friends who are willing to help you now."

"But I am quite able to take care of myself," Daphne protested.

"Of course you are, dear," Sophia said with a gentle smile. "But perhaps you misunderstood Ivy. What she means to say is, you have no choice in the matter. Our help is not negotiable. That's what friendship is all about."

Daphne was silent for a moment, processing what Sophia had just said.

She'd never had a true friend before, it was true. Many acquaintances, but aside from Nigel—and look what a bounder he'd turned out to be—she'd not had anyone to rely upon besides herself. Perhaps it was time she accepted a bit of help here and there. Just to see how it felt.

"Very well," Daphne said. "It would appear I have no choice." Though she could hear the hint of pride in her voice. Curious.

"If you are all finished giving Daphne the rules of friendship," she heard Maitland say from behind her, "then I would greatly appreciate it if you would give us the room."

Turning, she saw that he appeared none the worse for wear despite what must have been a most trying conversation with her father. She might have known Maitland would emerge unscathed from such a meeting.

Without protest, her newly sworn friends all slipped away from her and out the door, closing it behind them while Maitland moved to sit on the edge of the library table just across from her chair. So close he was able to cross his booted feet only inches from where her skirts rested just above the thick Aubusson carpet.

"Your father is quite an interesting man," he said without preamble. "I had thought perhaps the tales I'd heard about him in town were exaggerated. But only a few minutes in his company was enough to tell me they were likely toned down for credibility's sake. Any description of him as he is would be dismissed as utterly outlandish."

"Interesting is one way of describing him," Daphne said, not knowing whether she should apologize for her father's behavior or scold Maitland for telling the lie to Lord Forsyth that would surely cost him both money and a bit of his reputation. "Greedy is another, though not one I would use in polite company. At least he's asked me not to on more than one occasion."

Maitland laughed softly. "I'll wager he did not like having his own daughter tell the truth about him amongst the tea things after dinner."

"It was actually at Lady Beresford's dining table," Daphne said with a frown. "Though you are correct that he did not like it. Rather the opposite, in fact. I thought perhaps he would strike me when he scolded me later. One is never quite sure, you know, if verbal violence will turn to physical. But he never did."

The duke's amusement evaporated at that, and when Daphne dared to look at his face, his mouth was tight. "I only did it that once, you understand."

"I am not angry with you, Daphne," he said moving to kneel before her, which should have made her uncomfortable, but instead made her heart beat faster. "I am angry with him. For making you feel threatened. For using you to make money because he was too damned lousy with a hand of cards to make it for himself. But I am most enraged at him because he forced you to blackmail him in order to protect yourself from being sold like a brood mare to the highest bidder."

She was silent. Her father had done all of those things. And she was angry about them. But the notion that someone would feel angry on her behalf was so foreign she couldn't quite comprehend it.

"Is that why you told him we were betrothed?" she asked, wondering if those reasons he'd just named added up to his declaration before Lord Forsyth. "Because you were angry with him and wanted to thwart him?"

He dipped his head so that she had no choice but to look at him. As she'd noticed before, eye contact with Maitland did not fill her with the kind of anxiety as it did with other people. Still, her heart pounded harder.

"I told him we were betrothed," Maitland said in a low voice that vibrated along her spine like a struck tuning fork, "because I wanted to."

She blinked at that. Because he wanted to? But why?

As if he'd spoken the questions aloud, he continued. "Because I couldn't bear the thought of some rich social climber with piles of money but no appreciation for how special you are to have you."

She didn't know what to say.

And didn't need to, because he said finally, "I did it because I wanted you for myself, Daphne. I wanted you to be mine."

As he spoke, he moved his face closer to hers. So close that by the last word, she felt his breath on her lips. And a whisper of anticipation ran through her.

Just before he kissed her.

It wasn't as if Maitland had awoken that morning with the notion of proposing to Daphne before the day was through.

He'd actually been awakened by his nephew Jeremy— who had escaped his nanny's leash—jumping on the bed beside him asking if he'd come play soldiers with him. But almost as soon as he'd opened his eyes, the duke had recalled the moment when he'd seen Nigel Sommersby's dead body on the floor of the secret room.

Reluctantly, he'd told Jem he would come visit him in the nursery later, and dressed to go downstairs. If he was going to ensure that Northman's pursuit of Daphne as a suspect in Sommersby's murder went nowhere, he would need to get to work at once finding an alternative theory of the crime.

As it was, he'd been thrust almost immediately into that awful scene where Lord Forsyth had tried to bully his own daughter into giving up her inheritance at Beauchamp House and return to London with him.

Not mind you, so that she could return to the loving bosom of her family, but instead so that she might marry some strange fellow with little more to recommend him than the fact that he was possessed of enough funds to give Forsyth enough to pay off his debts and live in the style to which he'd become accustomed. Ironically, Daphne's father had confided all this to Maitland as they'd discussed terms for his own—that is, Maitland's—marriage to Daphne.

All of this was running through his head as he knelt before her in the library, trying to explain his reasons for making that impetuous pronouncement to Lord Forsyth.

But then he'd looked up into her big green eyes and lost all capacity for talk.

Knowing her history now, and wanting to give her comfort, his kiss was gentle.

With just the slightest pressure, he leaned into her.

Closing his eyes, he breathed her in, inhaling the lemony scent of her and the warmth of her skin. Giving himself up to the feel of her.

And when he deepened the kiss, licking at her with the tip of his tongue, she welcomed him in. Opened to him in a way that told him everything he needed to know. And then he was lost to the sensation of the moment. Of knowing just who it was he held against him, just whose lips he kissed.

Daphne, he thought with a flicker of satisfaction, sliding a hand up to cup her face in wonder. Daphne, whom he'd wanted from the moment he saw her. The beautiful, maddening, creature who shocked and amused him at every turn.

Her mouth was hot and soft and sweet, and as their kisses grew more intense—as she slipped her arms around his shoulders to pull him against her—Maitland had to fight his growing need to feel her hands on other parts of him. He'd meant to keep this kiss sweet, chaste even, but with each stroke of her tongue, he was growing more mindless.

He'd only just reversed their positions, settling Daphne in his lap so that he might kiss his way down her neck, when a knock sounded at the library door.

With a jolt, he realized just how close he'd come to taking her here in the library, and reluctantly, pulled back a little. Breathless, he buried his face in her neck, inhaling the sweet scent of her for the barest moment before lifting his head and resting it against the back of the chair. Daphne, who was also out of breath, rested her cheek against his shoulder.

"A moment if you please," he called out loudly, hoping that whoever it was would give it to them.

"Sorry old fellow," came Kerr's voice, sounding amused, "but Mr. Sommersby's friend, Foster has come. And he wishes to speak with Daphne. You won't be disturbed further. I just wished to let you know he was here." A sound that was suspiciously like laughter disguised as a cough followed. Then silence.

Daphne flattened her palm against where his heart was still pounding. "I knew I had chosen wisely," she said with the tone of one who had been proved right. "We are very compatible. Amorously speaking, I mean."

He huffed out a laugh. "My apologies for denying you, madam. I see now I was harming us both by refusing your offer the first time."

It felt as if decades had passed since that first awkward suggestion she'd made that they become lovers. He hadn't wanted her any less then. He saw now that his rejection had sprung from shock more than anything else. And bruised pride. Clearly it took him some time to get used to the force of nature that was Lady Daphne Forsyth.

"I accept your apology," she said regally. Then, sobering, she said, "I suppose we cannot stay here forever."

"I'm afraid not," he said, kissing the top of her head.

Reluctantly, she climbed off his lap, and righted her skirts. Her hair, he noted, was mussed from his hands. But he said nothing. In some primitive part of him, he liked that she looked as if she'd just been thoroughly kissed.

Straightening his own cuffs, he ran a hand through his own no doubt disordered hair.

When they were as tidy as they could get given the lack of professional assistance, he offered her his arm, and they left the sanctuary of the library and made their way to the drawing room.

Still a bit breathless from her interlude with Maitland, Daphne walked into the drawing room on his arm not knowing what to expect from Sommersby's traveling companion. Having only met him for those few minutes three days ago, she'd had little time to assess his emotional state. Though he'd seemed civil enough. If he was like other men, he was likely having a glass of brandy while he waited.

Mr. Ian Foster, however, was doing no such thing.

Instead he was pacing before the low fire, and muttering under his breath. Lord Kerr and Ivy stood together by the window and looked relieved when Daphne and Maitland walked in.

Foster, on the other hand looked aggrieved. "I was beginning to think you had fled the country, Lady Daphne." While his words might have been considered a jest from some men, in this one, they were deadly serious.

"Of course, I did not, Mr. Foster," she said, puzzled at his suggestion. "Why would I do such a thing?"

She felt Maitland's comforting hand on her lower back and was grateful for it. Something about Foster's demeanor made her nervous.

"Perhaps you'd best tell us why you're here," the duke said once Daphne had taken a seat on the settee. He took up a perch on the arm, a protective hand on her shoulder as if reminding her he was here if she needed him.

"Yes, do, Mr. Foster," said Sophia, who was seated with Gemma near the windows overlooking the garden. "He wouldn't tell us a thing until you got here," she said to the newcomers with a speaking look.

"I should think that was obvious," Foster said with a scowl. "My friend was found dead in this house three nights ago. And no one saw fit to inform me of that fact. I had to learn of it from the innkeeper when I returned from Pevensey. Surely it would not have been too much trouble to send a messenger for me?"

"Oh, I do apologize, Mr. Foster," Daphne said, knowing that in his situation she would be overset, too. "I had supposed that Squire Northman would do so, since he is the magistrate and was here to question us. And then . . . well, as you can imagine things have been rather at sixes and sevens, so we must have overlooked you."

"Well, Squire Northman did not, in fact, send for me," Foster continued, his face still red with pique.

"Lady Daphne has apologized, Foster," said Maitland firmly. "And we are all sorry for your loss. But I believe some of the blame for this must rest on you. It's not as if you left details of your direction with anyone. We will, of course, do what we can to assist the magistrate in his investigation of the murder. But I believe that is all we can do. Now, if you will excuse us, Lady Daphne has had a trying time as you can well imagine, and. . . ."

"I wish to see the room where he was found," Foster interrupted, his fists clenched at his sides. "I know he was here searching for the Cameron Cipher that night, and I wish to see the room where he was murdered.

I daresay one of you might have done the deed because he found it when you yourselves could not."

"Of course, we didn't kill him," Daphne said in an aggrieved tone before anyone else could speak. "And though I know he was your friend, so it might pain you to hear it, but Mr. Sommersby was not nearly as clever as he thought he was. Or really, as any of us gathered in this room. It's true he was no simpleton, but he was hardly the sort of mind capable of finding the Cameron Cipher. And even if by some miracle he did find the cipher, it would have been useless to him. He was terrible at unraveling ciphers. Always was."

Then, thinking to soften her words, she added, "Though he was quite good at geography, if that's any consolation."

Foster gaped.

Thinking that his silence denoted agreement, Daphne continued, "Perhaps you didn't know, but someone shot at the Duke of Maitland and myself the night Sommersby was killed. Perhaps the same person who killed him. I hardly think we would be capable of shooting at ourselves."

By this time, however, Foster had regained some of his composure. "He told me you had reason to wish him dead, Lady Daphne. So do not think to draw suspicion away from yourself with this tale of being shot at. If you are as clever as you say you are, then you would doubtless be smart enough to hire someone to shoot at you."

"You are offensive, sir," Maitland said coldly, his hand hard on her shoulder, which she interpreted to mean she should stop talking. "And I will remind you that you yourself are without anyone to verify where you were the night of your friend's murder. How do we know you weren't simply hiding out here with the intention of killing him while everyone thought you were out of town?"

"What is offensive, your grace," said Foster, "is the way you aristocrats stick together. Sommersby warned me it would be this way. That you would do whatever you could to discredit him. I simply didn't guess that it would mean you'd murder him."

"You are overset, Mr. Foster," said Lord Kerr, who had come to stand on Maitland's other side. "Perhaps after you have had time to grieve, you will come to realize how wrong you are. In the meantime, pray accept our condolences for your loss. Mr. Greaves will see you out. I'll be sure to let Squire Northman know you've returned so that he may question you about your whereabouts three nights ago."

And as if he'd been waiting there listening, the butler Greaves appeared and took Ian Foster by the arm and led him from the room.

As soon as the door closed behind them, Maitland turned to Lord Kerr. "What do you mean exposing the ladies to that fellow? Especially after everything that's happened to Daphne. She's had quite enough to upset her for the time being."

"It's hardly Quill's fault, Maitland," said Ivy coming to her husband's defense. "Mr. Foster seemed amiable enough when he arrived. But the longer he waited, the more overset he became. But the time you both arrived, he was showing signs of agitation."

"It was bad of us not to let him know what had happened to Sommersby," Daphne said ruefully. "I didn't

even think of him, though we met him on the trail with
Sommersby."

"None of us did," Maitland reassured her. "But that
still doesn't make his accusations against you appropriate."

"I wonder what he wished to see in the secret
room," Sophia asked, rising to stand before the fire, her
sketchbook in one hand, as if she'd forgotten she had
it with her. "It was almost as if he thought he'd find the
cipher there."

"Well, he'd be out of luck there," Daphne said with a
scowl. After the body had been removed from the inner
chamber, she and Maitland had searched the recess from
floor to ceiling, as well as the small chest that had been
lying open on the floor beside Sommersby's body. But
they'd found nothing. Whoever had killed Sommersby
had likely taken the cipher as well. "We certainly didn't
find it. And not for want of trying."

"Perhaps we weren't looking in the right place," Maitland said thoughtfully.

As if in response, Daphne's stomach growled. Loudly.
Thanks to her father's surprise visit, she'd missed breakfast.

"It's time for luncheon," she said sheepishly. The
events of the morning had given her an appetite.

"Then let's go have luncheon," Maitland said, taking
her hand. "Perhaps some fuel will help us figure out
where the cipher might be."

They were greeted by Serena in the dining room, and
Maitland was reminded that he'd never gotten back to
Jem with the promised game of soldiers. Making a

mental note to see the boy that afternoon, he gave his cousin a questioning glance as she stood behind her chair waiting for the others.

"Greaves told me there was some trouble with Mr. Foster," Serena said with a frown as she took her seat. "I cannot like how many dangerous situations you ladies have found yourselves in since your arrival here. And now a murder in this very house. I cannot think that this was what Aunt Celeste had in mind when she promised you adventures in Beauchamp House."

"Given that Aunt herself requested that Ivy find out who killed her," Kerr said dryly, "I suspect this is exactly what she had in mind, Serena. Though perhaps she did not anticipate a man being stabbed to death in the library. Even so, she was hardly one to wish young ladies to be wrapped in cotton wool. And I think they've handled things admirably."

"Indeed," Maitland agreed, lifting his glass to the table at large. "There's not a heartier group than the one assembled at this table. And I daresay Aunt chose them specifically for their strength."

Serena shook her head in exasperation. "It's all well and good for the two of you to sing their praises. You aren't the one who is supposed to be chaperoning them. And thus far, I've done a poor job of it. First Ivy was compromised into marrying Quill and now you, Maitland, my own brother, have faked a betrothal to Daphne in order to protect her from her father. At this rate, Sophia and Gemma will be embroiled in scandals with the vicar and his curate before the week is out. It's like living in a Sheridan play. With murder."

Maitland wanted to laugh off his sister's worries,

mostly because it was amusing when she laid it all out there like that. But he knew that she took her responsibilities seriously. And that her gratitude to Aunt Celeste for offering her this chance to get away from her drab life in the dower house colored her feelings about the current situation.

But before he could speak up to comfort her, Daphne broke in.

"Lady Serena, I can assure you that there is no need for you to worry so about our reputations. Indeed, Ivy needn't concern you at all now that she's married to Lord Kerr. And my reputation was never that much to begin with."

Serena blinked, as if trying to determine if Daphne was serious.

"But really," Daphne continued, patting her chaperone on the hand, "it is sensible for you to be overset about the murder of Sommersby. We have no notion of who might have done it. And they did shoot at Maitland and me the other night. There's no telling when he will strike next."

Maitland was overcome with a coughing fit as he watched his sister's eyes widen at Daphne's words. So much for comforting her, he thought with an inward sigh. At this rate, Serena would have guards stationed at every door.

But his sister was made of sterner stuff.

"Thank you for validating my fears, Daphne," she said, then with a speaking glance at Kerr and Maitland, she continued, "At least someone in this house doesn't think I'm overstating things when I say that we are all in danger."

Wincing, Maitland gave his sister a nod to indicate she'd made her point. "I apologize for minimizing your worries, Serena. It's only because I don't wish to alarm anyone. And I can assure you that we're safe as houses. In point of fact, I myself had Greaves post extra guards at all the entrances the morning after we found poor Sommersby."

At his words, he saw Serena's shoulders slump with relief. He felt a pang of guilt at not having noticed earlier how much this situation had bothered her.

"Thank you, my dear," she said with a genuine smile. "I might have known you would take charge. You were always ordering things to your liking. Even when you were a boy."

"You're just still angry that I ordered *you* around," Maitland said with a grin.

He had been a bit of a handful as a child. Especially since he had for a few years there taken his father as his role model. And the late duke was hardly the sort to take the feelings of others into consideration when he was making decisions. By the time Maitland had come into the dukedom at sixteen, he'd long since realized that it was far more pleasant to go through life with a smile on one's face than with a cold sneer.

It hadn't endeared him to his father, of course, who saw his son and heir's sunny disposition as a sign of weakness. But it had stood him in good stead. And he'd never inspired the kind of fear and loathing he'd seen enter the eyes of his father's circle as soon as the old duke approached.

"Of course, I am," Serena answered pertly, drawing his attention back to the table. "I was the elder, and you tried to lord your title over me like some sort of crown prince."

"You complain," Kerr said with a laugh, "but you were just as bad. And knew exactly the right place to pinch when we didn't bow to your wishes."

"He's right, Rena," the duke said to his sister with a shrug. "And I was manageable enough so long as I was allowed to visit the stables every day."

"You were fond of horses even as a boy, then?" Daphne asked, her eyes bright with curiosity.

"I wanted to live in the stables," Maitland said, a little wistful for those days before he'd realized the enormity of his position in the world. "Mr. Jacoby, the head groom at the Maitland estate, let me sneak in as much as I wanted until my father discovered it. I thought at one point—I was far too young to realize it was an impossibility—that I would become a groom myself when I was older. But Father quashed that flight of fancy soon enough. Fortunately, I was able to convince him not to take out his anger on Jacoby. But it meant less time among the horses for me."

"But you're able to do so now," Daphne said softly, as if she understood how difficult it had been for him to give up the shelter of the stables and the gentle guidance of Jacoby. Their eyes met and he saw recognition there. And sympathy. "That must be counted as an improvement."

"One of the first things I did when I came into the title was to have the stables fully renovated—father didn't have much use for animals or people. Or at least only so far as he could use them." He didn't say that his father had also neglected the buildings just because

Dalton had cared so much that they were so shabby. He'd been a cruel man, his father. But he liked to think that he'd got his revenge by living well.

"It's the home for elderly horses that I most love about your renovations, though," Serena said with a warm smile. She had been just as hurt by their father's neglect, but she'd never stopped supporting her brother. He was grateful for her, as he was for Quill and his aunt Celeste, who had shaped him into the man he was today.

"What's this?" Daphne looked from one Maitland sibling to the other.

"My cousin has dedicated a special area of his estates to housing elderly or infirm horses, who through no fault of their own find themselves on the way to the . . . er . . ." Maitland watched in amusement as Quill tried to come up with an alternative to the word "slaughterhouse."

"In straightened circumstances," Maitland finished for him. "And they are able to live out their days without fear of the lash or any other sort of cruelty."

"That's the most beautiful thing I've ever heard," Gemma said with a sniff. And as he glanced at the other ladies, Maitland felt himself redden under their scrutiny. Daphne was beaming at him, and he got the feeling she would have launched herself into his arms if there wasn't a tableful of people watching them.

"It's nothing," he protested, suddenly very interested in the pigeon pie before him. "Just a good use for that particular piece of land. That's all."

And that was all he had to say about the matter.

Chapter 7

Maitland and the ladies tried to convince Daphne to rest for a little, given the odd circumstances of the last day, but she steadfastly refused.

"There is too much to be done," she insisted, leading the way to the library. "A man was murdered. And if it was over the cipher, then I want to make certain that we haven't missed something in the secret room."

She was made of stern stuff, his Daphne, the duke thought as he and the others followed her down the hall to the book room.

His Daphne. For the time being at any rate. Until he convinced her to turn this betrothal begun in deceit into a real one.

Which would not be an easy task given what she'd said to her father about her feelings on the matter of matrimony in general. He'd known, because of his sister's horror of a union, that in the eyes of the law men held almost all the power in a marriage. But Daphne's wish for autonomy for the sake of her studies was another layer to the issue he'd not considered. With the wrong man, marriage could mean a total loss of freedom for a woman.

He'd just have to make sure Daphne knew he was the right man.

The library was bright with the early afternoon sun, and while the others wandered in, Maitland stood where Daphne had halted just inside the door.

"I know we were in here this morning," she said with a frown, "but I didn't go back in there." She stared at the now closed portal into the secret room."

They hadn't returned to the little room since Squire Northman had come to look at the crime scene. Despite the man's suspicions that Daphne might have had something to do with the murder, his sense of chivalry had prevented him from forcing her to return to the spot where she'd found the body.

She betrayed her apprehension only with her words. Her spine was straight and though she did not take her eyes off the other side of the room, her stance was one of determination. It took every ounce of self-control to stop himself from pulling her to him in a reassuring hug. Only because he knew her better now was he able to see how much she feared revisiting the scene of Sommersby's death.

He contented himself with a touch of his hand to hers. And to his surprise, she turned her hand over and squeezed, taking comfort from him, though she didn't glance his way.

"You needn't go in now," Maitland said, reluctantly

letting her go, and following her as she made her way to the secret door. "There are enough of us that the room can be easily searched again without your assistance. I daresay it will only fit a few of us at a time anyway. You needn't be one of them."

She'd stopped just before the shelf with the opening mechanism. The books that had been removed by Sommersby still lay where Daphne had begun organizing them last night. "I must go inside," she said, reaching out to depress the latch. "Lady Celeste left the secret of the Cameron Cipher's presence in the library to me. She wanted me to be the one to find it. And I won't let some beastly murderer keep me from fulfilling her wishes. I owe her too much."

As they watched, the bookshelf swung inward, revealing the darkness of the chamber within. Wordlessly, Maitland lit the wick of the lamp they'd left on the table the night before.

"I'm coming with you," he said, even as she stood in the open door. If she heard him, she gave no indication of it, only waited for him to follow her with the lamp.

Perhaps sensing that this was something Daphne did not need witnesses for, the others remained in the library, searching through the books and shelves for any further clues.

Recalling the hook in the wall just inside the doorway Maitland hung the lamp from it, which illuminated the silk hung walls. He hadn't noticed last night, but the chamber was furnished with every bit as much care as the rest of the house. On the floor, where they'd found Sommersby, was a thick carpet, similar to the one in the library itself, covering the wood floor. A portrait hung in a place of pride on the far wall. He had no memory of seeing it the night before. He'd been so focused on the dead man on the floor, the chamber might as well have been empty.

When he moved to look closer, he saw that the likeness was of Charles Edward Stuart, The Young Pretender, also known as the man for whom the Jacobite cause was fought and lost.

It had been over half a century since the 1745 uprising that had left the movement to put Bonnie Prince Charlie on the English throne in tatters. Prominent members of the cause had been put to death for treason.

Aunt Celeste hadn't even been born when the Jacobites were defeated. But that didn't mean she hadn't found something to admire in the movement. Had Aunt Celeste been a Jacobite sympathizer? Or did this décor simply reinforce the fact that the Cameron Cipher had been secreted here? Given his own knowledge of his late aunt, Maitland was inclined to believe it was the latter.

Daphne sat on her haunches, examining the small chest that still lay where Sommersby had dropped it. He watched as she gingerly lifted it from the floor and ran her fingers over the velvet lining. Searching for some other items contained there, no doubt.

Leaving her to it, he moved to the painting and carefully lifted it from the wall. It wasn't large. Like every other object d'art in the house, it looked as if it had been made for its particular placement.

He hadn't really been expecting to find anything there. He'd actually chosen to inspect the painting in an effort to distract himself from Daphne's close proximity. When he turned it over to look at the back, he almost missed it. If he had not taken a leaf from Daphne's book and run his hand over the back of the canvas, the frame, and the bits of wood wedged into each of the four corners, he'd not have felt the rolled bit of parchment hidden almost invisibly between the wooden stretcher and the canvas.

He must have made some noise of excitement because Daphne looked up at once. "What is it?" she demanded, her eyes shining in the lamplight. "What did you find?"

"Bring that," he told her, nodding to the box in her hands before carrying the painting back into the main room of the library.

At their quick reemergence, the others came crowding around.

"I hadn't realized there was a painting hidden in there," Sophia said with what sounded like pique. As the artist of the group, she would have a natural interest in such a find.

Daphne rested the box on the nearest table with a thump, while Maitland gently lay the painting face down next to it.

"Which of these are we meant to examine first?" Ivy asked, glancing from the chest to the back of the canvas.

"There is nothing more to the box than what you see," Daphne said with a frown. "I thought perhaps there would be something hidden in the lining, or maybe a secret compartment. But there's nothing here that I can find."

In the bright natural light of the library, Maitland was able to see the parchment wedged into the corner of the picture frame more clearly. "I may have discovered something useful," he said, pointing to the section in question. "Since you are the one my aunt chose to tell about the cipher, I thought I'd let you be the one to have the first look at it. We may have lost whatever was hidden in the trunk, but perhaps this can shed some light on who took—" He broke off as she reached out a hand to remove the rolled document and without ceremony, unraveled it.

When she did not speak, Ivy expressed the impatience they were all feeling. "For heaven's sake, tell us what it says!"

"Is it a clue?" Gemma demanded.

Sophia put her hands on her hips. "Does it tell anything about the cipher?"

Maitland's heart sank as she shook her head.

"It's blank," Daphne said turning the page to show them that there was indeed no visible writing on it. Her mouth was twisted with disappointment. "It was probably used as a wedge to hold the canvas in place. It's not a clue at all."

"I wouldn't be so sure," Sophia said, moving to examine the open structure of the frame, which exposed the back of the canvas it showcased. "It's far more common to use a bit of wood to secure a loose canvas. There is no reason I can think of for placing this page here."

She reached out to turn the frame so that the subject of the painting could be seen in the light, and gasped. "It's a Catherine Read," she said, awe in her voice. "I'm almost sure of it. Perhaps the best I've seen."

"And who is this Catherine Read, pray?" Gemma asked her sister with a touch of exasperation. "You forget, Sophia, that we do not all have your knowledge of obscure art."

"If you spent more time away from your fossils and bones, sister," retorted Sophia, "you might recognize the name. And she's most certainly not obscure. She's one of the best-known pastel artists of her generation, as well as the member of a prominent Jacobite family. It's no wonder Lady Celeste chose a Read for the room where she'd hidden the cipher. It fits perfectly, in fact."

"There's no signature," Daphne noted from where she peered down at the painting. "How do you know it's by this Catherine Read person? There's nothing at all that indicated who painted it."

"Notice the way the Prince leans his chin on his fist?" Sophia asked, pointing out the specific area on the painting. "Well, that is a characteristic in many of Miss Read's works. Not to mention that I recognize other elements of her style. It's not one particular brush stroke or element that makes me think it's hers. It's the thing as a whole."

Maitland frowned down at the portrait. "The chin thing," he said with a nod toward the work, "I've seen that at the National Gallery. Sir Joshua Reynolds, I believe."

At the mention of Reynolds, the diminutive artist drew herself up to her full height. "You are not alone," she scowled. "Miss Read's work has often been misattributed to Reynolds. Mostly by men who cannot possibly believe a woman capable of such skill. Which is absurd, of course. But when has misogyny ever been a surprise?"

All four ladies scowled in Maitland's direction, and he threw up his hands. "I meant nothing by it, Miss Hastings. It was merely an observation. I'm as familiar with art as any man in my position. But I'm hardly an expert. And knowing Aunt Celeste, she was probably making a point by choosing a Read painting to adorn the hiding place of the cipher.

"What's really of interest, here," Sophia said looking somewhat mollified, "is the fact that I've never seen mention of this painting in any collection. I've read through the catalogs of most of the better-known art collections in England and the continent, and I've made a particular study of Miss Read's work. And I cannot recall ever seeing it mentioned."

"What if it has never been made public?" Daphne asked. "If this Miss Read was a Jacobite herself, perhaps the painting accompanied the cipher. As a sort of talisman?"

"I'm not sure how practical it would have been for Cameron to travel across England carrying a portrait that all but shouted that he was a Jacobite sympathizer," Maitland argued. It was a romantic notion, he supposed, but a man hiding from the authorities would wish to keep from drawing attention to himself.

"It's quite impossible anyway," Sophia said. "Miss Read didn't travel to Europe, where she likely met the Prince, until after 'forty-five. And if Cameron brought the cipher through this area before 'forty-five, there's no way he could have even seen the portrait, much less carried it with him along with the cipher."

"So, Lady Celeste was the one who set up this secret room?" Daphne asked, puzzled. "But to what end? Why not simply tell me the location of the cipher in the letter she wrote me and be done with it?" She rubbed her forehead as if she were fighting a headache.

Unable to stop himself, Maitland placed a comforting hand on her back, which was turned away from him. "I know it's frustrating," he said in a soothing tone, "but there is a method to the madness."

"I'm sure I can't begin to guess what that might be," she said in a petulant tone.

"I hate to add to the growing list of questions without answers," Gemma added with an apologetic look, "but has anyone asked yet how Sommersby, who had, to our knowledge, never visited this part of England, knew precisely where to find this secret room? Can Lady Celeste have told someone who passed on the location of the cipher?"

They all stared at the painting, as if its subject would leap off the canvas and give them the answers they sought.

Finally, Daphne sighed. "I cannot imagine that Sommersby, who was not the most intelligent of men, could have discovered the room's location on his own. I spent most of my time since my arrival here searching the library and I never came across it. I think you're likely correct, Gemma, that someone else told him, but who?"

"Let us not get distracted from our current conundrum," Maitland said mildly. "If we begin pulling at every loose thread we'll have nothing but a tangle."

Daphne nodded. "You're right. First things first." She picked up the scroll and stared at it again.

"Aunt Celeste was quite fond of Gothic novels," Lord Kerr said into the glum silence. "I suspect she saw all of this . . . theatre, for want of a better word, as part of the puzzle."

"Perhaps it's just a painting," Sophia said with a shrug. "A significant one, by a female artist of some note, with Jacobite connections. But we may be attributing too much significance to it. And letting ourselves fall prey to the excitement of mysteries and secret codes and hidden messages."

Something about what Sophia said sparked a memory, and with a renewed sense of hope, Maitland turned to his cousin. "Kerr, do you recall how we used to send secret messages to one another when we were boys?"

The marquess met his gaze and frowned. Then realization dawned and he whistled. "I haven't thought about those things in ages," he said. "But she was the one who taught us how to do it, so of course Aunt Celeste would choose it as a way to include another clue here."

"What?" Daphne asked, turning to Maitland in puzzlement. "What are you two talking about?"

"Someone get me a candle," the duke said with a grin. "If I'm right, we're going to unravel at least one mystery today."

"Invisible ink," Daphne said as she watched the duke hold the scrap of seemingly blank parchment over the candle flame. "I should have guessed."

She had read about the use of lemon juice instead of ink years ago in a book about spies in the Colonial Wars in America. Why hadn't she thought of it as soon as they'd found the parchment? She was usually much quicker than that.

Clearly the excitement of the past few days was taking a toll on her intellect.

Leaning against Maitland's side so that she could see more clearly, she watched as writing in Lady Celeste's hand—which she knew well by now—appeared on the parchment in a brownish hue. A shiver of excitement ran through her.

"I knew our boyhood schemes would come in handy one day," Kerr said with satisfaction. Rolling her eyes, Ivy mock cuffed him on the ear.

"This is serious business, Quill," she chided, though her eyes were light with amusement.

Diverted from the matter at hand, Daphne's heart constricted at the interaction between the married couple. Would she and Maitland be that happy if they continued this hasty betrothal? She tried to imagine herself behaving with the easy affection that Ivy showed her husband. And failed.

Breaking into her reverie, Maitland handed her the message, which was still warm from the heat of the flame. "You should be the first one to read this."

She swallowed, suddenly nervous at the prospect. What if it was something mundane, like a shopping list?

Self-doubt wasn't something that Daphne was accustomed to. She was, most of the time, quite sure that she knew at the very least what the most logical course of action should be. But now she hardly knew up from down.

Taking the note from Maitland's hand, she read it aloud:

If someone steals the prize hid here
You may find it still, my dear.
Another version I have hid,
To find it just do as I bid.
Three clues I've stashed with trusted friends.
Each missive toward the map extends.
For your first clue you now must chase
The man whose help enhanced this place.

"That's it?" asked Gemma, scowling. "I've seen hiero-glyphs that were more specific."

"It's really only the last bit that's the puzzle," Daphne said with a shrug. "The rest is clear enough. She left more clues to the location of the cipher in case some-one else got to it first."

"How on earth could she have known it would go missing?" Kerr asked, clearly aggrieved by the notion. "Aunt was canny, but she hardly had the ability to pre-dict the future."

"She's been clever enough so far," Maitland reminded him. "She somehow managed to matchmake between you and Ivy from beyond the grave. And the Cameron Cipher is one of the most sought after treasures in all of England. It's only logical to think that someone would figure out where she'd hidden it. Aunt was nothing if not thorough."

"The note itself is straightforward enough," Daphne said, drawing their attention back to the matter at hand.

"But who does she mean by 'the man who helped enhance this place'?" Ivy asked. "A gardener? Or the decorator? Is this something perhaps Mr. Greaves would know?"

Maitland cleared his throat, and Daphne turned to look at him. "Are you ill?" she asked, frowning.

"I am not," he said with a grin. "It's just that I might be able to answer this riddle."

When he did not continue, Daphne tilted her head, as if to say, "Well?"

"I think she might be referring to Mr. Renfrew," he said, looking in Kerr's direction. "You recall him, don't you? The steward who was here when we were children?"

Lord Kerr stroked his chin. "I haven't thought about Old Renfrew in years," he said frowning. "Though he does fit the description, since he oversaw the design and work on the gardens. I wonder what happened to him? I must confess I didn't really pay much attention to his comings and goings."

He turned to the ladies. "Aunt went through several stewards after Renfrew left, as I recall, since many of them had a difficult time taking their orders from a lady who knew precisely what she wanted."

"Nor do I," Maitland agreed. "But I suspect Ivy is correct that Greaves will know. He's been here for decades."

Without waiting for the others, Daphne began walking toward the door.

"Where are you going?" Sophia called after her from where she stood with her hand on the bell pull.

"To speak to Greaves," Daphne said without turning back. She could wait for the butler to respond to the bell, but she was tired of inaction. She needed to do something proactive, instead of relying on others to solve the mystery Lady Celeste had left for her.

"If you'll just excuse us," she heard Maitland mutter from behind her.

He caught up to her in the hallway and followed as she strode toward the landing. "I take it this means you've decided which of our many mysteries you'd like to pursue?"

"It's the one that holds the key to all the others," Daphne responded as she hurried down the stairs toward the ground floor. "If we find the cipher, we are likely to find who killed Sommersby."

"I agree," he said trailing after her. "But the murderer might have already got to the cipher by now."

"I doubt that," Daphne said with a shake of her blond head. "Your aunt must have known someone else would try to steal the cipher. Otherwise she would not have left the second set of clues. I think now that whatever was in the box, it was not, in fact, the Cameron Cipher."

They reached the shining black-and-white marble-tiled floor of the entry hall, and Daphne turned toward the door leading into the servants' hall.

Before she could push through it, Maitland laid a staying hand on her arm. "How can you know that?" he asked, looking flummoxed. "You didn't see whatever it was that the killer removed from the box."

"No," she said with strained patience. Did he think she was a simpleton? There was a rational reason for every conclusion she'd drawn so far about the cipher and the trail Lady Celeste had left for her. "Of course I didn't see what was hidden in the box. How could I when I only saw it for the first time with you when we found Sommersby's body?"

"Then how do you know the cipher wasn't in it?" he persisted, looking as frustrated as she felt.

"Because she told me," Daphne said. "I just didn't realize it until a few moments ago."

When he only frowned at her, she sighed. "In the letter Lady Celeste left for me, she said 'I hope you'll find sanctuary here at Beauchamp House—where even Hypocrites could ne'er Soil Eden.'"

"What does that even mean?" Maitland asked with a frown. "It's . . . it makes no sense."

"When I first read the letter," Daphne said with a shrug, "I saw the first anagram referring to the Cameron Cipher, and thought that was the only message hidden there."

"All right," the duke said. "So I take it that means this other sentence contains a hidden meaning?"

"I assumed the bit about Hypocrites was some classical quotation I was unfamiliar with," Daphne said with a slight blush. "My classical education is not what it should be, since I insisted Mr. Sommersby, Senior, devote most of our studies to mathematics. And I did not wish to reveal my weakness, so I did not take it to Ivy, who would likely have told me at once that there was no such quote. And that the reference is religious and not classical."

Maitland sighed. "You are not supposed to know everything there is to know in the world, Daphne. You're allowed to ask for help sometimes."

His words made her stomach flip. It simply didn't feel right to rely on others when she was perfectly capable of finding out something for herself. But if Lady Celeste's quest had forced her to learn anything, it was that Maitland was correct. Sometimes one had to ask for help from others. And it wasn't shameful. It simply was.

And, coming from Maitland, the reminder held more importance than it would have otherwise. She was willing to admit that at least. But not aloud. Not yet.

"Just as with the message about the cipher," she continued, "this second message is a simple anagram of the three capitalized words. *Hypocrites, Soil,* and *Eden* can be rearranged to read . *Decoy in Priest's Hole.*"

"I'll be da—er, dashed," the duke said, shaking his head in wonderment. "You are never allowed to doubt your powers of deduction again," he said with a grin. "I would never have figured that out in a million years of trying."

A line appeared between her brows. "You could not possibly try for a million years. You'd very likely die after the first eighty or so. Or sixty, I suppose given your current age."

Maitland stared at her for a second before shaking his head. "You are a true original, Lady Daphne Forsyth," he said, his blue eyes crinkling at the corners, in that way she'd learned meant he was happy.

Which, in turn, made her feel happy. "Thank you, your grace," she said with a shy smile.

"Perhaps you could call me Dalton now?" he asked, dipping his head so that he could see her eyes. "We are, for better or worse, partners in this adventure. And even if it's only temporary, we're betrothed."

At the mention of the betrothal, Daphne's heart began to beat faster. "I suppose so, your . . . Dalton."

With an approving nod, he held out his arm for her. "Let's go see if Mr. Greaves can point us in the direction of Renfrew, now. Because unless I miss my guess, whoever took the decoy cipher is likely growing very frustrated just about now."

"Will he come back here, do you think?" she asked, alarmed at the prospect. After all, this man had been willing to kill Sommersby to get what he thought was the real cipher. What would he do if he came back?

"I don't know," Dalton said with a frown. "But if he does, we'll be ready for him."

Together they went down the servants' stairs in search of the major domo of Beauchamp House.

Chapter 8

"Yes, of course, your grace," said Greaves, whom they found in his office, going over the household ledgers. "I am in correspondence with Mr. Renfrew and know his direction well. He's gone to live with his daughter in Bexhill, no more than a day's drive from here."

"And he is in good health?" Maitland asked. It would be just their luck if they drove all the way to Bexhill only to find him at death's door.

"As far as I know, your grace," said the butler with a frown, as if the notion that an elderly man could be in ill health was troubling to him. Greaves was no spring chicken, after all. "Though now that you mention it, I haven't had a reply from my last letter, sent at Christmastime."

That had been over six months ago, Maitland thought with alarm. He hoped that wasn't an omen.

* * *

Seeing that he had upset the older man, he hastened to reassure him. "I'm sure he's quite well, but busy with his grandchildren," he said.

"How far is Bexhill from here?" Daphne asked, cutting to the heart of the matter, as usual.

"Only six miles or so, I should think," Greaves said to her coolly. The very proper upper servant clearly found Daphne's abrupt manner difficult, though he would never say so aloud. It was indicated only in a slight lessening of the warmth he'd shown Maitland. Still it was noticeable.

Raising his brows at the man he'd known since he was a boy, the duke was not displeased to see him color a little at the rebuke. Daphne might not be to everyone's taste, but she was one of the four owners of the house and an earl's daughter to boot, and as such deserved the man's cordiality as well as his respect.

"Perhaps I can ask cook to pack a picnic luncheon for your drive," the butler said, trying to make amends.

"Oh, but I don't think . . ." Daphne began.

"That would be perfect, thank you, Greaves," said Maitland at the same time.

Looking from one of them to the other, the butler seemed to decide that the duke outranked his new mistress. "Very good, your grace. I will inform her at once."

When he and Daphne had reached the ground floor again, Maitland said, "A kind word goes a long way with the servants, you know. Even if it's just to thank him for his time."

"But it is his job to give me his time," Daphne said,

looking puzzled. As if he'd suggested she th
ister for aiding her ascent of the stairs.

"Of course it is," he said patiently. "But everyone
likes to be appreciated. Don't you like to be told you're
clever?"

"I suppose," she said, giving the matter some thought.
"But I already know I'm clever. So it does me no good
to have someone else tell me. I'd be more pleased if they
told me I'd done something well that I am not generally
good at. Like needlepoint."

He hid a smile. "You're not fond of sewing, eh?" He
had a difficult time imaging her dutifully seated before
a needlepoint frame, plying her needle.

"I like it well enough," Daphne said with a sigh. "But
I am horrid at it. Which is why words of encouragement make me feel a bit better about my less-than-elegant
work. It goes against my logical side, of course. Truth
is important, but I am beginning to learn that there are
times when it hurts."

"Precisely. So you must simply think of thanking the
servants as a sort of encouragement for their version of
needlepoint."

"Your gr—Dalton," she corrected herself, much to
his pleasure. "That makes very little sense. They are
presumably excellent at their occupations, so, it doesn't
follow at all. Though I suppose I will try to do as you
say and simply thank the servants when the occasion
arises if, as you say, it makes them feel better."

"That's all I ask," he said with a nod.

Eager to be on to the next part of their quest, he took
her hand and pulled her toward the main staircase.

going now?" she asked, stifling a

we go back to the library and see if we

128 ything else?"

assuredly not," he said pulling her hand up to

the back of it, making her color up quite prettily. "You, madam, are going to take a nap."

"A nap?" she protested, though her exhaustion was evident in the shadows beneath her eyes. "I am not a child, Dalton."

"No, you are not," he said with a sigh. He was well aware of that fact every time he felt her brush against him. "But, you have had an eventful few days. And if we're to journey to Bexhill tomorrow, you need to get some rest."

When they reached the door to her bedchamber, he pulled her against his body and leaned his forehead against hers. Slowly and deliberately, he kissed her, infusing the caress with some of the passion he'd been holding in check all day.

She was breathless and looking a little dazed when he pulled away. She said nothing, only held a hand up to her lips as she blinked at him.

Sorely tempted to drag her into the bedroom beyond and continue what he'd started, Maitland got himself under control. When he had her for the first time, it would not be in the middle of the afternoon when anyone might disturb them.

"Sleep well, dear Daphne," he said as she continued to watch him.

She didn't speak until he'd already turned to go.

"I never feel it with you," she said softly.

Arrested by both her cryptic words and the touch of vulnerability in her tone, he turned back.

* * *

"The fear," she continued quietly. "Whenever I meet eyes with someone, I get this . . . this knot of fear in my stomach. Anxiety."

She looked down at the floor, then quite deliberately looked up and met his gaze. "But not with you. I can look at you, see you, without that feeling."

It was perhaps the saddest thing he'd ever heard. But also the most exhilarating.

He knew instinctively that he'd just been given a gift beyond price.

"Thank you," he said softly. Not daring to step closer to her lest he break his vow not to follow her in.

"Thank *you*, Dalton," she said with a sweet smile. "I didn't think I'd ever have that with anyone."

Then she stepped into her bedchamber and shut the door behind her.

Alone in the hall, Maitland slumped against the wall, staring at the now closed door.

Unless he very much mistook the matter, he was in serious danger of falling in love with her.

And maybe. Just maybe. She was falling for him, too.

Standing up straight, he strolled down the hallway, tempted to whistle a jaunty tune like a jubilant schoolboy.

The next morning, a picnic basket—put together by the cook at Greaves's request—tucked away beneath the seat, Daphne and Dalton set off in his blue-and-yellow trimmed curricle for Bexhill.

She'd informed the other ladies of their plan last evening when they met in their shared parlor before bed.

"I suppose it would look odd if we were all to go *en masse* to Bexhill to question him," Sophie said, though there was something in her tone that told Daphne she rather wished they could do so anyway.

Then she'd given a squeak, and rubbed her arm. As if someone had pinched her.

The Hastings sisters were quite odd sometimes, Daphne had reflected.

"It certainly would look odd," Ivy said firmly. "Besides, we have plenty to keep us occupied here. What with the number of calls we're sure to receive now that word of Mr. Sommersby's death has got out. I knew we could rely on Squire Northman's wife to tattle all over the village."

That lady had been quite rude to Ivy not long after she'd announced her betrothal to Lord Kerr, and Ivy had yet to forgive her.

"It would have gotten out sooner or later," Gemma said with a shrug. "And we can use the opportunity to question the neighbors about Sommersby's coming and goings. Whoever killed him could still be in the village, you know."

Daphne would like to be there to question the village ladies, but she knew that her talents lay elsewhere. She could never quite figure out what to say to that sort of woman, and always managed to insult them in some way or other. Even when that wasn't her intention. Truth be told she'd be far more comfortable with Maitland.

"Speaking of those who are 'still in the village,' Daphne," said Ivy with an apologetic look, "Quill told me earlier that your father is still in the neighborhood.

Staying with the Northmans, in fact. So perhaps it's a good thing that you and Maitland are leaving."

"I thought Maitland's ruse about the betrothal would have reassured him enough to make him go back to London," Daphne said, shocked despite knowing her father was nothing if not unpredictable.

"You don't think he has doubts about the validity of the betrothal, do you?" asked Sophia with a slight frown. "Perhaps he's remained here to make sure you weren't trying to fob him off."

That was something Daphne hadn't considered. She'd been so relieved—after the initial shock of Maitland's outlandish announcement—at the prospect of being freed of her father's demands, even if only temporarily, that she hadn't thought beyond his departure. And once they'd found the clue to the cipher, she hadn't thought of Lord Forsyth at all.

"Even if he is," Gemma said, trying to reassure her, "then we will simply need to spread word of your happy news to the gossip-hungry matrons who come to talk about Sommersby. A few congratulations from neighborhood busybodies will allay any doubts your father might have."

"And, your day trip with Maitland will lend credence as well," Ivy said. "A courting couple might go for an afternoon's drive together without incidenct, but an all-day journey must surely mark you as an engaged couple."

Somewhat mollified by their assurances, Daphne nodded. "I suppose you're right. And perhaps if we're lucky, by the time we return from Bexhill, Papa will have decided to go back to London."

"You don't suppose there's a possibility that you and the duke could decide to make your betrothal real, do you?" asked Sophia, tilting her head as if she were trying to see more clearly into Daphne's thoughts. "I couldn't help but notice how cozy the two of you were in the hallway."

At the mention of the hallway, Daphne's face flushed. Had their kiss been observed? In truth, she'd been too caught up in the moment to consider it.

"Don't tease, Sophie," chided her sister. "Besides, it's impolite to spy on betrothed couples. Everyone knows that."

"I'm just pointing out that it may not be so easy to dissolve this pretend betrothal as they think," Sophia said, ignoring Gemma's censure. "And it's not as if Daphne is immune to his charms. We all know about her indecent proposal to him the night of Ivy's shooting."

"I'm not sure you're aware of it," Daphne said in seriousness, "but I am still in the room. And I fear that I was carried away yesterday. But there's been no actual declaration from the duke. And aside from that I cannot consider any of this until we've found the cipher and learned who killed Sommersby. Some things are just far more important than . . ."

"Than love?" Sophia asked pertly. "Is that the word you were searching for?"

"Than fooling my father," Daphne returned. Whatever this newfound closeness she had with Dalton, it could hardly be called love. Friendship, maybe. But not love.

Looking disappointed, but thankfully seeing that she would get no more revelations from Daphne about her relationship with the duke, Sophia changed the subject.

"Do you think the duke will let you take the reins?" she asked, genuinely wanting to know. The petite brunette was quite fond of driving and had tried and failed to get Dalton to let her drive his curricle on more than one occasion. "His grays look like they're quite spirited."

"I shouldn't think so," Daphne said with a shake of her head. "I am quite content to let him drive, as you well know."

She paused, recalling what Dalton had said about thanking the servants. Perhaps if she complimented the other ladies about the things they were good at, it would make them feel as she did when someone complimented her terrible needlepoint. They likely knew what they were good at, of course, but it was something. "You are quite good at driving, Sophia."

The other three stared at her in astonishment.

"What?" she asked, when they remained silent. "Did I say something offensive?"

"Quite the opposite," Ivy said with a grin. "Do you realize you just paid Sophia a compliment?"

"So?"

"So," Gemma said, gleefully, "you have never paid any of us a compliment before. Never. In the three months of our acquaintance."

"I'm sure that's not true," Daphne said with a blush. Was she so difficult? It wasn't as if she did not respect them. Of course, she did. Lady Celeste would not have chosen them as her heirs if they were not experts in their fields.

"It is true, I'm afraid," Sophia said. "But clearly something has happened to bring about this change in your manner."

"Or some*one*," Ivy said with a raised brow.

Daphne's cheeks grew hot. So much for stopping their interest in romance. "Of course not. I simply wanted to make Sophia feel good about herself, so I told her she is an excellent driver. Though she likely knows that already."

Though they knew she did not like it, she felt all three girls move closer and hug her one by one.

"I did know," Sophia said as she drew away. "But it was nice to hear all the same."

Now, in the light of day, Daphne recalled the conversation with a small smile as she watched Maitland . . . that is, Dalton . . . handle the reins.

"You're quiet," he commented, as if sensing her scrutiny. It really was extraordinary how he seemed to know what she was thinking much of the time. If only she had a reciprocal ability to interpret his thoughts.

"Did you not sleep?" he asked, glancing at her before turning back to the road ahead of them. "'Journey proud' my old nanny used to call it."

"I slept quite well, thank you," she said, answering the question. She liked to do things in order.

The truth of the matter was that for the second night in a row, she'd slept soundly. She hadn't realized it before Sommersby's death, but even when she'd known he was thousands of miles away in Egypt, she never could quite trust that she wouldn't be jarred awake in the middle of the night by his unwanted advances. She'd even slept with a burning lamp in her bedchamber for a time, that is, until her father discovered the practice and scolded her for wasting fuel.

Before he could speak, and possibly question her more about her sleep habits, asked, "What is 'journey proud'?"

She'd had a nanny when she was small, but she'd been a dour woman who had disliked Daphne's impertinent questions and odd ways. When they'd no longer had the funds to pay her and she left, Daphne had not put up a fuss.

Now, seated beside this handsome man who had clearly enjoyed a different upbringing than she had, she was curious about what sort of nanny his had been. It hadn't really occurred to her before that some children held their nannies in great affection.

"It's the feeling one has," he explained, glancing over at her again with those green eyes that missed nothing, "the night before a trip. You have trouble falling asleep because you're anticipating the next day's traveling. You're far too excited at the prospect of an adventure."

Daphne frowned. "I never knew there was a name for it," she said. There was so much, she'd come to realize, that she didn't know. It was easy enough when she was in the world of numbers, and ciphers, and puzzles to think she knew all. But, she'd come to learn in the past months at Beauchamp House just how ignorant she was on some subjects. Even something as simple as this phrase Dalton's nanny had taught him. "I suppose that's one more thing I can add to my list."

That seemed to intrigue him. "What list?"

They were approaching the outskirts of Little Seaford.

But this bit of the road was deserted. And she was glad of it. She felt as if they were cocooned in their own private world where she could speak freely without fear of upsetting someone or saying the wrong thing.

Only with Dalton could she be this comfortable in her own skin. Silently, boldly, she slipped her arm through his and leaned into his body, already dangerously close on the narrow curricle seat. Daring even more, she leaned her head against his shoulder, the hard muscle beneath his arm making her feel protected. Safe.

She'd never imagined how addictive physically touching another person could be.

Rather than object to her forwardness, or questioning her unusual behavior, he instead seemed to welcome it. Silently, he took both reins in his left and used his right to stretch out her arm so that he could clasp her hand.

Then, as if nothing had happened, he said, "Tell me about this list of yours."

Relaxing against him, she said, "I keep a list of things I've learned since I arrived at Beauchamp House. It's getting quite long."

He was quiet for a beat, and she wondered for a fleeting moment if he was about to laugh at her foolish list. Her father certainly would. Mostly because he disliked the fact that she was able to calculate sums and gauge how many cards had been played before he could. He had no compunction about using her abilities for his own profit, but even so, the fact of it seemed to irritate him beyond bearing.

"And what have you learned in your months here?"

he asked, sounding intrigued. There was no hint of censure from him. Only curiosity. Still . . .

"It's silly. Forget I said anything."

"Of course, I won't forget it," he said lightly. "You've got me primed now. Besides, if we're going to make this false betrothal convincing then we need to know these things about one another."

His words were said in a teasing tone, but the fact that he used the word false told Daphne all she needed to know about the possibility of their turning the engagement into something more permanent. A pang of disappointment rang in her chest, before she tamped it down, reminding herself that she'd never wished for the betrothal in the first place.

Still, he did have a point about their being able to make it seem real. Especially if her father was lingering in the village in hopes of finding them out.

"Fine," she said grudgingly. "But it's not very exciting. Just a catalog of things I should have known but somehow did not."

Dalton tilted his head, but didn't turn to look at her. "Why are you keeping a list? And what sort of things have you put on it? Besides 'journey proud' of course."

"Before I came to Beauchamp House," Daphne admitted, "I thought I knew everything. Or at least, the most important things."

"Like what?"

Despite her nascent trust in him, she felt naked, but pressed on.

"Mostly information about mathematics and such,"

she said finally. "Monsieur Fourier's theory of infinite sums, for example. Wherein periodic functions can be expressed as the sum of an infinite series of sines and cosines. I was able to meet him when he came to England. Did you know? My tutor, Mr. Sommersby, had a colleague who knew him from somewhere and he arranged an introduction for me. A brilliant man. Truly."

"I shall have to take your word for it," Dalton said wryly. "I don't think I understand most of what you just said. Except for the bit about the introduction and this Fourier chap being brilliant. I'd guess, however, that you could give him a bit of competition."

Daphne laughed. "Hardly. I am gifted, but I'm hardly the equal of one of the best mathematicians of our time."

"I don't know about that," he said skeptically. "But if you will insist upon it, I must stand down since I know almost nothing about the subject."

They drove on in companionable silence for a few minutes more before they reached the road leading through the village of Little Seaford. Daphne wondered why he had chosen this route, since there seemed to be more traffic, which made for more difficult driving.

Not that Dalton seemed to notice as he skillfully steered the grays around the various obstacles along the way—an apple cart here, a wagon there, pausing so that its driver could ensure the security of its load.

As they moved farther into the center of town, the curricle slowed near the entrance of the Pig & Whistle, finally coming to a stop just behind a waiting carriage.

"Why are we stopping here?" Daphne asked. She'd thought they'd drive through to Bexhill without stopping. "Is there something amiss with the horses?"

She knew from experience in town that horses could cause all sorts of delays in travel. They seemed always to be throwing a shoe, or coming up lame. Really, it was a most inefficient means of travel, though she could think of no better with the exception of walking on one's own. Which carried its own drawbacks.

Handing the reins to a waiting ostler, Dalton leapt down and moved around to offer her his hand. She turned, and before she could speak, his strong hands were around her waist, and he lifted her easily from the seat and set her firmly on the ground. They stood front to front for a moment, and Daphne dared a peek up into his blue eyes. What she saw there made her look away again.

It was really quite illuminating to know how many occasions for improper thoughts there were in seemingly mundane acts.

"I thought we'd pay a call on Mr. Foster," he said, turning away at last, and offering her his arm.

Remembering how overset Foster had been yesterday, Daphne blinked. "Are you sure that's a good idea? He is very unhappy with us, though I suppose in his position, I would also have been angry. It must have been quite distressing to not know where his traveling companion had gone."

"Hopefully the chap is in a better mood today," Dalton said as the door of the inn swung open and they stepped into the darkened interior.

Chapter 9

He should have told her before they departed Beauchamp House that he wished to visit Sommersby's traveling companion, Maitland thought as he escorted Daphne into the inn. But it hadn't occurred to him until they were on the outskirts of the village and she mentioned her list.

Only Daphne would keep a list of the things she didn't know.

And one thing no one knew was who had killed Sommersby. The man who'd traveled to the coast with him must certainly know something about the matter.

They didn't have to wait long for the innkeeper, Mr. Allenby, to approach.

When one was a duke, it was always thus.

In his younger days, he would have thought glumly about his childhood dream of the anonymity of the stables and cursed his fate. As an adult, however, he saw and appreciated the privileges of his position, knowing that too much complaint spit in the face of the everyday difficulties people without his blessings had to endure. "Your grace," Allenby said with the broad smile of a man who wanted coin, "what a delight to see you. Please tell me at once how I may serve you. A private dining room, perhaps? A cup of tea for Lady Daphne?"

The man's speculative glance at Daphne told Dalton he was already wondering who he could tell about their presence here together.

"Though a pint would be appreciated, Allenby," Maitland said somewhat impatiently, "I'm afraid we are not here to partake of your excellent service. We'd like to speak to one of your guests. A Mr. Foster?"

Allenby's enthusiasm dimmed a bit at the demurral, but he didn't say as much. "Of course, of course, your grace. A bad business with his friend Sommersby." He turned to Daphne. "I hope you ladies were not too overset by the discovery, my lady. It must have been most distressing."

"As it was the first time I'd seen a dead body, sir," she said with her usual forthrightness, "it was indeed most disturbing. I do not recommend it."

The innkeeper's mouth dropped open. Maitland didn't know what he'd been expecting from her, but clearly Daphne's plain speaking hadn't been within his imaginings.

"Mr. Foster?" He prodded.

Allenby blinked. Then, regaining his powers of speech, he bounced back. "Yes, of course, your grace. Mr. Foster is in a private dining room just now, enjoying a late breakfast." In a lower voice, he confided, "He did not wish to be pestered with the questions of the curious masses."

Maitland wondered if the man included himself in that description.

"I'll just take you there, shall I?" Allenby asked, ushering them to a door just off the taproom.

As they walked, Maitland could feel the curious eyes of the patrons on them.

Allenby's brisk knock on the dining-room door was followed by an invitation to enter, and Maitland waved Daphne inside then shut the door behind them, shutting out the innkeeper.

"What is the meaning of this?" asked Ian Foster, rising from the table where he seemed to be partaking of a rabbit stew. "Your grace, I really must object to this intrusion."

"My apologies, Foster," the duke said easily, pulling out a chair for Daphne, who, looking unusually cowed by the man's outburst, sat. "Of course, you remember Lady Daphne Forsyth."

"Of course I remember her," Foster said with contempt, remaining on his feet despite the fact that the lady in the room was now seated. "She's the one who got my friend killed."

Despite her obvious discomfort, Daphne did not let that pass. "I did nothing of the sort. Sommersby had no right to break into Beauchamp House. And he certainly didn't learn of the Cameron Cipher's connection to the library there from me. I told no one of it. For all I know, you followed him there and stabbed him yourself, sir."

Though Foster scowled, he didn't repeat his accusation. Which told Dalton that he likely knew his allegations were without merit and had only lashed out because he was angry over his friend's death. It was, however, interesting that he also didn't refute the charge that he himself might be responsible.

Deciding to see how Foster would react to a second accusation, Maitland asked, "*Did* you kill your friend, Foster? It isn't uncommon for co-conspirators to fall out. Did he go to Beauchamp House without telling you of his plan to break in? Perhaps plan to take the cipher out from under your nose?"

"This is absurd," Foster said, collapsing into his chair, and shoving aside the plate of stew, clearly no longer hungry. "I cannot believe I'm embroiled in this mess."

"I'd have expected you would feel more sympathy for poor Sommersby," Maitland said mildly.

At that, Foster gave a harsh laugh. "Poor Sommersby. Hah. He got what he deserved."

Maitland stared. A glance at Daphne showed she seemed just as astonished.

Had the man just confessed to murdering Nigel Sommersby?

Carefully, so as not to alert the man to what he may have just said, Maitland said easily, "That's an odd thing to say about your friend, sir."

Sighing, Foster sat back in his chair and shook his head. The shadows beneath his eyes were prominent in his pale face. He looked as if he'd aged ten years since they'd first met him.

"He wasn't my friend, your grace," he said bitterly. "I could barely stand the fellow if you wish to know the truth. But I had a job to do, and so I accompanied him here. Much to the detriment of my own career."

Daphne shot a questioning look at Maitland, but he

had just as little explanation for Foster's confession as she did.

"What career is that, sir?" he asked Foster when the other man didn't continue.

Foster, who looked as if he would like to be anywhere but in his current position, said in a weary tone, "I am not an old school friend of Nigel Sommersby's. And I have no personal interest in finding the Cameron Cipher. In fact, I wish I'd never heard of the thing."

"Explain yourself, sir," Daphne said, any guilt she'd felt over the loss of his supposed friend now gone. "If you have no interest in the cipher then why did you come here with Nigel Sommersby? And why did he introduce you as his friend if you were not."

Sensing that this would not be the brief encounter he'd hoped it would be, Maitland took the chair on Daphne's other side and watched as Foster sat thinking. Whether to get his story straight or to recall the details, it was impossible to tell.

Finally, Foster leaned back and admitted, "I'm here because my superiors ordered me to be here. I work for a government . . ." he searched for the right word, finally settling on, "entity, that would like to find the Cameron Cipher and the gold it leads to so that it doesn't get into the wrong hands."

The duke's brows rose. "Home Office?" he guessed. "I should think they would dislike the idea of all that gold funding another rebellion. Though the Jacobites seem an unlikely possibility in this day and age."

Foster indicated that Maitland was right about the government connection with a slight inclination of his head. "I'd rather not say whom they wish to keep from acquiring the gold, but let us just agree that it would be a very bad thing if these people had that sort of largesse at their disposal."

"But how did you end up with Sommersby?" Daphne asked, clearly more interested in the man's connection to her former friend than in who might misuse the Cameron gold. "Surely he didn't agree to take you along if he knew you were working to take the treasure as soon as he found it?"

"That was little more than a few words in the ears of the right people," Foster admitted. "Sommersby wasn't particularly discreet about his plans to search for the cipher. And when I showed up on the scene with an introduction from one of his actual old school friends, and told him I'd heard the cipher was hidden in the library of Beauchamp House here on the coast, he invited me along."

Daphne stared. "You're the one who told him the cipher was hidden at Beauchamp House? But how did you know?"

Foster's eyes turned opaque. "That information is off limits, I'm afraid, Lady Daphne." He didn't sound particularly apologetic to Maitland's ear, no matter what he actually said.

"I'm guessing it was either someone who worked in government who was close to Aunt Celeste," the duke said to Daphne, though he didn't take his eyes off Foster, whom he trusted even less now that he knew his occupation. "Or, it was someone who'd already tracked down the cipher to Beauchamp House and offered the information to Foster's superiors. For a price."

Lady Daphne shook her head in amazement. "For a

supposedly secret cipher, it seems as if a great many people knew it was hidden in Beauchamp House. I wonder why they didn't simply break in before Sommersby did and take it themselves."

"It's a bit more difficult than you realize, Lady Daphne," Foster said snidely, "to infiltrate a private residence. Much less the private residence of the well-placed daughter of a duke who is more than usually cautious about the security of her home."

That hadn't stopped the person who killed Lady Celeste, Maitland thought bitterly. But then that had been poison, which was admittedly easier to slip into the house without anyone noticing than a large man with a gun would be.

"But Sommersby managed it," Daphne returned, undeterred by Foster's attitude. "I'll bet that didn't sit well with you at all, having a civilian succeed where you had not."

"Of course, it didn't," Foster snapped. "Because it allowed someone else to take the cipher, and it got that fool Sommersby killed to boot."

"Interesting you should place the two in that particular order," Maitland said thoughtfully.

Scowling, Foster said, "I will not lie and say that the disappearance of the cipher isn't the more pressing issue to me. I didn't wish Sommersby dead, but his loss is not nearly as dangerous for the well-being of the nation as that of the cipher. If the person who's taken it manages to find the gold and deliver it into the coffers of England's enemies, then we are in serious trouble. I won't apologize for seeing the big picture."

"I wonder, however," Maitland said, leaning forward

a little, "if it's not something less patriotic that makes you take this loss so hard. I can't imagine the upper echelons at the Home Office are very happy with you just now."

At the other man's flinch, he knew he'd hit his mark.

"I'm guessing you spent years of your life fighting the French, old man," he continued in a companionable tone that he could see Foster hated. "Then, once the war was over you came home and began working in a less-overt capacity. All those years of service, effectively erased by the rash actions of a man you didn't give a damn about. That must really infuriate you."

"If you're asking me again if I killed Sommersby," Foster said sourly, "the answer is still no. I might have disliked the man, and his childish wishes to find the gold at the end of some ridiculous mystery trail may have driven me almost mad, but I didn't want him dead. And I certainly would never have allowed the cipher to fall into enemy hands."

"But perhaps you didn't," Daphne said, looking at Foster like he was some curious specimen she'd found in a museum. "Perhaps you have the cipher. That would surely be a way of keeping it out of the hands of these dangerous people you seem to fear so much."

Before Foster could retort, Maitland spoke up. "An admirable theory, Daphne, but if that were the case, then I think Mr. Foster would be long gone. I believe he's here because he suspects the thief is still in the area. Isn't that right, Foster?"

The agent for the crown didn't respond either way. But his silence was an answer in itself.

Seeing that there was little more to be learned from

the man, Maitland rose. "Daphne, we should take our leave now. Mr. Foster very likely has a great deal of . . . searching to do."

With a last look at the spy, Daphne turned and took the duke's proffered arm. They were almost to the door when she turned and asked, "Why did you dislike him so much?"

"Because he was a braggart and a bore," Foster said coldly.

When she didn't turn and leave, he sighed. "Because he actually thought he would find that hidden cache of gold. After almost a century of searching by dozens and dozens of treasure hunters, Sommersby thought that he would be the one to finally do it when no one else could. It was ridiculous."

Maitland thought that said more about Foster's cynicism than it did about Sommersby's optimism.

"I mean to find it, Mr. Foster," Daphne said, her chin raised in defiance. "It's not ridiculous to have confidence. What is ridiculous is to despise someone for having it. If your reach extends your grasp at least some of the time, then what harm is there in having hopes all of the time?"

Turning back to Maitland, she said, "I am ready to leave now."

Without turning back to see Foster's reaction to her declaration, Dalton led her away.

They were more than halfway to their destination before Daphne spoke of Foster's admission again. As if by mutual consent, they'd talked of everything from

Dalton's childhood home to the weather, each of them avoiding the scene in the Pig & Whistle. But after she'd had time to think the confrontation over, Daphne was ready to discuss it.

"I should have known he wasn't Sommersby's true friend," she said, one hand on her hat to keep it from flying off in the increasingly turbulent wind. "I should have guessed, and then perhaps none of this would have happened."

"I do not know how," he said, glancing at her with a furrow between his brows. "You hadn't seen the man since you were a girl. A fellow can befriend any number of people over the course of several years."

She made a noise of dismissal.

"The fact remains that I let Foster fool me, just as he tricked Sommersby," she said mulishly. "I should at the very least have questioned him further about his interest in the cipher—what his own feelings were about the prospect of finding such a famous treasure. Given how little he seemed to care about the romance of it in our recent discussion, it's very likely I would have sussed out the truth with only a few pointed queries."

"If you are determined to find yourself at fault," Dalton said with a shake of his head, "then you may as well blame yourself for not knowing someone would shoot Sommersby that night. After all, the all-knowing Lady Daphne Forsyth must have been able to predict such an event, otherwise she is merely an ordinary person."

"You may poke fun," she said stiffly, feeling strangely vulnerable, "but I am not ordinary. And if I cannot understand the motives of ordinary people, then what good is my extraordinary talent? It isn't as if an encyclopedic knowledge of mathematics has contributed to the betterment of the world."

"Daphne," he said softly, "there is no reason you should have guessed what would happen. Especially not when your abilities in one area have clearly caused a deficit in another."

She gasped, not sure if she'd heard him right. "Did you say I am deficient in some way?" It mattered not that she'd just said essentially the same thing.

They'd been sitting pressed against each other as he drove. But at his words, she scooted as far as she could—which wasn't very far—to the other side of the narrow curricle seat. Rather than looking abashed, Dalton pressed on. "I'm not sure I'd use that term," he said mildly, "but do you deny that you sometimes have a hard time discerning what motives lay behind people's words? That you cannot understand whether something is meant to be taken seriously or in jest?"

She'd never really heard it expressed in such a way, but his explanation did come close to describing what she'd come to think of as her blindness.

"What of it?" she asked cautiously.

"I am simply saying that even with your extraordinary intellect, you were at a disadvantage when it came to catching on to Foster's ruse." Dalton took both reins in his left hand and placed his right one over hers where it lay in her lap. Though they were both wearing gloves, she could feel the warmth of him through the soft kid, and was comforted by the contact. "You are not responsible for what happened to Sommersby. No matter how guilty you feel at your relief that he is dead."

His words struck her like a blow, and she felt tears spring in her eyes. She wanted to deny his accusation, but she could not. Her blissful sleep in the nights since they'd discovered Sommersby's body was proof enough.

"I am horrid," she said, her voice thick with emotion. "Only a monster would rejoice in someone's demise."

"Only a monster would do to you what Sommersby did," he replied, reaching out to take her hand. "Only an unfeeling wretch would not feel some relief at knowing the man she feared for years was no longer a danger to her."

Perhaps he was right, she thought, though some part of her still had doubts.

"You are doing what you can to find his killer," Dalton continued in a soothing tone. "That is more than he has a right to. More than most would do for the man who tried to take her virtue."

"I suppose so," she said, wishing she could go back to her usual unflappable self. These past few weeks had turned her into one of those simpering ladies she'd once scorned. "I only wish I had been able to speak to him about . . . that night. Before he died, I mean. I wish I could have asked him why he did it. Why he broke my trust as he did."

Dalton didn't speak for a few moments, simply kept his eyes on the horses and the road ahead of them. Daphne had begun to wonder if he'd heard her at all when he finally spoke up. "I cannot pretend to know why a man would do such a thing to someone who trusted him. My sister's husband was often a brute to her, and then would come back to her with tears and promises never to do it again. Then a short time would pass and he would beat her, hurt her, again."

Daphne had not known this about Lady Serena's husband, though she'd somehow known that there was some darkness in her past. Were there so many of these men, then? Who hurt those who loved them with little or no compunction? The notion had never occurred to her. And it was chilling.

"I once asked him," Dalton continued, his steady voice and warm presence beside her giving her much needed succor, "why he did what he did to my sister, who once loved him beyond reason. Do you know what he said? What explanation he gave for brutalizing her again and again?"

She hardly dared ask, yet the words left her in almost a whisper. "What?"

"He said that he did not know. When it came to any sort of self-reflection, or ability to know his own motives, that was all he could say. He did not know."

She thought about Sommersby for a moment. Was he, too, incapable of knowing himself? Of understanding the impulse that led him to force himself upon his oldest friend? It was a supremely unsatisfactory idea.

Leaning against his shoulder again, she wondered at how different Dalton was from Sommersby. Or even her father. He was a different sort altogether.

Still, she was frustrated at knowing so little of the reasons for Sommersby and his ilk to behave as they did.

"I like to know the explanations for why things happen," she said into the silence. "Not knowing why is one of the things about Sommersby's betrayal that haunted me the most. Not knowing if it was something I said or did that led him to think he could do that to me. Or if he'd have behaved as he did regardless."

"I know Serena would have liked an answer, too," he said. "But I can tell you this, Lady Daphne Forsyth. You didn't make him hurt you. He made the choice to do what he did, and there's nothing you could have said or done that would have justified his actions. I have no respect for a man who takes advantage of a woman. And if I'd known about what he did to you before he had the good grace to get himself murdered, I'd have been tempted to do the thing myself."

There was a fierceness in his voice that was alien to his usual manner. A protectiveness that was both comforting and invigorating. She had once liked to think she could take care of herself—after Sommersby's assault, she'd forced herself to do so, lest he come for her again. But after a lifetime of not being able to rely upon any of the men in her life—excepting perhaps Sommersby, Sr. before he left so unexpectedly—it was bewitching to think that she could count on the Duke of Maitland to stand by her side if the need arose.

Not knowing how to express her gratitude, she went with her impulse and simply squeezed his hand where it grasped hers.

"Thank you."

That was all. Words inadequate to express the depth of her appreciation. But words were all she had at the moment.

Chapter 10

Once they reached Bexhill-on-Sea, or Bexhill as it was known familiarly, a brief stop at the local tavern was enough to give them direction to the Miller farm, where Lady Celeste's erstwhile steward Mr. Renfrew lived with his daughter and son-in-law.

It was a pretty-enough area, with the town itself situated on an elevation that allowed for a clear view in every direction. It was said that William the Conqueror had eaten his first meal in England near here, though Dalton had heard all sorts of tales relating to the King since it was so near the site of the Battle of Hastings. As boys, he and Kerr had come to Bexhill on any number of occasions, to watch the German soldiers who'd come here to escape Napoleon's occupation at the invitation of the Hanoverian, George III.

"It is convenient that Mr. Renfrew was able to retire so near to where he lived and worked for so many years," Daphne remarked as they turned onto a country lane not far from the town proper. "He must be able to keep in close contact with his friends, I think."

"I imagine that is correct," Dalton said as they came nearer to a rather impressive farm house with what appeared to be an extensive husbandry operation attached. "His daughter appears to have done well for herself, at any rate."

"Or rather, her husband has done well," Daphne said dryly. "Unless Renfrew's daughter runs this farm all by herself. It is rare, I think that a woman should be able to do so. Even with the assistance of someone as influential as your aunt."

"I suppose that's correct," he said ruefully. He forgot at times how much women were forced to rely upon their fathers and husbands for their subsistence. Daphne was helping to remind him.

As they neared the front door, a stable lad approached Dalton's side of the curricle to take the reins from him, and as soon as Maitland had helped Daphne to the ground, the entrance of the farm house was opened by a curtsying, mob-capped maid.

"Milord, milady," she said as she bowed and scraped, "how may I help ye?"

"The Duke of Maitland and Lady Daphne Forsyth to see Mr. Renfrew," said Maitland in an amused tone. He had become accustomed to the people around Beauchamp House, who, if they did not precisely treat him like just another resident of the neighborhood, at the very least didn't look as if they were somewhere between a faint and a seizure on greeting him, as this maid seemed to be.

At the mention of Renfrew, however she looked non-plussed.

Fortunately, a pretty woman of middle years entered the hallway and on seeing her visitors, gave an elegant curtsy. "That will be all, Molly," she said to the blushing maid, who looked half-relieved, half-disappointed to be supplanted by her mistress.

"Your grace," said the lady, whom Dalton assumed was Mrs. Miller, "my lady, I'm afraid my father is indisposed at the moment. Is there something I can help you with?"

Dalton's heart sank at the news. Had they driven all this way on a fool's errand?

"But we need to speak to him most urgently," Daphne said in a brusque tone that revealed her nervousness.

Looking surprised, but not particularly conciliatory, Mrs. Miller said, "Perhaps we can step into the parlor for a moment and discuss this. I shall ring for some tea."

Giving the woman his most charming smile, Dalton took Daphne's arm. "That would be most appreciated, Mrs. Miller."

The farmer's wife ushered them into a small but well-furnished parlor, which seemed to serve the dual purposes of comfort and illustration of prosperity.

Once there, he waited for Daphne to take a seat on a low sofa, while Mrs. Miller sat calmly in an armchair. He remained standing, taking up a position before the handsome marble fireplace.

"Now, perhaps you can tell me what it is you wish to speak to my father about?" Mrs. Miller appeared to be wholly unruffled by their appearance in her drawing room.

Before Dalton could answer, Daphne said, "It is a confidential matter. Having to do with his former employer, Lady Celeste Beauchamp."

"Perhaps you could tell us something about the nature of your father's illness, Mrs. Miller?" Dalton asked hurriedly, before the other lady could respond to Daphne's admission. "My aunt was quite fond of him as I recall, and I know she would wish me to inquire after his health. If there is anything we can do . . ."

The tense line between the matron's eyes eased at Dalton's words. "That is kind of you to ask, your grace. My father was fond of Lady Celeste as well. But I'm afraid he would not even remember her existence if I were to tell him you called." Her eyes grew shiny with unshed tears. "His mind has gone, you see. And he is not the man he once was."

At the news Mr. Renfrew was suffering from senility, Daphne emitted a distressed sound.

"We are quite sad to hear it, ma'am," Dalton said, not sure where to proceed from here. "Is he able to receive visitors at all, or does that distress him too much?" He could at the very least find out the degree to which the man suffered from his mental ailment.

"He has good days and bad days," Mrs. Miller said with a sad smile. "Unfortunately, today is not a good day. Though I know if he were well enough he would love to receive a visit from you, your grace. You were always one of his favorites. You and Lord Kerr."

"But we've come all this way," Daphne said in a weak voice. Clearly, she was not taking the news of their man's indisposition well.

Moving to take a seat beside her, Dalton hoped that

his nearness would give her comfort as it had done in the curricle.

Aloud, he said, "Mrs. Miller, perhaps you will be able to help us after all."

Looking from Daphne to Dalton and then back again, Mr. Renfrew's daughter said finally, "I will do what I can, your grace. Your aunt was quite good to my father."

He smiled at that concession. Aunt Celeste had also been fond of Renfrew.

"Did Mr. Renfrew ever make mention of a letter or a note that my aunt asked him to hold for her?" he asked, hoping that the old man had done something to safeguard the clue to the location of the cipher before he lapsed fully into madness.

Mrs. Miller frowned, thinking. "I'm not quite sure, your grace. He gave me a great many items to put up in the attics, but I can have no notion of whether or not the missive your aunt entrusted to him is there. I did not go through them myself, you understand. And he keeps very few things in his bedchamber with him. Papa has always been a man with few needs for creature comforts."

"Mrs. Miller," Daphne began, and Dalton was almost afraid of what she would say. He was growing fonder of her by the minute, but he'd be blind not to notice that she had a way of setting up people's backs with her words. "Do you suppose we could search through his things?"

Already he could see that Mrs. Miller was opening her mouth to deny them, but then Daphne continued, "It's just that a man was murdered in Beauchamp House, and we think that something Lady Celeste gave your father could help us find what the killer was looking for."

At the mention of murder, the other lady blanched, bringing a hand up to her throat. "How awful," she said on a gasp. "Who would do such a thing? And why?"

"The man who was murdered was searching for something we think the killer has already found," Daphne said, cleverly dancing around the truth of just what it was that Sommersby's murderer had been looking for. "And Lady Celeste, being as brilliant as she was, left a clue with your father to the location of this artifact. If we find the artifact, we will, hopefully, find the killer."

"I do not pretend to understand all that you just said, Lady Daphne," Mrs. Miller said with a shake of her head. "But if I understand the gist of it, you need this paper in my father's things in order to apprehend a murderer. In which case, I will be happy to let you look through his things. Though in his right mind, poor Papa would have been most put out to know you were doing so. Still, he was fond of Lady Celeste, and I should think he would be willing to help find the man bold enough to commit murder in her home."

Dalton bit back a sigh of relief, thanking Mrs. Miller profusely for her cooperation.

As she led them upstairs to the third floor, where the attics were located, he said under his breath to Daphne, who walked beside him, "Well done, my dear. You knew exactly what to say."

Her pleased smile told him that he, in turn, had known just what to say to her.

"I spoke from the heart," she said, "just as Ivy told me to do when trying to persuade someone. I never guessed that it would actually work." She sounded both surprised and pleased at her discovery.

They reached the door leading into the attic then. Handing a lit lamp to Dalton, then turning a large key in the antiquated lock, Mrs. Miller opened the door into the storage area. "I'll leave you to it, then," she said with a brisk nod. "Papa's things are just to the left, near the chimney. I'll send up a maid in an hour or so to see if you need any other help."

"Thank you, Mrs. Miller," Daphne told her with a smile that lit up her entire face. For a moment, Dalton was stunned by her beauty.

"I am happy to help, my dear," said the other woman, with a smile. "I hope you find what you're looking for."

When she was gone, Dalton turned to see Daphne staring after her.

"What is it?" he asked, concerned.

"It's nothing," she said with a slight shake of her head. "It's just that I usually do not get on with people so well. It felt . . ."

"Nice?" he asked with a grin.

"Yes," she said. "Nice." Which sounded like the most wonderful feeling in the world when she said it just so.

Then her eyes cleared and she turned to indicate that he should lead the way.

No fool, Dalton followed her orders, and lifting the lamp to shed light on their path, he stepped into the musty attic room.

Unfortunately for Daphne and the duke, Mr. Renfrew had been a man who did not like to throw things away. So the number of crates and trunks they were forced to wade through was more than they had at first thought.

Mixed in amongst a few decades worth of *The Farmers*

Journal, Daphne found stacks of letters exchanged between the steward and friends who appeared to be fellow stewards with interests in farming. Not to mention all the correspondence between the man and his eleven (Daphne counted) siblings and four children.

"For a man who didn't speak much," Dalton remarked wryly, as he removed another stack of letters from the trunk he was examining, "Renfrew had much to say when he put pen to paper. I don't know how he found time to work Aunt Celeste's farmland given the number of letters he wrote."

Daphne had wondered the same thing.

She also felt a pang of sympathy for the old man, who must have craved interaction with his peers if he was willing to put so much effort into writing them. Since she'd spent her whole life feeling as if she didn't quite fit in, not only because of her intellectual pursuits, but also because of her odd nature, she could relate. She wondered, suddenly, if when she was gone someone would find her own saved letters from her mathematician colleagues equally as pathetic.

Aloud she said, "I should think if your aunt had found fault with his work she would have done something about it."

She glanced over at him and saw that in his concentration on the task at hand, he'd disarranged his slightly overlong hair so that a golden lock of it fell onto his brow. He really was more handsome than a man should be allowed to be. What with his wide shoulders, trim waist, and face that might have been a Greek statue come to life, he was really more than she could have ever conjured from her imagination.

He must have felt her scrutiny then, because he looked up with a question in his eyes. "What is it? Did you find something?"

Blushing at having been caught staring, she shook her head. "No, I was just wondering if you had," she lied.

With a wry smile, he lifted a small painting and handed it to her. "Does this answer your question?"

She gazed down at the artist's rendering of what looked to be an exaggeratedly large ox. She knew it was an ox—for she'd never actually seen such a thing in her whole life—because affixed to the bottom of the simple frame was a brass plate that read "Beauchamp House Ox—Live weight 464 stone."

"Good heavens," Daphne said, aghast. "It must have been enormous!"

"Indeed." Dalton rubbed a hand over the back of his neck. "I cannot seem to have ever spoken to Mr. Renfrew about the cattle raised on the farms at Beauchamp House, but clearly there were some prize winners amongst them. My aunt certainly never spoke of it."

"It must have meant something to Mr. Renfrew," Daphne said handing the painting back to him, feeling a small jolt of electricity as their hands brushed. She couldn't help but be aware of their enforced proximity in the attic. In the curricle, they could talk, but he was forced to keep his attention on the road so they could do little more than hold hands. But here, alone, she couldn't help but imagine the possibilities. "For him to have kept the painting, I mean."

"Oh, as opposed to the rest of his things, which he threw away?" Dalton gave her a sardonic look, and she laughed. Was she mistaking the light in his eyes for something it was not, she wondered as they shared a look? "Well, when you put it that way." She hoped her voice didn't sound as flustered as she felt. She couldn't remember ever feeling so nervous around a man. Leaning back on his haunches, Dalton sighed as he surveyed the piles of detritus around them. "I don't know if we're ever going to find this letter my aunt gave into his care. Not unless we spend the next month or so rooting around through agricultural artifacts and prize cow paintings."

Moving from her kneeling position to sit on the trunk next to where he crouched, Daphne said, "Perhaps we're not being methodical enough about our search. So far, we've gone through most of Mr. Renfrew's correspondence and found nothing. But what if we look for items that are particular to his work for your aunt?"

"I thought that's what this was?" Dalton gestured to the stack of journals and prizes.

"If he discarded so few of his things," Daphne said, "then he must have also held onto his correspondence with your aunt, including records of payment, and so forth. But I've seen nothing like that thus far. Have you?"

"No," he said with a nod of approval. "I have not. Well done, Daphne."

"Don't congratulate me yet," she said, though she felt a burst of pride at his praise. Which was silly given that she'd always been a step ahead of most people she knew. But there was something about being lauded by Dalton that felt different. It mattered. And fed her soul in a way she hadn't even realized she needed. "It's simple logic. But at least we can surmise that it must be preserved somewhere."

"You're just being modest," he said. Getting to his

feet, he stretched a little, and Daphne couldn't help but admire the way his muscles moved beneath his clothes.

Tearing her gaze away, she stood, too, and looked round the room for likely hiding places for documents. Her gaze lit on a crate against the wall and she moved toward it. "I believe you're the first person ever to call me modest," she said over her shoulder as she attempted to remove the crate's lid.

"Oh, please,' Dalton said with a wave of his hand. "You can be quite modest. It's just that you're so busy trying to prove yourself to most people that you don't give anyone the chance to see your prowess for themselves."

That stopped her in the process of lifting out a stack of books.

She'd never thought of it that way, but he was right. She did spend much of her life trying to prove herself to people.

"I suppose I don't feel the need to do that with you," she said, feeling suddenly shy. This extended period of proximity to him was wreaking havoc on her usual sense of aplomb.

When he touched her hand, she jumped a little, startled at the touch. She hadn't heard him approach.

"I'm glad," he said softly. "I want you to be comfortable with me. To be yourself."

And then he moved back to the trunk beside her, which he'd apparently decided needed his attention, and left her to her thoughts.

Taking a deep breath, she looked down and noticed that the books she had before her were finely bound in leather. Far more expensive than even a prosperous steward would be able to afford. Flipping open the first one, she saw an inscription on the fly leaf. "To Mr. Renfrew, Christmas 1818." Beneath it, was the signature she'd come to know so well, that of Lady Celeste Beauchamp.

Turning the book over, she saw that it was a title on cattle breeding.

Not wanting to raise Dalton's hopes, she searched each of the books from the crate, which all seemed to be Christmas gifts from Lady Celeste to her steward. And it wasn't until she reached the one at the bottom of the stack that she found what she was looking for.

Tucked neatly into the middle of a bound volume of *The Sussex Herd Book,* she found a wax-sealed note.

She must have gasped, though she had no awareness of it.

Dalton was by her side in an instant, kneeling beside her before the crate, staring down in the lamplight at the page in her hand.

"I knew you'd find it," he said with a grin. "Clever girl."

"I feel awkward opening it," she admitted, not meeting his gaze. "What if it isn't what we think it is?"

"Mrs. Miller has given us permission to go through his things with the expectation that we would find the note," Dalton said. "And in his present state, I doubt Mr. Renfrew will object."

With a nod, Daphne slid her finger beneath the upper fold of the page and broke the seal.

Chapter 11

Maitland had begun to worry that they'd traveled to Bexhill for nothing when Daphne hit on the idea to look for things associated with his aunt. His praise for her idea had not been empty flattery.

She was clever, and if he'd been forced to perform this hunt on his own, he likely would have given up in frustration long ago.

And there was no denying that it was quite pleasant to spend so much time in the company of a beautiful lady who looked at him when she thought he couldn't see her as if he were some sort of Adonis. He'd been admired by women before, and was under no illusions about the fact that he was handsome, but there was something particularly gratifying to know that Daphne—who was the most intelligent woman he'd ever known, aside from his late aunt—thought him attractive.

Kneeling there beside her, it was difficult to keep his mind on the matter at hand, especially when he could feel the warmth of her while the lemon verbena on her skin seduced his senses. Forcing himself to focus, he watched as she broke the seal and read aloud the message on the folded page.

> Huzzah for you
> You've found this clue
> And deserve your due reward.
> So leave these cattle,
> It's off to Battle
> And Themis' shining sword.
> Secreted there
> You'll find a pair
> Who'll my next note reveal.
> Forget thee not
> This puzzled knot
> Romance's treasure doth conceal.

"I never knew my aunt had such a knack for penning such awful verse," Maitland said when Daphne finished. "I mean, sincerely, this is terrible."

"I should imagine it's difficult to write lines that rhyme as well as convey the message she wished to hide there," Daphne said, with what sounded like a bit of defensiveness for his aunt.

"Aside from congratulating us for finding this clue," he said taking the page from her to read it again, "what is this message she's trying to convey to us?"

Daphne examined the words, her head close to his as she read.

"Well, discounting the congratulatory note," she said, pointing to the words, "the first part is this bit about 'Battle' and 'Themis' shining sword.'"

" 'Battle' is capitalized," Dalton said, "so perhaps she's referring not to an actual battle, but the town of Battle, since it's so near to Beauchamp House."

"I agree," Daphne said. "She showed in her note to me that capitalization denotes something she wishes to call attention to, and in this case I cannot think of an anagram of Battle that would make any sense. And then moving on to Themis' shining sword, I'm afraid I'll need to ask Ivy. It looks like a classical reference, but my knowledge in that area is sadly lacking."

"Huzzah, indeed," Dalton said with a grin. "Finally, an area in which I know something that you do not!"

Daphne rolled her eyes, but he chose not to notice. "Themis," he explained to her with what he considered to be great dignity, "was a Hellenic goddess, who was said to represent the divine rightness of law."

He grinned at her. "I knew those years at Oxford would be useful to me one day."

"Congratulations," Daphne said, shaking her head at his foolishness. "You must be so proud."

He made a show of preening for a moment before she turned the subject back to the matter at hand. "So your aunt must in these two lines be telling us that we should go to Battle to see someone related to justice. A solicitor? A barrister? Perhaps some other sort of legal person?"

"If I recall correctly," he said, serious once more. "Aunt employed the services of a solicitor in Battle. I can't remember the man's name, but I feel sure Greaves will know."

"But she says 'a pair,' " Daphne reminded him. "Could

she have used a pair of solicitors? Or perhaps she means we should see more than one person there?"

"I'm afraid my powers of recall do not extend that far," he said with a frown. "We'll ask Greaves, and then perhaps if he has nothing to add, we can simply travel to Battle and see what we find there."

She nodded, looking down at the page again. As if the answer would materialize there.

Unable to resist, Maitland moved closer, taking the opportunity to rest his chin on her shoulder to look down at the note with her. It had been damned difficult to keep his hands to himself the whole afternoon. Especially given the way Daphne had of looking at him when she thought he wasn't looking.

"And what of 'Romance's treasure'?" he asked, feeling a tremor run through her at his voice in her ear.

"As in the letter she wrote to me on my inheritance," she said, her voice betraying with a slight tremor that she was not as unaffected by his closeness as she seemed, "R-r-romance is an anagram of Cameron."

As she spoke, he turned and took the lobe of her ear between his teeth. Rather than tell him to keep away, as he half-feared she would, Daphne instead let out a little exhale of want, and turned her head so that he could have more access to her neck.

He would have liked to shout with triumph but settled for smiling to himself as he did as she had indicated she would like, and kissed the spot behind her ear and then worked his way down toward the hollow of her collarbone.

Still, trying to keep them somewhat on topic, she

continued, "And . . . t-treasure, is self-explanatory, I sh-should think."

"You're a treasure, Lady Daphne Forsyth," he whispered as she gave up any attempt at ignoring him and slid up a hand to run her fingers through his hair.

He'd just moved to fit himself against her arched back, and taken her breast—still covered by the layers of clothing she wore—in his hand, when the sound of loud footsteps coming up the stairs startled them both.

When Mrs. Miller stepped into the room, there were three feet between them as they each made themself busy putting various items from Renfrew's lifetime of hoarding back into the crates and trunks from whence they came.

"I thought I should check in on the both of you," the lady of the house said cheerfully, clearly unaware of the scene of incipient debauchery she'd just interrupted. "It's been quiet, but I supposed if you found something you'd have come down by now."

"In fact, Mrs. Miller," said Maitland, closing the trunk he'd just pretended to work in, "we just moments ago found the letter we were looking for."

Daphne remained silent as she placed the books given as Christmas gifts to the steward back into the crate.

"I had my doubts, your grace," Mrs. Miller said with a shake of her head. "But I might have known that between you, you'd find something. I don't suppose you could let me see it?" Curiosity shone in her eyes, and he wondered if she knew more about their reasons for coming here than she revealed.

"I'm afraid that won't be possible, Mrs. Miller," Daphne said, rising from the floor and shaking out her skirts as she stood. "The letter involves a matter of the highest important to the government."

At the mention of the government, the farmer's wife's eyes widened. "Oh, I had no idea! To think that my father had something like that for all these years."

Not wanting the woman to be fearful, Maitland assured her, "It isn't as dangerous as it sounds, dear lady. Though more than that I cannot say. And I would please ask that you keep this information to yourself. It is not something that we wish to be known abroad at this time." He flashed her his most winning smile, the one he used to inveigle biscuits from the cook at Beauchamp House.

"Oh yes, of course, your grace." Mrs. Miller blushed at his attention. "I will tell no one. Except my husband if that's all right. We don't keep secrets."

"Of course, of course," Maitland said, taking Daphne's arm as she moved to stand next to him. "An admirable habit, ma'am. Your husband is a lucky man."

He heard Daphne give a slight snort next to him, but when he looked over, she seemed serene enough.

"We really cannot thank you enough, Mrs. Miller," she said with what he saw was genuine effort on her part to make their gratitude known.

"Lady Celeste was good to my father, Lady Daphne," said the other woman. "I know he'd want me to show the same kindness to her nephew and her . . ." she seemed to search for a term to describe Daphne's relationship to Lady Celeste, and settled on "friend."

The note tucked into the pocket of the duke's coat, they followed their hostess back downstairs. And with a promise to come back at a later time in hopes that Mr. Renfrew would be well enough to receive them, they made their way back to the waiting curricle and were soon back on the road east.

They were nearly a third of the way back to Little Seaford by Daphne's calculation when she noticed the dark clouds gathering.

Most of that time had been spent attempting to decipher the meaning of that interlude in the Miller attic. And the rest of the time was taken up by self-recrimination at how quickly she'd become distracted from their reasons for traveling to Bexhill in the first place—namely to search for the cipher and Sommersby's killer. Surely someone as intelligent as she could manage to keep on task without turning into a blushing ninny.

If she felt every shift of his body on the curricle seat, and if the pleasant sandalwood and male scent of him distracted her from the task at hand, well, she would simply have to be stronger. And mindful of the purpose for this drive, she determined to keep her hands to herself throughout the rest of it.

A jolt of the carriage as it crossed a depression in the road, however, brought her attention to more immediate concerns. A glance at the sky ahead of them made her inhale sharply and in turn to process.

It was, in fact, growing quite dark with clouds.

"Dalton," she said, trying not to sound managing. He was after all, a very good driver and had seen them quite safely over the journey thus far. "Have you noticed that there appears to be a storm on the horizon?"

Her companion gave a slight snort of laughter. "Yes, Daphne dear, I see it."

She felt her face warm at the endearment.

"But what are we to do about it? I do not mind getting wet, of course. But we are in an open carriage. Even animals know to come in from the rain."

There, those were reasonable-enough questions. She had not lost all her wits because of a kiss. Or two.

"If it looks as if it will overtake us," he said mildly, "then we will stop in the next village. There is a perfectly respectable inn there where we can wait it out. There's no reason we shouldn't be able to get back on the road once it's passed."

As if he could read her thoughts, he added, "I do have a plan. I won't let you come to harm, you know."

Her stomach gave a little flip at that simple reassurance. Was it possible to trust that someone else would see to her comfort? It was both enticing and a bit terrifying to let him make the decisions.

Of course, there were any number of things that were entirely out of her hands. She was a lady, after all, and thus subject to the rule of her father in one way or other from her infancy. But her maneuver in which she forced him to allow her a tutor had proven to Lord Forsyth that she was no longer going to blindly follow him. So had the incident with Sommersby. After that it had become important that she be the one to make the decisions about her day-to-day life.

Could she trust Dalton to ensure her safety now? He had given her no reason to doubt him thus far. But her experience with men told her that they were sometimes inconsistent. Trust was such a leap, and she wasn't sure she could make the leap yet.

At least not with her heart.

With the curricle, and her safety from the storm, however, she was willing to take the risk.

The rain began just as they arrived in the stable yard of The Bo Peep.

An odd name for a coaching house, but at this moment Daphne only cared that they had tea and a warm blanket on hand. The wind had picked up on the road, and combined with the rain and the chill of early summer, she was shivering in her wet clothes.

Tossing the reins to a stable hand, with orders to give the horses extra oats and a good rubdown, Dalton leapt down and was at Daphne's side before she could manage the step. His mouth a solid line of concern, Dalton reached up for her and when he felt her chill, he cursed, then shrugged out of his greatcoat and placed it around her. She would have argued, but there was something about his manner that kept her silent.

Inside the inn, even their bedraggled state was not enough to disguise the fact that a very important personage had arrived. No sooner had they stepped inside, than the proprietor was before them.

"Milord, milady," the little man said with an unctuous manner, "welcome to The Bo Peep. How may we serve you?"

"A private parlor, a pot of tea, and perhaps a room where the lady may repair to dry her clothes," Dalton said without his usual sangfroid.

The innkeeper, however, seemed used to dealing with high-handed aristocrats. "I'm afraid we are filled almost to the rafters, milord. A local family is having a wedding, and we've got quite a few guests here."

Dalton frowned. "What do you have available, then?"

"Only one bedchamber, milord," said the man, "and it is not the sort of room I would normally offer to someone like yourself. But I'm afraid it's all we have."

Just then raucous laughter erupted from the taproom behind him. Clearly the wedding party was spending the storm enjoying whatever spirits the establishment had on hand.

As if to emphasize their situation, a crack of thunder sounded outside.

Without looking to Daphne for assent, Dalton nodded. "Very well, we'll take it. But I do wish for tea and some food to be brought up as soon as possible."

With a nod, the man led them toward the stairs, where they passed several gentlemen coming down.

One in particular seemed to pause as he saw Dalton.

"I say, is that you, Maitland? What on earth are you doing in this hellhole?"

The innkeeper seemed to stiffen at the description, but did not object, clearly having learned to let his guests have their way.

Rather than greet his friend with his customary warmth, however, Dalton paused long enough for Daphne to see him close his eyes in frustration. Then almost as if it hadn't crossed his visage at all, it was gone and replaced with a friendly grin. "Pinky," he said, nodding to the fellow before indicating to his companions that they should proceed.

But Pinky was not to be ignored. "I should have known I'd see you here, though. Your aunt's place is just over near Hastings, isn't it?" He gave a quick but speculative scan of Daphne. "I might have guessed you'd find the best bit of fluff around. Always did have a good eye, eh?"

Daphne's eyes widened at the insult. She had been subjected to those sorts of glances before, of course, but had never been spoken of so blatantly. And certainly never mistaken for a lightskirt. She opened her mouth to give this Pinky a set down, but was forestalled by Dalton.

"And you always did have a way of mistaking matters, Pinky, old thing," he said in a drawl that sounded as foreign on him as a French accent would have done. "May I introduce my bride? Darling this is Lord Pinkerton. We were at school together."

It was difficult to say who was more shocked by this pronouncement, Daphne or the gaping Pinky. The innkeeper looked surprised as well, but kept his mouth shut.

One glance at Dalton showed his eyes boring into hers, heavy with a message she was quite able to read.

"A pleasure," she said, extending her hand toward Pinky, who bowed low over it.

"The pleasure is mine, your grace," the fop said with a grin. He seemed not to be in the least embarrassed by his earlier assumption about her. "Leave it to Maitland to find such a diamond."

"I'm sure you'll understand if we get upstairs now, Pinky," Dalton said before Daphne could speak. "We were caught in the storm, and I do not wish her to catch a chill."

Not waiting for his friend to respond, Dalton indicated to the innkeeper that he should proceed, and they hurried after him.

Once they reached the door to what was, indeed, a most unimpressive chamber, the innkeeper looked abashed. "Your grace," he said, as if seeing just how bare the little room was, "I can ask one of the other guests to exchange rooms with you. I feel sure once they learn who it is that wishes to use the chamber . . ."

"This is adequate, Mr. . . ."

"Woodley, your grace. George Woodley, at your service." He bowed.

"A pleasure, Mr. Woodley." Dalton's easy manner seemed to have returned with their removal from the crowded taproom. "I should like some hot water brought up for my wife, as well as the tea and food. And if you have any clothes that she might change into, that would be appreciated. We were caught unawares in the storm and had not planned to stay over."

With a promise that he would find something, Woodley left them then, closing the door behind him.

Daphne, who had moved to stand before the fire as soon as they walked in, turned to see Dalton watching her.

His hair was almost brown thanks to the rain, though wisps of gold stood up in places. And his mouth was tight as he watched her.

"You have a remarkable habit of making pronouncements about our relationship, your grace," she said with some asperity. "I have found myself betrothed, then married to you in the space of a few days. Both times without my recollection of ever having consented to the match."

"Pinky is one of the worst gossips in the *ton*," he said, stepping forward to take her hands in his. Feeling their coldness, he gave a curse and began rubbing them between his own ungloved hands. "I might have attempted to pass you off as my mistress, but the likelihood of him remembering your face if you were to meet later is strong. He never forgets a face, and worse, he never passes up the opportunity to spread tales."

"Surely he is just as likely to realize once some time has passed that there has been no announcement in the papers." Daphne tried to keep her mind on the matter at hand but she was very cold. And his hands were quite warm.

He was silent for a spell, and was saved from reply by the arrival of both a maid and a footman, bringing clothes, a pot of tea, and hot water.

Once they were gone, Dalton turned back to Daphne, his eyes never once wavering from her face. "There will be an announcement in the papers, Daphne. There's no help for it. We might have broken things off in front of your father without any sort of ramifications. But I'm afraid that this is one action that cannot be undone."

"But surely, we can simply tell Pinky what happened," she said, knowing as she said it that it was futile. She'd recognized Pinky from some card party or other in London. He was one of those men who traded on gossip for his own amusement as well as in exchange for invitations. There was no way he'd agree to keep quiet about finding the Duke of Maitland in such a compromising position.

"That wouldn't stop him from spreading gossip about it." Dalton sighed, and pulled her against him. "Your reputation would be in shreds."

As would his. Even so, marriage was not what she had foreseen for herself.

"I do not care overmuch for my reputation," she said softly. "I could withstand it."

But even as she said the words she doubted them. She thought of the women she'd seen in town. Who were spoken of in hushed tones, and dared not show their faces in public lest they set off a flurry of whispers. It wasn't as if she cared for the social rounds. But she'd always taken pride in the fact that despite her father's insistence she use her skills at the gaming tables, her personal reputation was flawless. She might be the daughter of a scoundrel, but she herself had escaped being marked with the same brand. Was she willing to sacrifice herself just to keep from marrying a man who had thus far proved to be the most trustworthy she'd ever met?

"But I won't let you," he said kissing her forehead. "There's nothing for it, Daphne. We must marry."

Chapter 12

Dalton waited. Watched as her every thought flashed through her eyes.

He had known, of course, that she saw their hasty betrothal for her father's sake as a temporary thing. A quickly erected levee to stop the flood of Lord Forsyth's demands from overwhelming to the point of destruction.

But his offer had been more sincere than he'd let on. Though he would not force her, he had intended to use every persuasive skill at his disposal to convince her that they should make a go of the match. Since she'd first approached him not long after they met with her scandalous proposal, followed by his rejection, Dalton had come to realize that he was unlikely to meet her equal should he live to be a hundred.

She was lovely, intelligent, determined, and, despite her appearance of arrogance, self-effacing when it came to those things she felt she did not excel at. She just so happened to recognize that she possessed some skills that far outshone the average person. It was perhaps not humble of her to declare the fact, but neither was it sensible for her to pretend to be less than she was.

In that, she reminded him of Aunt Celeste, who had also known her worth and did not pretend to be a simpering ninny for the sake of other (mostly male) sensibilities.

He wondered as he stood there holding her, waiting for her to accept the inevitability of their match, if Celeste had had some hand in this. If she had engineered the lives of her nephews by choosing ladies as her heirs whom she suspected they would find appealing. Though he hadn't considered it before now, the idea held some appeal. It was comforting somehow to think that Celeste had known just what sort of women he and Kerr needed. That she was still here caring for them long after she was gone.

Even so, Daphne was hardly predictable. And whatever he might wish regarding her decision, he knew she was quite capable of digging in her heels when she wished it. The notion of having her reputation thoroughly ruined was not appealing, he could tell, but if the alternative was something she did not want, she would endure it.

Whether he was willing to endure it was another matter altogether. He had always prided himself on maintaining a spotless reputation—especially when compared to that of his father. He might admit to wanting Daphne for himself, but a part of him wished her to marry him because he did not want to be known as yet another ill-reputed Duke of Maitland. It was selfish perhaps, but he was honest enough to admit it should she ask.

He was about to do so when she raised her eyes to him, dark green in the dim light of the modest chamber. "Not long after we met," she said softly, "I asked you to take me to bed."

Dalton blinked. He had not been expecting her to speak of that just now.

Curious about where she was going with this, he said, "I remember." He had done nothing but remember that moment ever since he turned her down. Any other man would have leapt at the chance to hold such a beautiful woman in his arms. And in the wee hours of the night, for weeks afterward, he'd considered going back to her, to tell her he'd changed his mind.

"It wasn't for the reasons you think," she said, lowering her eyes again, as if she could not speak the words while meeting his gaze.

"It doesn't matter, now." He stroked a hand over her back in a soothing gesture. "We know each other better now. I need no explanations."

"But I wish to explain," she said, pressing on. "You see, I was still unable to get past that . . . incident with Sommersby. I couldn't stand the thought of being touched by any man. Even one I wished to be with."

At the mention of the other blackguard's name, Dalton wished, not for the first time, that he'd known Daphne at the time. He would have made quite sure Sommersby never approached her again.

"But I was drawn to you from the moment we met," she continued. "It was the first time I'd found someone appealing since the incident with Sommersby, you see, and I thought perhaps if I asked you to be with me in that way that it would erase the memory of him, make me whole again."

Dalton was overwhelmed. There were so many things he wanted to say at that moment. He wanted to tell her how flattered, and humbled, he was that she trusted him. To assure her that all men weren't like the bastard who tried to hurt her. To say he wished he'd known all this when she first approached him.

But sensing that she was the one who needed to speak now, he kept silent.

"I know that I shocked you," she said, smiling a little. "You were rather like a scandalized maiden aunt."

"In my defense," he said, feeling his ears turn pink, "it was the first time an unmarried lady had ever approached me with such an offer. You took me by surprise."

That gave her pause. "Does that mean that married ladies have approached you with similar offers?" She looked rather shocked, as if the notion had never occurred to her. For all that she pretended worldliness, she was still innocent about such matters, he surmised.

"We are not speaking about other ladies," Dalton said, deciding that they perhaps needed to make use of the lumpy settee behind them. He for one did not know if his knees would hold out for much more of this sort of talk.

Pulling her with him, he waited until they were seated, his arm holding her close to his side, before he said, "Go on."

In this position, she did not have to look into his eyes, which he thought she would prefer, given how difficult it was at times for her to endure eye contact. But once again, Daphne surprised him. Turning to face him, she lifted a hand to his face, as if she needed to see his eyes as she spoke. "I am asking you again, your grace. We may not have another opportunity like this, when we are away from the prying eyes of your sister and cousin and my friends."

He should have known she was leading up to this. But like before, he found himself caught off guard. If he did marry her, he could envision a lifetime of such surprises. And though he once would have said he longed for a life of calm and content, there was something about the idea of such a life with Daphne that appealed more than he could have imagined.

Taking her hand, he kissed her palm and moved it to rest on his heart, which was beating like mad with anticipation now. "That was not my intention in bringing you here, Daphne. I truly did just mean to wait out the storm for a bit before returning to Beauchamp House."

She smiled. "I know that. You are the most honorable man I have ever known aside from the elder Mr. Sommersby."

Knowing how much she admired her tutor, he felt humbled by the comparison.

"But, I need to know if this is something I can do— endure your touch, any man," she said, looking down again. "I need to know that I will be able to give you what you need if we do marry. Because if not, then I won't force you into a marriage with someone who is broken. Your title requires an heir—and more children to carry on the family name. It is an antiquated system, but I am well aware of how much it means to a man to know that his name will carry on."

Likely she knew this at her father's knee. He was not the sort who would refrain from chastising his daughter for not being born the son he wished for. Yet another reason to despise Forsyth. Especially since his own reputation was the probable reason he had not married again.

"It is true that my title does mean that I would like an heir," he said to her, knowing that he must choose his words carefully if he didn't wish to bungle things, "but I have a cousin, who is not a bad fellow, who will inherit if I should die without issue. He is more than capable of taking the reins of the dukedom. And even if that were not the case, I have given you my word. Honor dictates that even if it were not my choice—and I assure you it is—I would still be required to keep it."

"Such an honorable man," she said, without irony. "That is why I must make sure that I do not trap you."

"And what if I don't see it as a trap?" he asked, the possible consequences of her experiment's failure sending a jolt of fear through him. "What if I promise to marry you regardless of your ability to give me an heir. After all, there are any number of marriages that do not produce sons. Or produce no children at all. Why can we not leave it to fate to decide?"

"Because I need to know," she said firmly. "Either you make love to me here, now, or I must have your word that you will release me from this match."

He pulled away, needing to get away from her for a moment. To think without the nearness of her clouding his judgment.

"You must agree it's the only sensible way," she said, her tone brisk. Just as if she were trying to persuade him of some mathematical principle rather than a decision that could keep them apart forever. "If I am able to be a proper wife to you, then we will wed. If I am not, then we will agree to part ways."

"And what of finding the cipher?" he asked, knowing it was unfair, but grasping at the thing she wanted more than any other in an effort to persuade her. "What of finding Sommersby's killer?"

"Of course we will continue to search for both." She frowned, as if the notion they would no longer search for both was absurd.

At her expression, he couldn't help himself. He laughed. "Daphne, you are the most maddening woman!" He shook his head in amazement. Only she would consider a broken engagement as something to be brushed aside while they worked closely together to search for a murderer.

She didn't reply, only sat patiently watching him. Seeing that he would never be able to persuade her to change her mind, he sighed.

"Very well. We will perform this experiment as you call it. And if for whatever reason you are uncomfortable, we will stop."

Daphne beamed. "I knew you would see things my way. You are a reasonable man, after all."

But he wasn't finished. "However, I demand that you give me another chance to . . . er . . . convince you, if this attempt doesn't work."

He couldn't believe he was speaking about such a delicate matter as if it were some sort of laboratory exercise. Given the amount of pressure he now felt himself under, he was even beginning to doubt his ability to perform. Which had never been an issue for him in the past.

Perhaps sensing his hesitation, she stood and placed her hands on his chest. Leaning forward, she kissed him softly on the lips.

And that decided it. Unable to resist her any longer, he pulled her against him and kissed her back.

Daphne had known from the moment she met him that Maitland had the potential to hurt her. It had been there in his golden good looks and charming manner. In his easy way with everyone—so different from her own often fraught interactions with friends as well as foes.

Even so, she'd wanted him.

And all these months later, with a storm raging around their cozy room, she gave herself over to the need she'd felt deep within her that day.

His mouth was firm, but gentle, as she explored it with her own. He tasted of sin and salvation, and she gave herself over to the heady intoxication of knowing he'd let her take what she needed from him. She was the one who tested, tasted, pressed her tongue into his mouth. Led each step of their dance.

But he was no passive partner. Once she introduced something, he would reply in kind. A taste for a taste. A touch for a touch. A stroke for a stroke.

When she gave her hands license to thread through his hair, he caressed up the curve of her waist to cup her eager breast, straining against the confinement of her stays as he stroked a thumb over the peak. When she bit lightly at his lip, he took that as an invitation to suckle his way down her chin to that place near her collarbone that made her writhe against him.

Somehow he'd managed to lower the bodice of her gown and when his mouth met the sensitive skin of her bosom, she nearly wept at the way he teased the edge of her nipple. The deprivation stirred that place at her core, where she needed him.

She must have made some protest, for Dalton paused, and asked, a little breathless, "Yes?"

"Yes," she exhaled as he loosened the laces of her stays and put his mouth where she most desperately needed it, covering her straining peak with warm heat. "Yes."

And even as she gave herself up to the caresses there, she felt his other hand sliding up her stockinged calf to her knee, and when instinctively she moved to kneel, opening herself to him, he did not disappoint. The soft touch of his caress against that aching place combined with the deep pulls of his mouth almost sent her over the edge.

There was no need for him to ask her consent now, for she was all too eager for his touch. And when he stroked a finger into her, then followed it with two, she could not stop herself from rocking into his touch. She found his mouth so that they could mirror the motion of his hand with their tongues. Higher, higher she seemed to soar with every thrust of his hand, and when finally she went over, it was with a cry of elation as she closed her eyes against the bright burst of her release.

She was gone for no more than a moment and came back to feel his sweet kiss on her forehead as she sprawled against his chest.

"Are you well?" His voice was strained, and an experimental shift against him revealed the cause pressing against her still sensitive body.

"Yes," she said, moving against him.

But he caught her hips and stilled her. "We needn't go any farther," he said, even as he closed his eyes against his desire. "We can wait. I still wish to marry you, but if you aren't ready for the rest . . ." He left the words hanging in the air between them.

She considered the offer. She knew now that she would not flinch at his touch, and they could have a full marriage without the memory of what had happened with Sommersby between them.

But now they were almost there, and in the wake of what he'd just given her, she didn't want to wait. She wanted him to feel the same bliss she had.

And if truth be told, she wanted him, too. All of him.

Pulling away from him, and moving to stand, she saw a flicker of disappointment in his eyes before he quickly masked it with understanding.

He rose, and ran a hand over his mussed hair. "I'll just go check on the horses," he said.

He made to turn and leave, but she stopped him with a hand on his arm. "Stay," she said. And when he'd turned to look at her fully, she removed her gown and finished unlacing her stays, letting the boning fall to the floor until she was standing before him in nothing but her shift and stockings and boots.

The knock on the door forced a very foul word indeed from him.

"The food and clothes," he said closing his eyes in frustration. To his relief, it was mirrored in Daphne's face.

Unable to resist, he crossed the room and kissed her hard. "One minute."

It took only a brief exchange to send the innkeeper away, and when he turned back, he saw that she hadn't moved.

There was something so vulnerable and brave about her standing there, nearly naked, waiting. When he moved toward her, he stopped just far enough away to let her make the choice.

But he needn't have bothered.

"You're sure?" he asked as she stepped close to press herself against him. With a nod, and meeting his gaze with trembling courage, she began unwinding his cravat.

But once he realized she was serious, he pushed her hands away and led her to the bed and threw back the bedclothes. Quickly, he finished removing his cravat, and coats and boots, and when she was seated on the edge of the bed, made haste to remove her boots and stockings. Touching her tenderly every step of the way.

When he stood to pull his shirt over his head, she leaned back against the pillows to admire him.

His body was muscled without being bulky, and she loved the width of his shoulders, the way they tapered down to his waist.

Maitland caught her watching him, and his hands paused at the fall of his breeches. She glanced down to where that hard part of him strained against the placket. And suddenly this moment between them was more real than anything she'd ever known.

Swallowing her apprehension, she gave him a slight nod, and thinking to distract herself from the moment, she rose up and pulled her shift up and over her head.

When she emerged from the lawn fabric, he was kneeling on the bed beside her, and then they were skin to skin.

"I've heard there is some pain for the lady the first time," he said against her ear, even as he caressed over her naked skin. "I will try to be gentle, but I don't know if once I begin I'll be able to . . ."

She stopped his words with a kiss. "I trust you" was all she said. And then she gave herself up to the overwhelming surge of bliss that came from feeling his warmth against her from head to toe.

And when he kissed her now, there was no diffidence, no hesitation, only desire. She opened herself to his touch, and reveled in the primal sensation of his weight against her.

His hands, calloused from driving, were rough against her bare skin as they teased their way over her belly.

When he shifted to kiss his way from her neck to her breasts, then downward, she let him. Only when she felt his arms slide under her knees did she gasp in surprise. "What are you doing?" she asked, both breathless and puzzled.

Maitland looked up at her, every inch the decadent lord sprawled naked in her bed. But also patient. Tender.

"Will you trust me?" he asked, his eyes imploring. She sensed that he wanted this as much as he wanted it for her.

Since he was clearly the more experienced between them, and he hadn't yet broken her trust, she nodded.

Given free rein, he continued his movements, hooking his elbows beneath her knees and opening her wide to his gaze. She closed her eyes in embarrassment at the thought of him seeing her thus. But when she felt his warm breath on her mound, she gasped in a mixture of shock and sensation.

It was thoroughly wanton, but she was unable to stop herself from straining against him where he stroked his tongue against her, reigniting the flames his fingers had lit earlier. And when he sucked the peak, then teased his fingers over her molten core, it had her panting, begging, pleading with him to give her what she needed.

She almost wept when she felt him slide up over her, but just as quickly he placed his thumb where his mouth had been and propping himself over her on one arm, guided himself to that part of her that desperately needed to be filled.

With one strong thrust, he gave it to her.

Chapter 13

He'd tried to hold back. Tried to be gentle. He'd tried his damnedest to make sure she was as prepared as a woman can be for her first time.

But still that first thrust almost send Maitland over the edge.

He clenched his teeth against the need to pound himself into her, to let go of the desire he'd tried desperately to keep banked while tending to her needs. She was worth it, he knew, but dear God, he was desperate to let go.

"Yes?" he asked, echoing his earlier question to her, praying that her response would be affirmative. If he had to stop now, it might kill him.

He'd do it. He had to. But he would weep.

"Yes," she said, and whether consciously or not, her hot, sweet sheath clenched around him, and before she even finished the approving syllable he was lost.

Moving against her, struggling to keep his thrusts

decorous—if such a thing were even possible—he felt beads of sweat roll down his back as he pressed into her. Again and again, then needing to be closer, he brought his arms beneath her knees again, this time pressing her wide so that there was not even a breath of space between them.

And all the while, Daphne, moved beneath him. If there was pain, she gave no indication of it. Instead she writhed and bucked as much as she could in the position, and with each thrust he felt her clench around him.

He tried to hold out as long as he could, but after months of waiting and wanting, the feel of her tight body clasping him was too much for finesse. He sped up his thrusts, and when he stroked his thumb over her sensitive nub, she cried out, trembling beneath him as her crisis took her. Free to let go at last, he pounded into her three more times before he emptied himself within her in a shout of relief.

He came back to himself slowly, but fully aware that the soft body cushioning him was Daphne.

Daphne.

Reluctantly, he withdrew and eased onto his back beside her. "I'm sorry." Keeping her in the circle of his arms, unable to stop himself from touching her, he stroked a thumb across the soft skin of her shoulder. "I must have been heavy."

But she must not have minded, because she curled into his side, and stroked a hand over his chest, toying with the light dusting of hair there.

"Is it always like that?" she asked, her breath soft against his skin as she spoke.

He huffed out a laugh, still a bit breathless. "It most

definitely is not." He thought back to his previous lovers, though the very act felt disloyal somehow. But he could never recall being so . . . drunk . . . with passion before. Certainly, he hadn't felt the sort of protectiveness he did for the woman in his arms.

What that said about his chivalry, he didn't like to think.

When he didn't elaborate, she went on, "Ivy seems to think she and Lord Kerr are quite good at it."

Dalton raised his eyelids and found her watching him. He wasn't sure he wished to think about his cousin and his wife together.

No, he was certain he didn't wish to think of it.

Though considering that he and Kerr were cousins, it stood to reason that . . .

"I think we are better," Daphne said, breaking into his thoughts. Then her words sank in.

"You're quite the competitive little thing, aren't you?" He met her mouth for a kiss.

She settled her head back down upon his shoulder. "I'm better than all the other ladies at mathematics of course, but I did think that because Ivy is married she would have surpassed the rest of us at lovemaking. Especially considering that her husband clearly has a great deal of exp—"

He stopped her mouth with a kiss. "Perhaps we shouldn't talk about such things, my dear. It could make things rather awkward for me the next time my cousin and I are left to our port after dinner if I'm thinking about him in bed with his wife."

And that statement reminded him of Beauchamp House and all the changes awaiting them as soon as they left the cocoon of this room and returned to their normal lives. He sighed into her hair.

Before she could continue with her speculation about Lord and Lady Kerr, he said, "When we return home, I'll set out for London to obtain a special license. It shouldn't take above a day or so if the weather holds."

She pulled back a little, eyes wide. "So soon? We still have to visit your aunt's solicitor in Hastings. And there is the matter of informing the magistrate of what we've found."

And just like that, the spell was broken, and they were thrust back into the everyday world.

He sat up against the pillows as she held the sheet to cover her nudity. She'd never been more beautiful.

"There's nothing to be done for it," he said, watching as she examined her hands, not meeting his eyes. "We can't risk Pinky spreading word of seeing us here. The new vicar has been established at the church, so we can marry in a few days' time I should think."

He could tell that she didn't like the idea, though whether because it was sooner than she wished or because she didn't wish it at all he couldn't guess. Either way she would have to adapt. Because marry they would. On that matter, at least, he would not budge for one reason that was of the utmost importance.

"There might be a child, Daphne," he said. They could both endure ruined reputations if necessary, but he would not place that sort of burden on an innocent.

Her eyes widened, and instinctively she rested a hand on her softly curved belly. "I hadn't considered that," she admitted with troubled eyes.

He didn't like worrying her, but she was an intelligent

woman. She deserved to know all of his reasons for wishing to marry her.

"Come," he said kissing her one last time before he began gathering his clothes from the floor, "we should have time to get back before dinner."

He pulled on his breeches and watched shamelessly as she followed suit, though the sheet covered her spectacular bottom as she bent to retrieve her chemise.

Pity, that.

Slipping into her stays, Daphne said thoughtfully, "If we had a child, it would very likely be quite intelligent. And beautiful."

"With my stunning good looks and your brain," he said with a grin, "how could it possibly be otherwise?"

As luck would have it, they were met at the entrance to Beauchamp House by Ivy, who took one look at their disheveled state and called for hot baths and tea for them both. And soon Daphne found herself in her dressing room, soaking in a lavender-scented tub. Her maid fussed over her tangled hair and damp clothes and made sure that her robe was warmed by the fire before she wrapped herself in it.

Though she would have liked some time alone to consider what had happened with Dalton at the inn, she found her fellow bluestockings waiting for her in the seating area of her bedchamber.

"Here," said Sophia, handing her a cup of tea as she took the overstuffed chair they'd obviously left vacant for her. "Summer might be at hand, but these storms can be quite chilling. We don't wish you to catch your death."

"I am quite warm, thank you," Daphne said, though

she took the proffered tea and drank. Dalton had done a thorough job of warding off any chill the rain had left her with. Though she was oddly reluctant to tell her friends that. Their response to her confession that she'd propositioned him before had been swift and scandalized.

"What did you learn?" Ivy asked, settling back with her own tea. For the barest moment, Daphne thought she was talking about that interlude with Dalton, and her eyes widened.

"Did you find the clue with Mr. Renfrew as you'd hoped?" Gemma clarified.

Relieved, Daphne nodded. "Yes, we did. It took a bit of doing because Mr. Renfrew is suffering from the effects of old age, but we did manage after a bit."

She explained how the former steward's daughter had let them search the man's belongings until they found the clue from Lady Celeste. Dalton had the actual note, but she'd memorized it and recited it for the other ladies now.

"So you believe she means the next clue is with her solicitor in Battle?" Ivy asked, after they'd discussed the likely interpretation of "Themis' shining sword." "I can't help but agree. Themis is often used to symbolize justice and the law. Well done, both of you."

Daphne blushed a little at the praise. "It was mostly Dalt . . . um, the duke, who guessed the meaning. As you know my classical knowledge is not what yours is."

"Dalton, is it?" Sophia asked with a sly smile. "Do I take it the two of you grew a bit closer on your journey?"

"Hush, Sophia," her sister chided. "They are betrothed—even if it's only a temporary ruse. It's hardly shocking that she would use his Christian name."

"About that," Ivy said with an inquisitive look. "Was I mistaken or did Maitland not eschew the hot bath I had brought up for him and call for his horse to be saddled and his valet to pack a bag? Surely he isn't going to Battle on his own?"

Daphne didn't bother trying to dissemble. "I believe he is traveling to London for a special license."

Silence fell on the usually chatty group.

"It must have been a very eventful journey, indeed," Sophia said with a speaking look at her sister for chiding her earlier.

"I must say," Gemma said with a little shake of her head, "if my sister and I do not wish to become betrothed, we must of necessity avoid going out in a gentleman's company when a storm is likely."

She referred, Daphne knew, to Ivy's betrothal to Lord Kerr following their being caught out during a rainstorm. Daphne wondered if her friend and her husband had spent their rainstorm in a similar activity. Curious.

Ivy pursed her lips, but ignored them. Instead, she turned to Daphne and touched her lightly on the arm. "Is all well? Are you agreeable to the match? Because if not, I can speak to Kerr and have him put his cousin off for a bit."

But despite her reluctance when Dalton had mention a special license earlier, she was determined to go through with the marriage. Her own reputation might not be of primary importance to her, but she knew that Maitland took his gentlemanly honor quite seriously.

She may not have considered marriage to be something she wanted before, but if she was being honest with herself, she wasn't exactly dreading marriage to the duke. If anything, she was rather looking forward to it. She cared nothing for his title or wealth. But the fact that he was able to rouse fire in her with barely a look was certainly an enticement.

If what they shared in bed was as unusual as all that, she was reluctant to give it up for a life of lonely solitude. That only a few months ago she'd looked forward to such a life was an irony she found amusing.

And she had come, in the past weeks, to value his reliability and even temper. If he'd been a different sort of man, one like her father, for instance, she could have ignored the other benefits. But his passion coupled with his personality made the match that much more appealing.

Then there was the matter of a possible child. Something far too monumental for her to consider as anything more than an abstraction now. Though the very idea made her chest tighten with emotion she dared not name.

So, in answer to Ivy's question, she didn't need to be rescued.

"There is no need for anything like that," she told Lady Kerr with a shake of her head. "We are agreed upon the matter. Indeed, I am sanguine."

"Did you . . . ?" Gemma looked troubled. "That is to say, did you tell him about what Mr. Sommersby did to you?"

At the mention of Sommersby, Daphne was surprised

to find that she no longer felt the same sort of dread on hearing his name as before. Had Dalton managed to exorcise the demon of the other man's assault once and for all?

"He knows," she said with a small nod. "And it is likely a very good thing that Sommersby was dead before he learned of it."

"Speaking of Sommersby's death," Ivy said, "I believe the magistrate wished to speak to you again this afternoon. He called while you were both still gone. He would not tell Quill why he'd called however. Though I suppose that has more to do with their history than anything else."

Quill had had a liaison with the other man's wife in his salad days.

"Perhaps tomorrow we can call upon him," Daphne said, thinking that since Maitland would be away, and it felt somehow disloyal to travel to Battle without him, this would be a way for her to continue their investigation without breaking his trust. "He very likely will not be able to shed any light on the search for the cipher, but he should be aware that the killer likely has another clue."

From downstairs, the dinner gong sounded, and Ivy, Sophia, and Gemma rose.

"I believe I'll have a tray in my room," Daphne said, suddenly feeling exhausted from the events of the day. And if she were honest, dinner without Maitland there to entertain her with amusing stories and silly teases sounded dreadfully dull.

Hanging back from the others, Ivy waited until the Hastings sisters were gone before saying in a low voice,

"If you have any questions, Daphne, or would like to know if anything is . . . irregular . . ."

Daphne's brows drew together. It took her a moment to catch the other lady's meaning. And when she did, she felt her whole face turn red.

"Oh, no!" she said with a shake of her head. "There is nothing . . . that is to say I do not have any . . ."

Ivy nodded. "I thought I'd offer my counsel, nonetheless. It can be unsettling at first, but it can be quite enjoyable if you let it."

"I'm not sure I understand you," Daphne said with a frown. Her experience with Dalton had been more than simply enjoyable. "It was . . . magnificent."

At her pronouncement, Ivy grinned. "I am relieved to hear it. I don't mind telling you Kerr was brilliant that first time, too, but my mama refused to hear it. I thought perhaps my experience was singular. And feared yours would prove to be more as she described."

Daphne shrugged. "Perhaps it is a generational difference?"

Ivy nodded. "I confess I don't like to think of it too closely since it means thinking about my parents together like that." She gave a delicate shudder.

Having never met Ivy's parents, Daphne couldn't say one way or the other.

"In any event," Ivy continued, "I am glad to hear you are content with that aspect of the relationship. But I do hope you'll come to me if that should change. I like to think we ladies should stick together in such matters, though there seems to be a societal taboo about talking openly about them."

"I will keep that in mind," Daphne said. "Though

I am perhaps not the one who needs to be encouraged to strive for more candor."

"And on that note," Ivy said with a laugh, "I'll be off."

When she was gone, Daphne crawled into her bed, and as soon as she closed her eyes she was back in the little room at The Bo Peep.

She fell asleep remembering just how safe she'd felt in Dalton's arms.

Chapter 14

Maitland made good time to London, and though it meant rousing the sleeping servants, he decided to stay the rest of the night at his London house rather than going to a hotel. His mother slept soundly, so he didn't see her until the next morning when he stepped into the breakfast room and found her eating her customary toast and tea.

"Maitland," she said with surprise as he stepped over to kiss her cheek. "I wasn't expecting you. Though I suppose I should have guessed given the amount of food on the sideboard."

His mother disliked excess, which made her a most unlikely duchess. Especially given his late father's love of it.

He filled a plate for himself and sat down near her. "I arrived quite late," he told his mother. "And didn't wish to wake you."

Her blond brows rose in question. "Was there some reason for you to ride in haste?" He watched as she considered the matter. Before he could speak, she said, "There's nothing amiss with Serena or Jeremy is there?"

"No," he assured her, feeling like a cad for letting her worry. In truth, he'd been trying to come up with a way to explain his actual reason for coming to town, but it hadn't occurred to him that she'd interpret his silence as dire. "Both Serena and Jem were well when I left them, I assure you."

She relaxed at his words. "I don't believe I'll ever stop worrying about her after what that monster Fanning did to her," she said with a scowl. "Horrid man. Your father was a fool to let her marry him."

Not wishing to rehash the circumstances of his sister's marriage, Maitland was silent, and took a bite of eggs.

When he looked up he found the duchess watching him. "Why did you come back in such a hurry?" she asked again, scanning his face for an answer. "Has another of Celeste's bluestockings got herself into trouble? I hope she knows better than to try to trap you into marriage!"

The duchess had been rather jealous of her children's close relationship with her sister, and the news that one of them had actually married Quill, her nephew, in haste had only served to prove that Celeste's choice of heirs had been faulty.

At her choice of words, Dalton winced. He had imagined this conversation in a more comfortable setting than at the breakfast table while she interrogated him like a cardinal of the Spanish Inquisition.

"I would hardly call Kerr's happy marriage a trap, Mama," he said with a frown. "Indeed, Quill and Ivy are quite blissful, which you would know if you had accepted their invitation to come for a visit at Beauchamp House."

"Oh, piffle," the duchess said with a wave of her hand. "I have no wish to travel to the seaside unless it's Brighton. And you may make all the assurances you like about the happiness of your cousin's marriage, but your Aunt Estelle is convinced that that hussy lured him into a trap. A mother knows these things, Maitland."

Estelle was Lord Kerr's mother, the dowager Lady Kerr, and incidentally the sister of Celeste and the Duchess of Maitland.

Pushing aside his plate, Dalton took a fortifying gulp of tea before saying, "I wish you would not speak of Ivy in that manner, Mama. She is a lovely lady and has made Quill very happy, I assure you."

At her grunt of disbelief, he sighed before pressing on. "As it happens, my reason for coming to town is somewhat tangentially related to Quill's recent marriage. I have come to procure a special license, in fact. For myself and Lady Daphne Forsyth, another of Aunt Celeste's heiresses."

The Duchess of Maitland's jaw dropped. "What? I was only engaging in a bit of hyperbole when I asked if you'd been trapped into marriage. Maitland, please tell me this is some jest on your part!"

"I'm delighted to say it is not," he said firmly. "Lady Daphne and I will be married as soon as I return to Beauchamp House." Despite his fervent wish that she would reject the invitation, he added, "I hope you will return with me to celebrate the nuptials."

"I most certainly will not!" she said, her eyes wide and her back ramrod straight. "Because you will not be marrying the daughter of that . . . that rapscallion Lord Forsyth. Do you know who the man is?"

"He is currently in Little Nodding, so yes, I do," Dalton said through clenched teeth, not wanting to admit that her assessment of Daphne's father was not far off his own. "And it makes no difference to me who her father is. I am marrying *her,* not the earl."

"It is a *mésalliance* of gigantic proportions," the duchess said, her voice rising with every syllable. "Even worse than your cousin's marriage to that scholar's daughter. At least her father is respected and conducts himself with dignity. The Earl of Forsyth is a drunkard and a gamester. And he has made a practice of carting the chit all over town to play cards at his behest. Like some sort of gambling pander."

At her slander of Daphne, Maitland stood, glaring down at his mother. "Hear me well, Mama," he said, his voice barely controlled in his anger. "You will speak that way again about Lady Daphne Forsyth at the risk of damaging our relationship forever. She is not her father, and she is not to blame for his bad acts. No more than Serena or I are to blame for our father's."

At the mention of the late duke, his mother flinched.

"Yes," he said with a feral smile, "remembering now, are we, that the previous Duke of Maitland was also a rapscallion?"

"Maitland," she said, looking contrite, but unbowed, "I never meant to say that Lady Daphne was—"

He cut her off with a gesture. "I do not wish to hear you say it again. I am quite serious about the consequences should you defy me on this matter, Mama. I am the head of this household, and I have chosen my bride.

If she does not please you, then that is lamentable, but it is my choice to make."

"But her reputation," the duchess said with a shake of her head. "Your father's reputation makes it doubly necessary for you to behave like . . ."

"Like a gentleman?" he asked with a raised brow. "That is precisely what I am doing. I have compromised her, Mama. And my own scruples mean that I must marry her. But aside from that, I wish to marry her. She is quite the most intelligent person I have ever had the pleasure to know. And the loveliest."

At the word "compromise" the duchess raised a hand to her chest in horror. "Oh Maitland, did you not heed my warnings about the schemes young ladies will try on an eligible nobleman? How could you have let this happen?"

Seeing that she found it impossible to believe that he could have been the one to do the compromising, Maitland sighed. Pinching the bridge of his nose, he said, "Mama, I will not go into the details with you, but rest assured that every step of the way, I was the one at fault. Not Lady Daphne."

His words must have given her pause, because she shut her mouth on whatever it was she was about to say, and nodded.

With a sigh of relief, he continued. "Now, I hope that you will write a cordial letter to Lady Daphne welcoming her to the family if you still refuse to return to Beauchamp House with me for the wedding."

He thought for a moment that she would change her mind—something he very much did not want to happen—but fortunately, she said with a shake of her head, "I truly cannot leave town at the moment, my dear. Though I hope you will bring her to meet me as soon as you think you are able. I will oversee her introduction at court. And doubtless she will need a new wardrobe."

Though he was a grown man capable of making his own decisions, he would not put it past his mother to attempt some sort of intervention to keep the wedding from happening.

"I have little doubt that Daphne will welcome your assistance," he lied. Daphne would very likely chafe under his mother's guidance, but that was a bridge he'd cross when he came to it. "Now, I would like to discuss this further"—another lie—"but I must go find the bishop so that I can get back to the coast."

"I am sorry I reacted so badly, my dear," she said with a sad smile. "I suppose I do not only worry about your sister. It is quite hard to accept that my children are all grown up now and able to take care of themselves."

He looked at her, noticed the threads of silver in her blond hair that was so like his own. Her marriage to his father had not been a happy one. And she considered Serena's disaster of a marriage as something she should have been able to prevent. It was little wonder she greeted with shock and dismay the news that he was to be married by special license to someone she knew only by reputation.

"I know," he told her, bending to kiss her on the head. "But we are quite grown. Though it doesn't mean we don't need your affection and guidance."

She nodded and surreptitiously dabbed at her eyes with a lace-edged handkerchief.

When he left to find the bishop, she was bent over her escritoire, penning a letter to Daphne.

He could only hope it did not include references to Lord Forsyth.

When it came to speaking frankly, his mother and Daphne had that trait in common.

"I'll inquire as to whether the Squire is available to receive visitors," said the Northman's butler with a scowl.

Daphne and Ivy had risen early and set out after breakfast for the magistrate's house. After yesterday's storms, the sky above them was clear and blue, and they decided to walk rather than take the carriage.

"Perhaps I wasn't the best person to accompany you," Ivy said as they watched the dour man leave. "I still don't think I've been forgiven for the scene at their dinner party."

Ivy and Mrs. Northman had argued over something having to do with Lord Kerr, Daphne recalled. And the elder lady had been quite angry about the fact that Lord Kerr had become engaged to Ivy—though from Daphne's point of view, the woman had no right since she was already married herself.

"We are not here to see the lady of the house," Daphne reminded her. "And even if we were she would be obliged to be polite to me since I outrank her rather significantly." Daphne found that reminding unpleasant people of her due as an earl's daughter sometimes led to an improvement in their attitude.

Ivy hissed a laugh. "You should not say that," she said in a low voice, shaking her head. "And yet, I would very much like to see you tell Mrs. Northman that to her face."

"Where else would I tell it to?" Daphne asked, puzzled. Why did people insist upon speaking words that made no sense? It was most frustrating.

Then the butler returned to inform them that the magistrate would see them, and soon Daphne and Ivy found themselves seated before a very large desk in the Squire's study.

"I was quite displeased to find you gone from home yesterday, Lady Daphne," he said once they were settled. "I needed to ask you some questions about Sommersby's death, and you were not there."

"Yes," Daphne said, puzzled. "Because, as you say, I was gone from home."

"There is no need to be flippant, Lady Daphne," he said, his heavy brow furrowed. "This is a serious business. A man was killed in your home, and it seems very likely it was related to an artifact you yourself are searching for."

If he was going to investigate the matter, Daphne thought petulantly, then he should use the proper terms. "As it happens I am searching for a coded message, a cipher, if you will. Not an artifact. Though it is around seventy years old so it is not precisely of current origin. A cipher is a . . ."

Ivy touched Daphne on the arm, startling her into pausing in her explanation. Ivy was quite good at placating men when necessary, Daphne thought with a touch of jealousy,

"I think what my friend is trying to say, Mr. Northman," Ivy said with a sweet smile, "is that she is very sorry for not being available when you wished to speak to her. But she has some news that might help in your investigation."

Daphne scowled. That was not what she had meant to say at all, but her friend's placating tone must have worked, for the Squire sat up straighter.

"What is this news? I've had my men search high and low for this other man whom you and the duke say shot at you," he said with frustration, "but if he is still here, he's hidden himself well."

Ignoring the magistrate's complaint, Daphne quickly outlined how they'd found the note from Lady Celeste behind the painting and how it had led them to visit Mr. Renfrew in Bexhill.

"Why in the blazes would Lady Celeste hide all of these bits of verse across the county?" the Squire asked with a moue of distaste. "If you ask me it's a havey-cavey business. She should have just left the coded message with her will and had her solicitor hand it over when you inherited. Then there would have been no need for Sommersby to search high and low for it, breaking into other people's homes, and what not."

Though it felt disloyal to her benefactress, Daphne tended to agree with the man. Except for one particular point. "At the time, secrecy about the location was quite necessary because the gold was intended for treasonous purposes," she said, trying to be polite. But really, was the man so foolish that he didn't know as much?

"And," Ivy added, with a speaking look her friend, "Lady Celeste enjoyed creating puzzles. She thought she was leaving a game for one of her heirs to solve. I'm sure she had no notion that Mr. Sommersby would come to harm in the course of searching for it."

"Hmph." The Squire didn't argue, but nor did he seem convinced. "So you intend to follow these clues until you locate the cipher?" He folded his arms across his chest, the picture of skepticism.

"I do, indeed, sir." Daphne raised her chin a bit. "And I will solve it, and find the gold."

"And what of the murderer? He has the original version of the cipher. What if he beats you to the treasure?"

Daphne couldn't stop herself. She laughed.

"I don't see anything amusing about this matter, Lady Daphne." The Squire leaned forward. "A man is dead."

"I am well aware of that fact, Mr. Northman," she said before Ivy could intervene. "But I find it very hard to believe that the murderer has my mathematical and ciphering abilities. If he is able to unravel the message, then I shall be very, very surprised."

The magistrate just stared at her for a moment. Daphne was used to this reaction to her pronouncements about her abilities, and did not flinch.

"I'll say this for you, my lady," the man said with a shake of his head. "You've got bottle. I only hope you've got someone looking after you while you're haring about the countryside searching for Lady Celeste's bits of paper."

"I am perfectly capable of—" Daphne began, but was interrupted by Ivy, who rose and locked arms with her.

"Thank you so much for your time, Squire Northman," Ivy said inclining her head. "We will keep you informed of our progress. As we hope you will do with your own progress in finding Mr. Sommersby's killer."

Once they were in the hall, Ivy whispered, "I thought we'd agreed you would not argue with the man overmuch. He already is suspicious about this entire affair. We do not wish him to decide that you are acting strangely or had reason to want Sommersby dead yourself."

"But I did," Daphne said in an answering whisper. "Though not because of the cipher, you realize."

"I'm not a mathematical genius, Daphne," said Ivy with a huff, "but I am not a simpleton. Of course I know you had other reasons. But we haven't told the Squire about that, and if you intend to keep it that way then you had best not speak of it here in his hall where the servants might be listening."

That gave Daphne pause. She truly didn't want to explain what had gone on with her and Sommersby in the past. And Ivy was right. It would give him reason to suspect she had even more reason to kill him.

They were almost to the bottom of the main stairs when Daphne heard a familiar guffaw coming from below.

As she and Ivy reached the ground floor, she was shocked to see her father there, with Mrs. Northman's arm in his, as if they had just returned from a walk.

"Father," she said as the couple handed their hats and coats to the waiting footman, "I didn't expect to see you here."

As if he'd only just seen her, the Earl of Forsyth gave a theatrical start. "My dear daughter," he said. "What a pleasant surprise."

That was a lie, she knew, since he could hardly be surprised to see her in the home of a neighbor.

"I thought you'd returned to London but imagine my surprise when I learned through gossip you were still here," she said, watching as Mrs. Northman's glance flitted from one Forsyth to the other in barely disguised glee. "Why did you not tell me you were staying in the neighborhood?"

"Did I not?" Forsyth asked. "It must have slipped my mind after our disagreement the other day. Though I must admit that I was able to come to quite agreeable terms with your betrothed. How is Maitland?"

At the mention of Maitland, Daphne felt herself color. "Maitland is none of your concern. And he told me that he gave you enough funds that you shouldn't bother us again anytime soon. Which makes me ask again, why are you still here?"

If he felt the sting of her rebuke he did not let it show. "If you must know, I was at school with Northman. And when I met him on the road to Little Seaford, he was kind enough to invite me to stay. And since I would like to be here for your nuptials, I thought I would accept."

His eyes narrowed. "You are going to wed soon, are you not? A little bird told me that you were seen at The Bo Peep looking very cozy indeed. In fact, someone said that Maitland claimed you were already wed, which I know cannot be true. Why it takes a day's hard riding at least to get to London for a special license."

Before Daphne could respond, Mrs. Northman spoke up. "Lady Daphne," she said with a catlike smile. "I was rather shocked to hear of your hasty betrothal. Though I suppose that is becoming quite typical of the way things work at Beauchamp House. If we are to go by the precedent set by Lord and Lady Kerr, that is." She nodded in Ivy's direction.

"Now listen here, Mrs. Northman—" Ivy began with a scowl.

Daphne, knowing that no good could come of a sentence begun that way accepted their pelisses and hats from the butler and led her friend to the door.

"Good-bye, Father," she said over her shoulder as she hurried her friend away from danger.

"But what of your wedding?" he called after her.

"Why didn't you let me speak my mind to her?" Ivy complained as they hurried away from the Northman home and toward the lane leading back to Beauchamp House. "I'm a Marchioness now and outrank her. Didn't you say that reminding people you outrank them helps?"

"Not when Mrs. Northman loathes you as much as she does," Daphne explained. "And besides that, you shouldn't get overexcited. Lord Kerr won't like it."

"Oh piffle," Ivy said with a scowl. "Kerr knows how I feel about her. And I'm not an invalid."

Daphne thought about the possibility that she might soon be saying the same thing. If Lord Kerr was any indication, men became quite overprotective when their wives were breeding. "Very well," she said, stopping as they reached the end of the Northman's drive. "Would you like to go back and rip up at her?"

"No," Ivy replied grumpily. "I'm no longer in the mood. Besides I do not wish you to have to see your father again. What on earth was he thinking to stay in the neighborhood without informing you?"

"I don't know," Daphne replied. "But it can't be good."

Chapter 15

"I'm afraid his lordship and the ladies have walked over to the vicarage to meet the new vicar, your grace," Greaves informed Maitland when he arrived back at Beauchamp House the following day.

He was bone tired, and still troubled over his conversation with his mother the day before. But he needed to see Daphne before he could rest—because, truth be told, he missed her.

Handing his hat, gloves, and greatcoat to the butler, he asked for hot water to be sent to his room. Then, recalling what Lady Celeste's note in Renfrew's belongings had said, he asked the older man if he could recall the name of his aunt's solicitor in Battle.

"Yes, your grace," Greaves said with a nod. "It was a Mr. Hargrave."

A flash of some emotion Maitland couldn't read crossed the butler's face, and something about how quickly the man was able to recall the name told him it wasn't the first time he'd heard the question. "Lady

Daphne asked after Hargrave while I was away, didn't she?"

"Indeed, your grace. Though she did not ask for the man's direction." He gave a small smile. "I believe she was waiting for your return, if I may say so."

Well, thank heavens for that, at least. Maitland had been half expecting to learn Daphne had traveled to Battle on her own when the butler told him she was home.

With thanks to the man, he hurried upstairs to wash off the worst of his travel dirt and change clothes, then because he was mindful of getting to the vicarage before the others left, slipped through the secret passageway off the kitchens and took the shortcut along the shore.

"When the vicar's housekeeper showed him into the comfortable drawing room of the tidy manor house, his cousin, sister, and the four bluestockings looked up in surprise at his entrance. Daphne was seated beside a handsome man with curling light brown hair and smiling eyes.

Maitland hated him on sight.

"Your grace," the man, who must be the new vicar, said with a warm smile. "I am glad to meet you. From what your sister and her friends have said, you are a most amusing fellow."

The duke glanced at Lord Kerr, who gave a slight shrug as if to say "What did you expect?"

Then his cousin stood and performed the introductions. "Reverend Lord Benedick Lisle, may I introduce my cousin the Duke of Maitland?"

"That sounds rather imposing, doesn't it?" said Lisle after he and the duke exchanged bows. "Among friends, I am just Ben."

"And are you?" Maitland asked, with a raised brow. Something about the fellow set his back up. Perhaps the fact that he'd seemed so cozy sitting next to Daphne when he arrived. "Among friends, I mean. You've only just met us all today, as I understand."

Before the vicar could respond, Lady Serena spoke from where she was seated beside Daphne on a rather hideous green chintz settee. "We have actually determined that Benedick shares many acquaintances in common with us, Maitland. And he is the brother of Lord Freddy Lisle. Were you not at school with him?"

On closer inspection, Lisle did bear a striking resemblance to his brother Freddy, whom Maitland had known at university. And in that context, his good looks and charm made absolute sense. The Lisle brothers were known for their way with the ladies.

"Indeed, I was," he said. "Though Freddy was a year ahead of me. We did run in some of the same circles."

"Freddy knows everyone," the vicar said with a laugh. "I have yet to visit any part of England where I haven't met someone who has at the very least heard of him."

"But surely it is your brother Lord Cameron Lisle who is the more famous of the two," Gemma said from where she was examining a shelf of books. "He is quite well known as one of England's foremost natural scientists. I've read all of his treatises. They're quite fascinating."

Benedick hid a smile. "I would promise to tell my

brother of your praise in my next letter," he said, "but I'm afraid his sense of his own importance is already quite outsized enough."

"One cannot blame him for being proud of his achievements," Daphne said, coming to the absent man's defense. "There is nothing wrong with being aware of one's own strengths."

Further conversation was stalled by the arrival of the tea tray, which Lady Serena offered to preside over.

"Your cousin and the ladies were telling me a bit about what happened here before my predecessor retired," the vicar said as cups were handed around. "I must confess, it does not sound like the sort of thing I am used to as a general rule. Most parish scandals are rather dull."

He was referring, of course, to Ivy's kidnapping and the former vicar's harm at the hands of Lady Celeste's killer.

"Unfortunately, we seem to be prone to some rather unusual happenings in the area," Lord Kerr said, taking a seat on the divan beside Ivy. "I suppose you've heard by now about the business with Sommersby at Beauchamp House?"

"A bad business," Lord Benedick agreed. "Mrs. Northman was quite happy to fill me in on the particulars." He gave a slight grimace. Clearly, he had not been charmed by the magistrate's wife, Maitland thought wryly. The matron would be quite disappointed.

"She is a very unpleasant woman," Daphne said with her customary certainty.

Maitland was prepared to defend her to the clergyman, but he only said mildly, "I cannot disagree, Lady

Daphne. Though it is perhaps un-Christian of me to say so."

"She is hardly in a position to cast judgment." Sophia turned from her examination of a small landscape hanging above the fireplace. "Mrs. Northman, I mean. She who is without sin and all that, after all."

The vicar raised a brow. "I hope no one here will be casting stones any time soon."

"Only into the sea, Lord Benedick," said Sophia with a hint of color in her cheeks. "Much as it would satisfy me to take Mrs. Northman down a peg. She has been quite unpleasant to several of my friends now. And I do not tolerate such for long."

"Most loyal of you," replied the vicar with an approving glance.

The conversation then turned to other, less-inflammatory topics, like the local congregation and how the newcomer was settling in. Before long Lady Serena rose, as did the others, to take their leave.

When Maitland lingered behind the others, Daphne did as well, telling them that they would be along soon.

"I had hoped for a word alone with the vicar," he said in a low voice as she placed her hand on his arm.

"But this involves me as well as you," she said with a frown. "Why should I not be here when you speak to him?"

Lord Benedick, who watched them with some amusement in his eyes from his place before the mantle, bit back a grin. "I take it you wish to speak to me about performing a marriage?"

Startled, Maitland turned to him. "What makes you

guess that?" Perhaps he and Daphne wished to speak to the fellow on some arcane matter of theological importance. Or they wished to invite him to supper at Beauchamp House. They could be here for any number of reasons.

"For one thing," the vicar said, looking from one to the other, "as soon as you entered the room, your grace, Lady Daphne's entire demeanor lightened."

Daphne frowned, and placed a hand to her cheek as if to verify the statement.

"And you, Maitland," he said to the duke, "scanned the room until you found her, then relaxed, as if knowing her location allowed you to be calm again."

Maitland wasn't sure if he was pleased or annoyed at the other man's assessment.

"The duke has just returned from London where he acquired a special license," Daphne said. "That is, I presume you were successful?"

"Of course." Maitland was not a mathematics genius, but he was quite able to exert his ducal influence when necessary. "And, as you guessed, we should like you to perform the ceremony. Here in your church preferably."

He hadn't discussed the matter with Daphne, but Maitland had fond memories of sitting beside his aunt in the family pew here as a boy.

But the idea seemed to appeal to Daphne, and she nodded her agreement.

"I would be delighted," said the vicar with a warm smile.

They made plans for ceremony in three days' time with just their friends in attendance.

As he walked them to the door, however, Lord Benedick

stopped. "I just remembered. There was something I found while going through some papers my predecessor left behind. If you'll wait for just a moment?"

And before they could protest, he hurried from the room, returning a moment later carrying a sealed letter.

"I didn't make the connection until you arrived this afternoon, Lady Daphne," the vicar said as he handed it to her. "And then there was no convenient moment to bring it into the conversation. I suppose you met the old vicar before he departed and he wished you to have it?"

But when Daphne held out the missive, her scrawled name was in Celeste's handwriting.

"Thank you very much," she said, staring down at the page. She made no mention of what the note could pertain to. Noting the seriousness of her expression, the vicar didn't ask.

Ready to get her alone so that they could open it, Maitland bowed to the clergyman and they made their farewells.

They made their way to the path leading from the vicarage to the sea stairs in silence.

As if by mutual agreement, they didn't stop to read the note until they were at the bottom of the stairs, out of sight of both the vicarage and Beauchamp House, which loomed over the cliffside cave entrance that served as the portal to the secret passageway.

There, Maitland handed Daphne down to sit on one of the lower steps, and he sat down beside her.

She slid a finger beneath the seal and opened the folded page.

* * *

Daphne had felt such a cavalcade of emotions since arriving at the vicarage that morning, she almost suspected she was sickening with something.

If the Reverend Lord Benedick Lisle was to be believed, she was love sick, though she knew very well that whatever it was she felt for Maitland was something far less hysterical. She wasn't even sure she was capable of such a thing as love. Affection? Absolutely. Attraction? Certainly. But love implied flights of fancy and public declarations. And she was as prosaic as ever.

Even so, when he'd arrived in the parlor of the vicarage, she had felt a spark of elation to see him after his absence. Had it only been a day or so? If one measured by how much she'd missed him, it would have been a month at least.

She hadn't realized just how transparent her affection for him had become—for that was what it was—until the vicar mentioned how she'd looked on seeing Maitland's arrival. She wasn't normally one to wear her emotions on her sleeve. But then the past few days had been far from normal.

She'd been so pleased to see him, in fact, she hadn't even argued with him over his decision for their wedding to take place in the church. It wasn't that she was against having it there, but she had thought perhaps the gardens of Beauchamp House would be pleasant. The wedding was just a legal formality, however, so it hardly mattered where it took place. And Maitland seemed to be sentimental about the area, so he likely had his reasons for wanting it in the tiny church.

Their silence on their walk back toward Beauchamp

House was comfortable, rather than awkward, as silences could sometimes be. And she was pleased to have him beside her, feeling the pleasant zing of attraction between them even as they did something as ordinary as walk home.

Now, seated beside him on the sea stairs, Daphne read aloud from Celeste's letter.

> *My dear Lady Daphne,*
>
> *I gave this letter to the vicar to, in turn, give to you should you come to him for assistance in the quest I left for you.*
>
> *It is my hope that if someone should get the cipher before you, you will find the second set of clues I've left for you. I have always believed it is better to prepare for the worst while hoping for the best, and unfortunately, there are those who would like very much to know the location of the prize I left for you. One of the paths to it is more straightforward than the other, but I have faith that no matter which you take you will emerge the victor in my little game. Certainly no other is as quick with numbers and ciphers as you are.*
>
> *It is also my hope, though he will not thank me for meddling, that my nephew Maitland will be of some use to you in this matter. He has never considered himself to be a good student, but I know him to be quite clever when it comes to handling people. And you, my dear, for all that you are an intelligent woman, are not. I have left instructions for him to take charge of your comfort at Beauchamp House and to assist you in any*

way he sees fit in your quest. Please allow him to help you should you need it.

You are a bright and lovely lady, Daphne. And I trust you to do whatever is best when you reach the prize. It's why I chose this particular puzzle with you in mind.

Yours affectionately,
Lady Celeste Beauchamp

"What does she mean she 'left instructions' for you?" Daphne asked a sheepish Maitland. "You never mentioned anything about that?"

As she watched, he rubbed a hand over the back of his neck. "It never came up," he said in a defensive tone. "And I did not think you would be particularly pleased to learn my aunt was concerned about your lack of . . . that is to say your problems with . . ."

"My brusque manner?" Daphne asked sweetly. She was rather enjoying seeing the normally self-assured duke off his pedestal.

"That isn't what I said," Maitland returned with a frown. "Though you must admit that I do have a charming way about me. And I'm not nearly as good as you are at maths."

"The fact that I am your superior when it comes to calculations is beside the point," Daphne said with a huff. "I am more concerned about the fact that you kept your aunt's message to you from me, when I have been thoroughly honest with you."

"I thought she was meddling, as she said," the duke replied, staring out at the rolling waves. "And I didn't wish you to think I was helping you only because of what my aunt said."

"But weren't you?" Daphne asked. She suddenly wasn't quite so sure that the connection she'd felt between them was as strong as she'd at first thought. Had he sought her out only because his aunt had suggested it?

She felt her heart constrict at the thought.

Folding the letter, she stood and hurried toward the cave entrance, suddenly needing to be alone to think the matter over.

"Daphne, wait!"

She heard him behind her as she stepped into the coolness of the cave. After the brightness of the seaside, her eyes took a minute to adjust to the dark, though the others had left a pair of lamps burning where they hung from hooks on the wall.

To her surprise, she felt tears well in her eyes. She hadn't realized how much she had trusted Maitland's attraction to her before it was in doubt.

"It isn't what you think," he said softly, stopping her with a hand on her arm. "My aunt's letter had nothing to do with my interest in you."

"I don't see how that can be true," she said, turning to face him, though she once again found herself unable to meet his gaze. "Indeed, your initial rejection of my advances seems to indicate that you could not see me as a potential lover because your aunt had already got you thinking of me as someone for you to look after."

"That had nothing to do with it," he said, grasping her by the shoulders. "Daphne, look at me."

She swallowed, terrified at what she would see if she let her eyes meet his. But when he asked again, she looked up.

"I rejected you for the reasons I gave you at the time," he said, his eyes intense with some emotion she couldn't read. "Because I do not debauch innocents. And because you were my aunt's heir, and as such off limits to such things. That is not to say that I wasn't attracted. You know I was, from that first moment we met."

"But I don't know what to believe, now," she said with a shake of her head. She looked down at the front of his coat, unable to meet his gaze any longer. "And this calls all of your actions into question. Your announcement of our betrothal to my father. Your ruse with Pinky at The Bo Peep. How do I know this wasn't all part of some plan you concocted at your aunt's behest?"

"All of that was genuine," he said, tipping up her chin with his finger. "All of it. Daphne, I've never been more drawn to a woman than I am to you. I think of you every moment of the day. I rode for almost twenty-four hours straight just so that I could get back to you."

She wanted to believe him. She truly did. Before Maitland she'd come to believe that she would never find a man she could truly trust—not outside of her tutor Mr. Sommersby. And there were so many things about him she had come to appreciate. His warm smile. His—yes—his charm. Even the crooked grin he seemed to save only for her.

"But what if I trust you and you let me down?" she asked in a voice so low he had to lean down to hear her.

"Oh, sweetheart." He wrapped her in his arms, and unable to resist his nearness, she went willingly, slipping her arms around his neck and lifting her face to his. "I will let you down. Because that's what it means to be human. But I promise you, I will try not to."

He bent his forehead to touch hers.

"I don't know if that's enough," she whispered.

"Then perhaps what's between us can be," he said, just before he took her mouth.

Chapter 16

Daphne felt the cave wall at her back as he worshiped her mouth, every touch more devastating than the last.

She'd missed him while he was gone. Far more than she could ever have imagined.

It wasn't just that she enjoyed his company, but she admitted to herself, as she reveled in the feel of his hard body beneath her hands, that she craved him physically. Like the perfect equation, there was something about his particular combination of body and soul that, when combined with hers, rendered the most elegant solution.

"I missed you," he said against her throat as she slid her hands beneath his coats, to feel the warmth of his skin through the fine lawn of his shirt. "Missed this."

She replied with a sigh as he tugged down the top of her gown and put his mouth where she most needed it, on her exposed breast. Bold in the circle of his arms, she grasped his buttocks and pulled him closer, the jut of his erection pressing into her belly, reminding her of how much he wanted her.

As if he could sense her need for contact there, Maitland shifted, lifting her skirts with one arm as he kept suckling her peak. When she felt his fingers at her aching center, she gave a whimper of relief. Desperate now, she moved restlessly against his hand and almost cried out her disappointment when he drew away. She bit her lip as she followed him with her hand, stroking where he pressed against the falls of his breeches.

"I'm coming back," he said in a strained voice, making quick work of the buttons there, before raising her gown to her waist. "Hold on," he said, lifting her in his arms.

Instinctively, she wrapped her legs around his waist, fitting him against the aching heart of her. With one thrust he plunged into her, and Daphne cried out with the rightness of it.

They clung together for what felt like hours like that, Maitland's breath warm against her neck as she felt a tremble run through him, like a racehorse eager to sprint away. Then when the stillness was almost unbearable, he began to move. Slowly at first, so that she felt every inch of him as he withdrew from her clasping body. But soon they were both writhing together in an erotic dance, Daphne welcoming his every surge forward with a rising sense of urgency.

At last, before she even knew it was upon her, she felt herself hurtling over the edge as she seemed to splinter into a thousand pieces of profound joy. Aware only in some distant part of her consciousness of the pulsing waves of her body where he claimed her with his own. Still clinging to him, she felt his rush toward his own release, until with a strangled cry he thrust one last time before relaxing against her.

They clung there to one another for several minutes, both trying to catch their breaths. When she let her feet drop to the ground, she found that her knees were a bit wobbly and was grateful for his steadying arms around her.

"Easy," he said with a smile in his voice. "I wouldn't want to follow up the most incredible experience of my life with a visit from the doctor. It tends to reflect poorly on a man's sense of his own lovemaking skills when his partner ends up with broken bones."

He was absurd, she knew. But it was one of the things she most loved about . . .

She stiffened as she realized what she'd just thought.

Loved? Why had her mind gone to that word?

Which Maitland misinterpreted as offense at his joke. "Not that that's ever happened before, of course. I wouldn't wish you think that I . . ."

Shaking off her momentary lapse, Daphne forced herself to smile. "Of course I don't think that."

He seemed to be skeptical of her reassurance for a moment before he smiled back and stepped away. "Good."

While they both began setting their clothing to rights, Daphne reflected on her lapse in thought.

Perhaps it was perfectly natural for a lady to fancy herself in love with the man who'd just brought her such carnal bliss. That was what it was, she decided. Gratitude. She'd mistaken her natural response to his very considerable skills at bringing her pleasure for love.

Relief at having found a likely explanation for her

momentary slip, she pulled up the sleeve of her gown and straightened her bodice.

Just because she was going to marry Maitland, she reasoned as she watched him turn his back so that he could discreetly refasten his breeches, did not mean that she had to give him her heart. Before this week, she'd been content to think of spending her life as a spinster bluestocking. While other women were toiling as wives and mothers, she would use her superior intelligence to blaze trails where no lady had gone before.

Circumstance and necessity had changed those plans, and she had agreed that marriage to the duke was now necessary both to protect their reputations and that of their as-yet hypothetical child. But that didn't mean she had to give all of herself to him. Surely it was allowed for her to hold some part of herself back from him. No matter how much she trusted and admired him, there was some resistant corner of her mind that did not, might not, ever fully believe he could remain such a paragon as he seemed now.

And, she couldn't help reminding herself, he had kept his aunt's letter to him from her. As betrayals went, it was small, but it could be the first in a series. Or worse, might lead to larger and larger ones.

"You're quiet," Maitland said as they walked in single file through the hidden passageway leading from the cave up into the kitchens of the main house. "I wasn't too rough, was I?"

She heard the concern in his voice and felt a pang of affection—that's what she'd call it—for this man who seemed so careful not to do her harm.

"Not at all," she said, glancing back to give him a

reassuring smile. She'd never been overly concerned about the feelings of others—mostly because she managed to hurt them without meaning to again and again. If she allowed herself to care too much, she'd be always in tears—but perhaps because of his gentleness with her, she wanted desperately not to hurt him. Hopefully, there would be no reason to do so.

She couldn't help but recall his words to her earlier about letting people down being part of the human condition.

Not really giving a damn if the whole household guessed what they'd got up to in the cave, Maitland left Daphne at her bedchamber door with a kiss before going in search of Kerr.

Unfortunately, he was forestalled by the appearance of his sister, Lady Serena, bearing down upon him in the hallway leading to the study.

"I'd like a word please, Maitland," she said with a speaking look that reminded him of their mother in one of her moods.

Without waiting for him to agree or disagree, she stalked down the hall past the study, where he'd hoped to find Kerr, and toward her own little parlor.

By the time he stepped into his sister's *demesne*, she had already taken up a position behind her writing desk, reminding him of a father about to reprimand his heir. Their father had been particularly fond of the pose, though he'd often employed a birch as well. Fortunately, he needn't worry about any sort of corporal punishment from Serena.

Closing the door behind him, he couldn't help straightening his coats before he perched on one of the painfully small chairs before her desk. Really, had it been too much to ask that his aunt, who had furnished the entire house, would ensure at least one man-sized chair per room?

"I trust your trip to London was a success?" Serena asked. "I know you at least were able to speak to Mama, because she sent a letter informing me of her intention to come down for the wedding. Which, by the by, she has instructed me to tell you, should really be at St. George's Hanover Square."

Maitland gaped. "How the devil did she get a letter here so quickly? I only made it there and back in such haste because I rode as if the hounds of hell were on my heels."

"I daresay she told her messenger to do the same," Serena said with a shake of her head. "You know when Mama is determined, she can make whatever she wants happen."

"She told me she would not attend the wedding," he continued, wanting to tug his hair from its roots. "That she was far too busy. I should have known it was a feint. Just once I'd like her to do what she says she'll do."

"You had just as well wish for the moon to fall to the earth to be bowled like a ball," his sister said. "She will always do as she pleases, as you well know."

"Then so shall I," he said with a scowl. "Daphne and I have arranged to be married in the village church in three days' time. If Mama is not here by then, she'll simply have to settle for meeting my duchess after the fact."

Serena, who had come to respect their mother's whims

like the unpredictable imps they were, made a tsking noise. "Are you sure you want to do that? She can be most disagreeable when she's been thwarted."

"So can I," he said simply. "And I am more concerned with disappointing Daphne, who must be my main concern now. Mama will just have to adjust."

"Speaking of Daphne," Serena said with a chiding tone, "I would prefer it if you could manage to behave yourself until you are wed. It's bad enough that Ivy and Quill compromised themselves into marriage on my watch, but now my own brother has got himself a bride in the same way. Beauchamp House is beginning to get a reputation in the neighborhood for mayhem."

He felt his ears turning red. He had thought Kerr might tease him about the extra time they'd taken on the return from the vicarage, but not Serena.

Still, he felt a need to defend himself, if only to preserve the upper hand as a sibling. "I would think that finding a dead man's body in the library would do more damage to Beauchamp House's reputation than the hasty marriages of two of Aunt Celeste's protégés."

His sister scoffed. "You know full well that sex is far more scandalous than murder, Dalton." She only used his Christian name when she was truly annoyed. "And if you had the decency to keep your . . . um . . . escapades confined to other places besides the house, I would perhaps be less incensed."

"But we did," he protested, because technically the cave was not inside the house. At least not the part of it where he and Daphne had . . . escapaded.

But his words fell on deaf ears. "I don't wish to hear it. I know what I heard when I was in the wine cellar looking for something for dinner tonight, and it was not the soothing sound of the sea, let me tell you." She gave him a pointed look.

If possible, his ears got redder. He had never enjoyed the sort of relationship with his sister—or any family member aside from Quill—where he felt comfortable discussing his sexual exploits. And certainly he didn't relish the thought of his sister overhearing him with Daphne.

He shuddered. He couldn't help it.

"Oh, I heartily agree," Serena said with a pained expression. "So, perhaps now you'll agree with me that at the very least you should confine your amours to the bedchamber?"

"But you just said you didn't want us doing it in the house!" He couldn't help pointing out her inconsistency.

"I don't want to know about 'it' at all," she said, her voice rising with exasperation. "But at least in either of your bedchambers, I won't be in danger of overhearing you."

She had a point there. Being overheard by his sister was about as strong a cockstand killer as he could imagine. In fact, some of the afterglow from the cave had been destroyed knowing she'd heard them.

"Very well," he said with some remorse. "You've made your point. I apologize for scandalizing you. It's just that Daphne and I are . . ."

There was no way he could describe just how impossible it was to keep his hands off his betrothed without embarrassing them both. So he settled for saying, "very compatible."

Serena smirked at the euphemism. "I could have told

you that from the first day you met," she said with a shake of her head. "I am happy for you, Dalton. More than I can say."

Her smile was genuine, and he felt the warmth of her affection in a way that had been missing from his interview with their mother. It was Serena whose support he wanted most.

"I will admit," she went on, "that at first I was not overly fond of Daphne. She can be quite abrasive at times. And her insistence upon her own intelligence was grating before I realized that it is her insecurity about all her other abilities that makes her flout it so."

"And she is correct that she knows more about maths than the rest of us will ever forget," he said wryly. It should perhaps be a bit intimidating for him to contemplate marrying a woman who could think circles around him, but he sensed that there was something about *him* that she was drawn to. Something only he could give her. Something she needed—and not just carnally, though that was one connection between them certainly.

"But I think she's beginning to realize there is more to life than just intellectual pursuits," Serena said. "And you are not a simpleton, brother. Just because you haven't devoted your life to scholarship doesn't mean you know nothing."

It was true he'd been rather good at school, but Dalton knew that his true skill lay in his ability to read people. And to navigate the sometimes troubled waters of personal relationships, be they business or social. He was good at people.

He said as much to Serena.

"I think that's why you complement one another," his

sister said with a smile. "Though I do worry about how she'll manage the political intricacies of being a duchess."

At that, he laughed. "Are you mad? She already behaves like a duchess. All she lacks is the title and power to follow it through. She'll be far more successful than Mama has ever been. With the difference being that she won't be manipulating people for the sake of her own ends. And if she offends anyone it will be accidental rather than purposely."

"You truly are in love," his sister said with a laugh.

At the mention of love, he shook his head. What he and Daphne had together was powerful, and he felt great affection for her, but he wasn't ready to call it love. Not yet when they'd only given in to their desires three days ago. "I wouldn't go that far," he said, "but perhaps it will grow into love. At least that is my hope. At the very least I want our marriage to be more affectionate than that of our parents."

"Or mine," Serena said with a sad smile. "Do not apologize for thinking it. I was, too. In fact, I sometimes look at Ivy and Quill, and you and Daphne and wonder if I will ever find that sort of happiness for myself."

Dalton's chest hurt for his sister. Her marriage had been, with the exception of Jeremy, a nightmare. But the very fact that she was even considering the possibility of finding love meant that she'd healed in some way. And he counted that as a blessing.

"I know you will, my dear," he said, grasping her hand where it lay on the desk. "I have every faith that there is some man out there who will appreciate and love you as much as Jeremy and I do. Indeed, as the whole of Beauchamp House does."

"Even Daphne?" Serena asked skeptically.

"Especially Daphne," he replied with a grin. "How can she not love the lax chaperone who allowed her to go cross-country with me?"

Her shout of offended laughter rang in his ears for a long time afterward.

Chapter 17

The next morning found Daphne and Maitland riding in Lady Celeste's ancient barouche with Ivy and Kerr, on their way to the town of Battle only a few miles from Beauchamp House.

That they bring along the marquess and marchioness had been Lady Serena's suggestion that morning at breakfast, and Daphne had seen some silent communication pass between Maitland and his sister before he declared it to be a fine idea.

She'd not seen him again after their encounter in the cave. Maitland having declared himself exhausted after nearly twenty-four hours in the saddle, retired early. Daphne had missed him at dinner, but had taken the opportunity to continue her organization of the library. And somehow, she'd been calmer knowing he was in the house, even if they weren't in one another's pockets.

"It was rather clever of Lady Celeste to engineer another way for you to obtain the cipher," Ivy said as the carriage rumbled along the road overlooking the sea. "It's almost as if she knew someone else would get to it before you did."

Daphne considered the notion. She didn't believe in premonitions, or anything of the sort, but she thought it very likely that Lady Celeste had used her reasoning powers to make the deduction. "It's not as if the existence of the cipher was a complete secret," she said aloud. "Though it was considered by many to be a romantic legend, I think there were an equal number of those who thought the legend was rooted in some truth. I first learned of it from my tutor, who said he heard of it while he was at school. So, it was known in mathematics circles."

"Aunt Celeste was at the very least concerned about ensuring you would be the one to eventually solve it, however," Maitland argued. "She must have chosen you as one of her heirs because she thought you could figure it out."

"I wonder that she didn't attempt to solve it herself," Lord Kerr said from where he sat beside his cousin in the rear-facing seat. "She was quite formidable at solving puzzles and the like."

"She did," Daphne responded, putting a hand on her hat to keep it from flying off in the wind. "She told me as much in her initial letter to me. I do believe that's why she sought me out. She wished her heirs to be good at different areas of expertise, but she wanted a mathematician in particular because she thought it would make the cipher easier to solve."

"If only we could find the blasted thing," Ivy said, holding on to her own hat. "I do appreciate Lady Celeste's attention to detail, but I do hope this other trail she left is shorter. If we reach the solicitor's office only to find another clue that leads to more clues, I will be most put out."

"I am more concerned that whoever killed Sommersby and found the other cipher has already unraveled it and found the gold," Daphne said. It was something she worried about more than she let on. Because if he'd found the gold, they might never know who had killed Sommersby. And though Squire Northman seemed to accept the notion that someone outside the household had killed the man, Daphne couldn't help but fear that their lack of success in finding the murderer would lead the magistrate to turn his suspicions back to her. Especially if he ever learned of Sommersby's assault on her.

"If it was too difficult for my aunt to solve," Maitland said in a reassuring tone, "then I doubt the killer has managed it either. It's said that Cameron was fond of maths and codes himself. So it's likely that he created something that was difficult for anyone but a truly gifted scholar to solve."

"I hope you're right," Daphne said with a sigh. "Otherwise we're wasting our time haring about the countryside."

"I wouldn't say that," Ivy said, grinning. "It's rather exciting to be on the hunt. Especially if we manage to catch a murderer at the end of it as well as find the lost gold."

"I fear your success in unmasking my aunt's murderer has made you bloodthirsty, Ivy," said Lord Kerr in mock exasperation.

Daphne watched as they shared one of those looks

that seemed to convey hours of conversation in a single glance. What must it be like to be so in tune with another person that you could read their feelings as easily as she could read the pattern in a series of numbers? She'd only just learned to meet Maitland's eyes without looking hurriedly away. She certainly couldn't tell what he was thinking.

But the same could not necessarily be said for Maitland when it came to him fathoming her thoughts. When she chanced a look at him, he raised a brow in question. He knew something was bothering her. She was able to read that at least, she thought, as she gave a small shake of her head in reply.

When they reached the village of Battle, so named because it was the site of the Battle of Hastings that put William, Duke of Normandy on the throne, it took only a few moments to find the office of Mr. J. Hargrave, Esq.

At the news that not one, but four noble visitors wished to see his master, the pale-faced clerk, a Mr. Fleet, in the outer office turned even whiter. "One moment please, your grace, Lady Daphne, Lord and Lady Kerr."

Alone with the clerk's underling, a thin young man who stood gaping at them like a circus exhibition, they waited.

"I take it Mr. Hargrave's clientele does not generally hail from the aristocracy," Kerr said in a low, amused voice. "I wonder what possessed Aunt Celeste to give him her business."

It was a well-appointed office, Daphne noticed, but hardly the sort of place one would expect of someone who enjoyed a thriving trade. At least, not that she imagined. She'd never had occasion to visit a solicitor's office before.

Before any of them could respond to Kerr's remarks, they heard a shout from the back room where the clerk had gone. Daphne looked at Maitland, who said, "Wait here." And though she chafed at the order, she and Ivy stood where they were as they watched the gentlemen, followed by the assistant clerk, disappear into the back office.

"I hope all is well," Ivy said nervously. "I wish I hadn't said that about this exciting me. I don't wish people to be harmed. Goodness knows."

Wanting to comfort her friend, and perhaps needing a bit of comfort herself, Daphne placed a hand on Ivy's shoulder. "I know you don't. And perhaps it was nothing. A book falling on someone's foot. The clerk tripping over his own feet."

But the longer they waited for the gentlemen to return, the more she knew it couldn't be anything as benign as she'd described.

When Lord Kerr came back alone, her heart caught in her throat. Where was Maitland?

"I'm afraid Mr. Hargrave has met with an accident," said Kerr without preamble. "I'm going to find the local physician, though I fear the man is no longer able to benefit from his services."

Daphne clasped a hand to her chest. "He's dead?" she asked, horrified.

"What happened?" Ivy asked.

"We're not sure," Kerr said. "I'd better go find the doctor. Maitland will be out in a moment to tell you more."

And with a quick kiss for his wife, Lord Kerr was out the door.

Not content to stay where he'd left them, Daphne and Ivy moved as one to the door and stepped into the office.

Maitland, who knelt beside an unconscious man behind the desk, looked up at their arrival. "I told Kerr to keep you out of here," he said with a frown. "Go back outside."

"We aren't children, Maitland," Daphne said with a firmness she did not feel. "Perhaps we can help."

Brushing past Ivy and Fleet, the clerk, who stood wringing his hands, she moved to kneel beside the duke and saw that Mr. Hargrave was bleeding from a rather large gash in his forehead. Beside him lay an open box, the twin of the one they'd found in the secret room in the library at Beauchamp House—and it was glaringly empty.

Ignoring the clue for a moment, she concentrated on the bleeding man. "Give me your cravat," she said to Maitland, who unwrapped the cloth from his neck and handed it to her.

Taking the starched linen, she folded it into a pad and placed it against Hargrave's bleeding wound. He had lost a great deal of blood, which ran down the side of his head to pool on the carpet beside him. "What can have happened, Mr. Fleet?"

When the clerk didn't respond to her question, Maitland turned to the man. "You there, Lady Daphne asked you a question. I know you're overset by finding your master in this state, but we must find out who did this."

Blinking, the clerk turned to look away from the pool

of blood at Daphne. "I don't know. I left to visit the stationers and I sent Henry here to collect the post. We were only gone for a half hour or so. Someone must have come in while we were gone.

The man left off with a broken sound. "If only I'd thought to check on him sooner."

"You can have had no notion of what happened," Ivy said in a soothing voice. "It's not your fault. It's the fault of whoever did this."

"Has your master had any visitors in the past couple of days?" Maitland asked, rising to begin looking through the papers on the unconscious man's desk. "Anyone you might have found suspicious?"

"There are always strange characters in and out of the office," Fleet said with a shake of his head. "It's part and parcel of the work. Mr. Hargrave isn't snobbish like some. He will take on work so long as the client's coin is real."

"So, you cannot think of anyone who might have done this?" Daphne asked, looking up from where she held the cravat to Hargrave's bleeding head. "Has anyone else been here asking about Mr. Hargrave's work for Lady Celeste Beauchamp?"

The clerk blinked. "Yes, there was a man here this morning before we left. But Mr. Hargrave sent him away."

Daphne and Maitland exchanged a look.

"What did he look like?" Maitland asked, turning from his search of the desk to look more closely at the clerk. "Describe him."

Sagging a little on his feet, the clerk said, "He was of middle years. Respectable-like, but his clothes weren't so fine as yours. I knew he wasn't from around here, though. I didn't recognize his name."

"He gave you his name?" Daphne asked, surprised.

"Yes," the clerk said shakily. "Sommersby. Mr. Richard Sommersby."

Maitland watched, arrested, as Daphne gasped at the clerk's pronouncement.

"Are you sure that's the name the man gave?" she asked, her face losing all color. "Richard Sommersby?"

Moving to her side, and indicating with a nod that the underclerk, Henry, come tend to his master's wound, Maitland pulled Daphne to her feet and saw her to a chair. "What did this person look like?" he asked once she was settled.

Fleet took a deep breath and closed his eyes for moment, as if trying to recall. Finally he said, "Not quite as tall as you, your grace. Dark hair with some gray mixed in. And spectacles."

"That's him," Daphne said with a helpless shake of her head. "My former tutor. Perhaps it's only a coincidence that he was here this morning."

Hearing the hope in her voice, Maitland's heart ached for her. It was possible that two men had called upon Hargrave that morning, but unlikely. The man who had assaulted the solicitor was almost certainly the elder Mr. Sommersby.

Ivy, who had been watching aghast from the other side of the desk, came forward and lay a hand on Daphne's shoulder. "I see some brandy, there," she said in a soothing voice. "Perhaps Maitland will pour you some?"

Grateful to have something to do, Maitland moved to the sideboard against the wall, and set about unstoppering the decanter and pouring a glass.

"I'm perfectly fine," Daphne protested, even as she took the glass from him. Their eyes met, and he saw how upset she was at the idea her mentor was tied up in all of this business. Even so, she squared her shoulders and took a sip, closing her eyes against the fiery taste. "I haven't seen Mr. Sommersby in a long time," she continued. "We're practically strangers now."

But Maitland couldn't help but remember what she'd said about her tutor being the one man she'd been able to trust in her life. Of course, that had been before he left their home unexpectedly, but she'd seemed to explain that away, blaming it on her father. What would she do if she discovered that he'd turned out to be just as unreliable as everyone else?

He didn't like to imagine the effect that would have on her.

On them.

Just then, the door leading into the office opened and Lord Kerr entered, followed by a man of middle years carrying the black bag that denoted his profession.

"Dr. Eustace," Kerr said to them as the physician hurried to the prone man's side and began examining him. "We've arranged for a couple of men to come with a litter to carry him to the surgery if necessary."

"Perhaps we should get out of their way," Maitland said, moving to offer Daphne his arm. She looked over to where the doctor was examining Hargrave's wounds, then with a sigh, she rose and allowed him to lead her out.

Fleet, who had regained some of his composure, remained behind to assist the doctor, sending his assistant, Henry, back to watch over the outer office.

Once they were back out in the outer room, Maitland explained in a low voice what they'd learned about the solicitor's visitor that morning

"Sommersby's father?" Kerr asked in surprise. "What is he doing in Battle? Wouldn't he have come to Beauchamp House or Little Seaford to collect his son's things?"

"I'm afraid it appears as if Mr. Sommersby is searching for the cipher," Daphne said, her disappointment evident.

"We still don't know that he is the one who hurt Hargrave," Maitland said, trying to reassure her.

"But logically, it's the only explanation that makes sense," Daphne said. She ticked off her points one by one using her fingers. "First, he is the one who initially told his son and me about the Cameron Cipher. Second, he may very well have been the one to encourage Nigel to go in search of the cipher. Third, he was not a wealthy man, and certainly would benefit from the hidden cache of gold.

"Most damning of all, however," she continued, "is that he could have had no reason to visit Mr. Hargrave other than to see if Lady Celeste left any other clues about the cipher with him. He was her solicitor—and people often leave important papers in the care of their solicitor."

"But why attack the man?" Maitland asked, not sure he understood the connections Daphne made between the tutor and the attorney. "It certainly doesn't help him find a solution for the cipher."

"We can have no idea what actually happened until we talk to one of them," Daphne said, "but the fact that the box was lying empty beside Mr. Hargrave seems to indicate that Sommersby took what was inside."

"I saw some blood on it," Maitland said. He'd wanted to keep the information from Daphne for as long as possible, but she was already leaping to the same conclusions he was. "Before you came into the room, I examined it. I'm quite sure it's what was used to bludgeon him."

"Dear God," Ivy said, raising a hand to her chest.

They'd all seen how strong the blow had been that cracked Hargrave's skull. It had taken a great deal of strength, and perhaps anger, to do that sort of damage.

"He would be quite frustrated," Daphne said softly from where she stared out the window. "He's likely already tried and failed to solve the decoy he stole from the hidden room. And I suspect he hoped that whatever was in the second box would make his task easier. If it was the real cipher, then he was met with just another puzzle impossible for him to solve."

"Why impossible?" Ivy asked, from where she perched on Kerr's chair. "I thought he taught you everything you know about mathematics and ciphers and the like?"

Daphne, turned, and gave a bitter laugh. "Actually, that's not correct. I did learn a great deal from Mr. Sommersby, it's true. But he was only my tutor for a year or so before I surpassed his ability to instruct me. He guided my studies, of course, but he didn't fully understand everything I worked on."

"But if you believe he's been after the cipher all along . . ." Maitland began. He stopped because to finish would mean putting into words what was for Daphne a horrific discovery.

She pressed on. "If he is the one who's now in possession of the cipher," she said in a sad voice, "then it is almost certainly the case that he murdered his own son."

Chapter 18

After ensuring that Mr. Hargrave, who was still clinging to life, was safely settled into Dr. Eustace's surgery, the party from Beauchamp House made the journey back home in a much more somber mood.

Without discussing the matter, Maitland and Ivy had switched seats, so that he could ride the entire way back with his arm holding Daphne close. She felt as if she should protest, but she had to admit that she needed the comfort of his nearness. Perhaps she had learned that the one person she thought she could trust above all was a murderer, but she still had Maitland.

When they reached Beauchamp House, they were met at the door by Serena, who informed them that Mr. Ian Foster was waiting to see Daphne in the drawing room. Wondering what the crown agent could want, Daphne hurried upstairs with Maitland hard on her heels. When she stepped into the blue-and-white room, it was to find Foster impatiently tapping his fingers on the mantle.

"Finally," he said without greeting as they stepped into the room, Maitland closing the door behind them. "I thought you'd eloped to Gretna."

Ignoring the man's complaint, Daphne stalked over to where he was standing with his back to the fire. "We're here now, Mr. Foster. And it's been a trying morning, so I hope you will get on with whatever it is you wish to say."

She knew she was being unforgivably rude, but what she'd said was true. It *had* been a trying morning. And she wanted nothing more than to hide away in her bedchamber and think about what she'd discovered about her tutor.

Foster frowned and turned to Maitland for support, but he didn't get it, because he said, "Well, I suppose I should have known you'd not exactly welcome me with open arms."

"How clever of you, Foster," said the duke with a pointed look. "But then, I daresay you Home Office spies are used to being given the cold shoulder. That happens when you lie to everyone around you and get a man killed in the process."

"For the last time," Foster said with a grimace, "I didn't tell Sommersby he should break into Beauchamp House. If I'd known what he was planning, I'd have warned him against it. And I certainly didn't stab the fellow to death."

"But it was your information that made him think the cipher was hidden there," Daphne retorted, feeling all the anger and frustration of what they'd found that morning bubbling up within her. "You are just as responsible for Sommersby's murder as the man who actually killed him. If not more so, because as a representative of His Majesty's government you're supposed to protect the lives of his citizens."

"I can't be responsible for every damned fool who decides to go in search of hidden treasure," Foster protested, looking aggrieved. "I wasn't even sure the tip about the cipher being hidden in Lady Celeste's library was even true."

"Where did you get that tip, by the by?" Maitland asked from where he'd stopped beside Daphne. "As far as we know, Lady Celeste told no one but Daphne, and that was in a letter she didn't receive until after my aunt's death."

Foster looked defiant for a moment, then as if coming to some decision, he gave a short nod. "Fine, but if I tell you, you must promise not to hold it against the man. He's been useful to us in the past. And he is actually quite good at his profession."

Daphne, who hadn't expected Foster to tell them anything caught her breath.

"I learned of it from Lady Celeste's solicitor. A man who keeps offices in Battle, by the name of Hargrave."

"What?" Daphne and Maitland asked in unison.

Thinking they were shocked because of the breach of ethics on Hargrave's part, Foster raised a hand. "I know it sounds as if the man broke his client's trust, but in matters of national security such as this, it's not unusual for a solicitor to give us information about his clients. In this case, Hargrave was privy to Lady Celeste's possession of the cipher because he was also her man of business. So he knew about all of her assets. And it was his idea that she create the secret room—a playful replica of a Priest's Hole as the Catholics used during the Reformation, and later the secret rooms Jacobites used during the rebellion."

"Who else knew about this?" demanded Maitland, while Daphne looked on in horror. Was it possible that Foster was indirectly responsible for both Sommersby's murder and Mr. Hargrave's attack?

Foster frowned. "I told only Sommersby," he said, some of his defiance seeping away. "Though I have no idea whom he might have told. I didn't say so before, but I suspected he had an accomplice. I mean, it's obvious, I suppose, considering his murder."

"Hargraves was assaulted this morning in his offices in Battle," Daphne said coldly. "That is where we've been this morning. Picking up the pieces of another man who was harmed as a result of your callous disregard of the safety of others."

Ian Foster paled. "What?" he asked, his voice strained. "That's not possible. I only spoke to Hargrave the day before Sommersby's murder. He was fine."

"I hope I don't have to tell you that there is a difference between then and now," Maitland said severely. "I daresay whoever it was that killed Sommersby sought out Hargrave thinking he might have more information about the cipher."

"But I don't understand," Foster said, oddly deflated. "If he has the cipher, what more does he need? He only needs to solve it and find the gold. There's no need to search for more information."

"We believe that the man who stole the cipher from Sommersby is unable to decode it," Daphne said wearily. Was it really only a week ago that she'd been excited at the prospect of finding the cipher and discovering the treasure? It seemed like a lifetime ago.

"Then why did he seek it out in the first place?" Foster asked, clearly baffled by the idea. "I was planning to take it to an expert the government consults with sometimes at Oxford. I certainly know my limitations and that there's little to no possibility that I'd be able to crack it. Though I'd likely give it a try for a bit at first.

"This man may have an elevated sense of his own abilities," Maitland said, exchanging a look with Daphne. He seemed to be asking how much she wished to tell Foster about her tutor's involvement.

"Who is it, for God's sake?" the agent demanded. "I can have the man taken into custody in a day's time. Or less, if the weather holds."

"We don't know where he is," Daphne said tightly. "If we did, we would have turned him over to the authorities ourselves when we found Mr. Hargrave."

"But who is it?" Foster pressed. "Is there some reason you're not telling me? Is it someone you're close to?"

Daphne sighed. She wasn't sure why she still felt any loyalty to Mr. Sommersby, considering all he'd done, but somehow she did.

Then, before she could even decide whether or what to tell, Foster's eyes grew wide. "It's Richard Sommersby, isn't it?"

She must have revealed he'd guessed correctly through her expression, for Foster's mouth gaped. "I knew it was no coincidence that Sommersby's father was visiting the seaside when we arrived in Little Seaford."

"Why didn't you tell us the elder Sommersby was

here before?" Maitland demanded, looking as if he wanted to lift Foster by the cravat and shake him. "He's the one who told Daphne about the cipher in the first place, years ago. He's likely been on the hunt for it for decades."

"He went on his way—or seemed to—after we met him in the village that day," Foster said, looking ill. "But it's quite possible he came back while I was traveling to Battle to visit his son. And I did tell Sommersby where I was going and whom I was planning to see."

Daphne said the foulest curse word she could think of, and far from looking shocked, Maitland nodded.

"Agreed."

"I've made a mess of this from the beginning," Foster said with a groan. "The Home Office will never trust me with anything again."

The duke scowled. "We aren't concerned about your career with the government, just now, Foster. A man is dead. And another is fighting for his life. In part because you conducted yourself with all the circumspection of a circus performer."

To his credit, Foster looked abashed. "What can I do to make it right?"

But the thing was, Daphne, who had always prided herself on her intellectual abilities, simply had no idea.

Once Foster had gone, Maitland watched helplessly as Daphne, all but vibrating with nervous energy, paced the area between the window overlooking the gardens and the fireplace.

And unfortunately, what he had to say would not make her any less agitated.

"Daphne," he said, stopping her motion with a hand on her arm, "I want you to go to London."

She stopped, her body stiff with shock. "Why on earth would I do that? I'm the only one here who really knows Sommersby. How he thinks. I cannot possibly leave now."

"You are also the only one who can solve the cipher," he said carefully. He'd known she would object to his plan, but knowing Sommersby had been brazen enough to kill his own son, he couldn't risk allowing him to get to Daphne. What if, somehow, she was unable to solve the cipher? He had every faith in her quick mind, but in times of stress, surely even she would falter. And the consequences would be fatal. "I don't want you here, at risk of being kidnapped by Sommersby so that he can use your mental acumen to solve the damned cipher."

It was a testament to his degree of concern that he swore in front of her. Like most gentlemen, he'd been raised to refrain from coarse language around ladies. But these were trying times.

"Who's to say he won't follow me to London?" Daphne was clearly not going to meekly do as he asked, it would seem. "Much better that I stay here in case he does decide to seek me out. At least here, I know I'm among friends."

"You're being ridiculous," Maitland said, knowing it was the wrong thing to say, but past the point of finesse. "He has killed his own son. He won't stop at killing you, should you fail to give him what he wants. Sommersby is a dangerous man and he knows how capable you are of unraveling the cipher. He knows first-hand how brilliant you are. It's only a matter of time before he comes to you with the cipher. I am only shocked that he hasn't done so sooner."

He moved closer to her, but when he tried to pull her to him, she resisted.

"You seem to think that I am unable to work that out for myself," Daphne said, mouth tight with anger. "I am well aware that I am in danger. In fact, the only reason I would go to London is because leaving here would remove the rest of you from danger. But the fact remains that Mr. Sommersby needs me. His own skills are not up to the challenge, and he needs help. And if he can't get that help from me, he will go to some other great mind for it. I cannot in good conscience allow that to happen. Besides," she continued, her eyes meeting his, pleading for understanding, "there's no guarantee that he won't figure it out on his own. It is a small chance, but if he found some clues at Hargrave's office, then he may even now have found the gold.

He heaved a sigh. "You're never going to agree to leaving, are you?" he asked, torn between admiration for her bravery and exasperation at her refusal to see sense.

"I can't, Dalton," she said stepping closer so that he could pull her into the circle of his arms. "And I wouldn't want to be separated from you, anyway. We are at our best when we're working together. Haven't you realized that yet?"

It was hard to maintain his anger when she said things like that. Dash it all. He needed his anger to keep her safe.

"I don't want to be away from you either," he said,

resting his forehead against hers. "But just for clarity's sake, if you'd agreed to go to London I would have gone with you. There's no way I'm letting you out of my sight while there's a murderer on your trail."

She was silent but did not argue. Instead she lifted her face to touch her mouth to his, and Maitland lost himself in the maelstrom of passion that swept over them whenever they touched. But they had work to do, so after a few moments, he pulled back. "We should go tell the others what Foster said."

Nodding, Daphne walked over toward the door, but Maitland almost ran into her when she stopped just short of the threshold. "What's wrong?"

"Look at this painting," Daphne said, pointing to a still life he'd always thought rather ugly. It depicted an ancient Greek man, complete with toga and a wreath of leaves in his hair, holding a scroll.

"What about it?" he asked, puzzled.

"There's a message written on the scroll," Daphne said as if that would explain everything. Then, to his further surprise, she flung open the door and all but ran down the carpeted hallway toward the library doors.

When he followed her at a jog, his cousin Ivy, Sophia, and Gemma all looked up from where they were each poring over separate tomes. They'd been searching for clues to where Lady Celeste might have hidden the second cipher while he and Daphne met with Foster.

"What's amiss?" Ivy asked, frowning as Daphne hurried to the shelf that served as the door to the secret room. She didn't respond to Ivy's question, so Maitland answered for her. "She's found a clue, I think. Or something." He wished he knew more, but he was as puzzled as they were.

He made his way toward the secret room, and met Daphne coming back out, the painting of Bonnie Prince Charlie in her hands.

"Bring the lamp," Daphne said, laying the painting flat on one of the wide library tables.

Kerr, who had hung back from the rest, picked up the lamp he'd been using to read by and brought it over. When it was close enough to illuminate the painting, Daphne pointed to a plaque in the background of the scene. "Look there. At the inscription on the wall."

Squinting, Maitland leaned down to examine the section she'd pointed out. But there didn't appear to be any meaning to the jumble of letters there.

"It's nonsense words," he said, standing up to look at Daphne quizzically.

"It's the cipher," Daphne said, barely able to contain her excitement. "It was hidden here in plain sight the whole time."

He looked down at the painting again, then back at Daphne. "You're serious? But if the cipher is there, why leave clues leading us around the coast on a wild goose chase in search of it?"

But Daphne was already sitting down at the table holding her notebooks and pencils.

"I daresay she was doing a bit of matchmaking," his cousin said from behind him. "From what you said about the note Aunt Celeste left for you, Daphne, she wanted you both to spend a great deal of time together. Not unlike her scheme with Ivy and me. What better way to bring you together than on the hunt for a cipher that was here all along?"

"It's mad," Maitland said, though he had to admit the theory made some sense. "Why couldn't she introduce us while she was alive and let nature take its course?"

"I daresay because planning all this was a great deal more amusing for her," Kerr said with a grin. "Aunt always did enjoy plotting."

With a sigh, Maitland walked over to where Daphne had begun scribbling in the margins of the page where she'd written the code. She didn't look up, and appeared to be lost in thought as she attempted to work out a solution for the cipher.

"Perhaps we'd best leave her to it, then?" Sophia asked from where she stood beside her sister. They all were watching Daphne as she worked, as if they would miss something if they looked away.

"You all may go," Maitland said with a nod in the direction of the door. "I'll stay here and keep watch."

But, clearly not as wrapped up in her thoughts as she seemed, Daphne looked up then. "You must have something to keep you occupied," she said to him with a sheepish smile. "I'm afraid I'll be at this for a while. It's as difficult as I could have hoped." Then she looked a little stricken. "I suppose that's awful of me when it's caused so much heartache."

Maitland, however, could understand her excitement. It gave her the opportunity to use her gift, and perhaps that was why his aunt had left the cipher to Daphne in the first place. "Not awful," he said aloud. "Just competitive. Which isn't a bad thing."

She gave him a thankful smile, and said, "You really

may go. I will be perfectly safe here. And my table is far from the French doors, so there's no danger of flying bullets."

If she thought the jest would make him feel better, she was mistaken. "He was able to break into this room before," he reminded her. "There's nothing to say he won't do it again."

"Fine," Daphne said, throwing up her hands. "Stay. But you must be quiet and still. Otherwise I won't be able to concentrate."

Hiding his satisfaction at convincing her, Maitland watched as the others left, and mindful of her admonition about bothering her, he picked up a volume of Byron's poetry and settled into the only comfortable chair, which happened to be on the other side of the room.

And waited.

He'd only got a short way into the first canto when the door opened to reveal a nervous-looking Greaves.

"Your grace," the older man said with a glance in Daphne's direction, "I'm afraid Lord Forsyth is below asking for you."

Maitland's eyes also went to Daphne, who was in deep concentration. "He didn't ask for Lady Daphne?" he asked the butler in a low voice.

"No, your grace. You specifically." The butler looked as if he would like to say more, but clearly having been warned that Daphne needed quiet, he said in a low whisper, "Please, your grace. He says if you do not come he will come up. And Lord Kerr told me how important it is that Lady Daphne is not disturbed."

With a sigh, Maitland called to Daphne, "I'm just

going downstairs for a moment. I'll be right back. Don't move."

But if she heard him, she gave no sign of it. Clearly, when she was immersed in her work, Daphne was deaf to anything else.

Following Greaves from the room, he prepared himself for a difficult conversation.

Chapter 19

Daphne stared at the series of letters she'd jotted down from memory from the painting of The Young Pretender.

As had happened since she was a small child and first began to notice patterns, she let herself go to the place she thought of as the aether. Where everything else ceased to exist. It was just her and the numbers.

She found it impossible to explain how it happened. Her tutor and her father had both tried to have her explain it to them—perhaps so that they could do it themselves? But she honestly had no notion of how it happened. It just did.

And it worked with other patterns as well. Cards for example.

When she was dealt a hand at whist, a glance at the cards in her hand was enough to set her mind calculating odds and possibilities. And every play set her to recalculation, reassessing, mentally building a list of which cards had yet to be dealt.

With codes, it was a bit more complicated. Instead of letters on the page, she saw numbers that were the sum of two other numbers. The first corresponded to a letter of the alphabet. "A" was equal to "0," "B" was equal to "1," and so on. The second was added to each of the letters in the solution. So, if she were to add 3 to every letter of the alphabet, "A" would be represented by 0 + 3, "B" would be 1 + 3, and so on.

It fell to Daphne to figure out what the second number or, perish the thought, numbers were that had been added to the original message's letters.

Of course, this was if Cameron had used a substitution code. It was entirely possible he'd done something else entirely. But Daphne thought not. Substitution codes had been used for centuries, and the fact that the message in the painting had been composed of letters only told her it was not a symbolic code or anything more complex. The true challenge would be to determine if more than two numbers had been added together to come up with the coded message. It was a typical form of substitution code—the type of code she hoped Cameron had used to write the location of his treasure.

The cipher in the painting had read:

Gdbpc Opiw Hjbbtgatp Thipit

She set to work, trying out various combinations and subtracting important numbers in Jacobite history from the letters in the message.

So engrossed in her work was she, that she was completely unaware of the silent figure creeping up behind her.

One minute, she was scribbling a notation in pencil. The next, she was unconscious.

Maitland found Lord Forsyth pacing the same path between the window and the drawing room fireplace that Daphne had so recently walked.

As soon as he stepped into the room, the earl looked up with ill-disguised impatience. "You took your time," he said with a scowl. "Am I not to be afforded the courtesy of prompt attention? I am to be your father-in-law, Duke."

Biting back a sharp retort, Maitland said, "What is it you want from me, Forsyth? I gather you wished to speak to me, and only me about this matter? What is it you cannot share with your daughter, pray?"

The earl pokered up. "It is a matter of my daughter's safety," he said with a touch of asperity, "which I thought would better be handled by her betrothed than her father. I am not, after all, in her good graces at the moment, and I doubt she'd listen to me."

That was an understatement, Maitland thought wryly. He doubted Lord Forsyth had been in Daphne's good books since she was a babe and had no way of knowing how corrupt the man was. "By all means, tell me. I will do what I can to see that she is kept safe. Though by demanding to see me in person you took me from that very task."

"You will know much better how to protect her when

you learn the man's identity," Forsyth assured him
with a flourish. Clearly the man had a flair for the
dramatic.

"Who?" Maitland asked, prepared to hear the name
that had been racing through his own mind ever since
they'd learned of Sommersby's visit to Hargrave's office.

"He has been passing himself off as an agent of the
Home Office," Lord Forsyth said, his nostrils flaring in
annoyance. "A Mr. Ian Foster."

Maitland felt a frisson of alarm. "But surely Foster
is who he says he is. Squire Northman assured me he
knew the man as such from his own dealings with the
Home Office."

"Perhaps it once was true," Lord Forsyth said, his ve-
hemence convincing Maitland of his sincerity, "but no
longer. I had dealings with the man on a separate matter
some years ago, and the fellow assured me he was no
longer in their employ."

"What 'separate matter'?" Maitland asked, suspicious.
He doubted it was anything aboveboard or Daphne's
father would have told him as part of the explanation of
how he knew Foster.

"That is neither here nor there," Lord Forsyth said
pettishly. "What I am telling you is that Foster is likely
the man responsible for the murder of Nigel Sommersby. If you had been more forthcoming with me
about the matter, I might have made the connection
earlier. As it is, I only learned from Northman this morning that Ian Foster was traveling with Sommersby, at
which point I knew he was responsible."

"Is it not possible that he only told you he was no

longer working for the Home Office in order to gain your trust?" Maitland asked, not quite sure he was ready to follow Forsyth down this particular avenue of speculation. He accounted himself a rather good judge of character, and he'd seen no hint that the man was lying.

Of course, he was not infallible.

"It's possible," Forsyth said. "If you must know the truth, I bought some claret and brandy from free traders through him. I do like a good brandy, you know. And his name was given to me by a friend, who said he'd once worked for the government, but now wished to get a bit of his own against them. He had the connections on the coast, and saw that I received the items I asked for.

"But surely," he continued, "I would have been taken into custody, or at the very least fined, if he was attempting some sort of trap. And there was none. I got my claret and brandy, and never thought of the man again until Northman mentioned him today."

Maitland didn't bother asking why Northman had been speaking to Forsyth about the murder at Beauchamp House. Northman didn't strike him as the most discreet of fellows, and he likely wanted to tell his old school chum the details of the murder that had taken place in his daughter's new home.

"What makes you think he poses a threat to Daphne?" Maitland asked. "We already believe that Nigel Sommersby's father is the one who killed him. And attacked a solicitor in Battle."

"Richard Sommersby?" Lord Forsyth asked, looking pale. "Of course—it makes perfect sense."

"What does?"

"It was from Richard Sommersby that I got Foster's name." Lord Forsyth looked grim.

"Are you sure you don't mean Nigel Sommersby?" Maitland asked.

"No, I'm quite positive," the earl said with a quick shake of his head. "I had little to do with the son. He showed a bit too much interest in my daughter, if you must know. It was impossible to convince the lad that he was beneath her, however. I tried to drive the message home by treating him in the manner his station deserved."

And perhaps stirred resentment against the girl who was so far above him, Maitland thought with a pang of contempt for Daphne's father.

"Why not forbid him from taking his lessons with her?" he asked.

"I had an agreement with Daphne that I wouldn't interfere in her lessons," Forsyth said curtly. "That included who was present for them."

He wanted to know more about this arrangement, but Maitland had a fair idea that it involved the blackmail she'd used to get a tutor in the first place.

"How did you find Sommersby?" he asked, realizing it had never occurred to him to wonder just how the man had ended up in Forsyth's employ.

"Daphne met him at some sort of meeting for scholars." Forsyth furrowed his brow. "I don't think it was the Royal Society or anything official. To be honest, I didn't ask many questions given the circumstances."

Which the duke took to mean that Lord Forsyth had

done exactly what Daphne told him for fear she'd reveal that she was his secret weapon in the card room. If he hadn't already despised the man, he would have begun now.

"I don't suppose you've had any luck finding this missing cipher that Northman told me about," Lord Forsyth said with a hopeful note in his voice. "It's been the cause of a great deal of trouble, but I must admit that the idea of finding a cache of lost gold is tempting. I can see why Sommersby and Foster would be so desperate to get their hands on it."

Maitland stared at the man in disgust. "Did you even come here to warn Daphne?" he asked. "Or did you come to pump me for information about the hidden gold? Because if that was your reason, then you can take yourself off now."

Turning, he began to leave the room, but was stopped by Forsyth's plea. "Maitland, I do want to find the gold. I won't lie. But I also wished to warn you about Foster. There was a vicious streak that the fellow only showed me once. But it was enough to confirm that I never wanted to see him again."

At the door, the duke looked back and saw that Lord Forsyth did indeed appear to be sincere. His face, which showed signs of the dissipated life he'd led, was no longer wearing his usual mask of ennui. "Protect my daughter, Duke," he said. "Don't let that villain kill her like he killed Sommersby."

Something was wrong, she was sure of it.

Consciousness came back to Daphne slowly, like the

sun creeping up over the horizon. First one thought, then another, then another, until she was fully awake and aware of the fact that she was no longer in the library at Beauchamp House.

Her head ached terribly, and she had some vague recollection of being transported across rough ground in some sort of cart.

"So," a familiar voice said from nearby, "you're rousing at last. I am afraid I was a bit rough when I hit you. But I couldn't take the chance that you would run. Fortunately I was able to let a strong fellow I hired in the side door and he carried you out to the cart. It's amazing what a man will do for a few pounds. And he earned his money. As I'm sure you know, you're no featherweight, my dear."

Her eyes were still closed, and she didn't need to open them to know the speaker's identity, but she slowly raised her lids anyway. She preferred to confront her captor face to face, rather than cower before him with her eyes closed against her inner terror.

Mr. Ian Foster, looking somewhat the worse for wear since her meeting with him that morning—had it truly only been a few hours ago?—stood before her, a glass of water in his hand. Stepping closer, he lifted the glass to her lips, and made her drink. Daphne wanted to take it from him and toss the liquid in his face, but her limbs weren't cooperating. Frowning, she realized that was because her hands were tied behind her back.

"Drink it," he ordered when she pulled away a little. "You need to be in some semblance of comfort so that you can use that lovely quick brain of yours."

Despite the nausea roiling in her gut, she took a small sip. Then realizing how dry her mouth was, she drank more.

Satisfied that she'd complied, Foster took the cup away and placed it on a nearby table.

Blinking, Daphne scanned her surroundings, careful not to turn her head too quickly. They were in a small chamber in what looked to be a cottage. The furnishings were neither very elegant nor too mean. The walls were painted in a pleasant light green shade that reminded her of the sea. And from where she was sitting she saw a seascape hanging over the fireplace. On the other side of the room, however, there was a tester bed. At the sight of it, she gave an involuntary gasp and couldn't help turning her eyes to her captor.

"As lovely as your person is," Foster said with a slight shake of his head, "I have no interest in harming you that way. That was more Nigel Sommersby's line than mine."

Despite the overall awfulness of the situation, Daphne heaved a sigh of relief. She could withstand anything, she knew that now. But she couldn't deny that his assurance gave her some little comfort.

"I want you instead for your mental acumen, Lady Daphne," he said, turning to leaf through some pages on a low desk in the corner. Over his shoulder, he said, "I knew when Nigel first told me about your skills at ciphering and calculating odds and numbers with such speed and accuracy that it would come in handy someday. I just wasn't sure how."

She wasn't sure what to say to that.

"When he told me what your father was doing with

you—sending you into the card rooms of the *ton* for fun and profit—I was awed, I must admit. Lord Forsyth has always struck me as a bit of a rapscallion, but I must say that he was able to harness your abilities in that way, well, it was quite admirable. He even bragged about it to me."

That gave her pause. "When did you have dealings with my father?" she asked, her mind racing at the thought. "And won't this scheme of yours put you in the bad books of your superiors at the Home Office? I should think they frown on kidnapping."

Turning, a single page in his hand, he gave her a rueful smile. "I'm afraid I misled you about my connection with the Home Office. We parted ways some years ago when they took issue with my too-friendly relations with some free traders here on the coast."

So much for using his government connections as a deterrent, Daphne thought with an inner grimace. "But that doesn't explain how you know my father," she pressed him. Perhaps if she could keep him talking to her, someone would realize she was missing from Beauchamp House.

Foster moved to stand before her. "He bought some claret and brandy from me," he said with a shrug, as if that should explain everything. "I had no use for him at the time. He really is a rather stupid fellow. But, I'd known about you for some time, and I was eager to learn if he too possessed your skills. So much easier to deal with men than ladies, I find. Even intelligent ladies like yourself can be ninnies at times, you must admit. Alas, however, Lord Forsyth was a sad disappointment."

She ignored his complaint about women. Much as she

abhorred his words, there were more important things to think of just now.

"Fortunately, I found another gentleman who seemed to possess your abilities with numbers," Forsyth continued conversationally as he got behind her chair and began to push it across the floor so that it faced the writing desk where he'd placed the page. When he was satisfied with the position, he went on. "Mr. Sommersby, the elder, was much more reliable than Nigel ever was. And he claimed to be far better at figures than even you were. It's too bad that turned out to be a gross falsehood."

Daphne's eyes widened as she stared up at him, just over her left shoulder. It made sense that he knew Nigel Sommersby's father, but the idea of her tutor discussing her maths skills with this man she hadn't even known at the time made her skin crawl. And the way he spoke of Richard Sommersby made her worry for her former tutor, Hargrave's attacker or not.

"Why would Mr. Sommersby say that?" she asked, trying to draw him further into the conversation.

"I thought at first," Foster said, annoyed, "that it was an overdeveloped sense of his own importance. But later I came to realize that he was only being gallant. Trying to divert my attention away from you. I needed the Cameron Cipher, you see, and I needed it to be translated."

"How did you learn the cipher was located at Beauchamp House in the first place?" Daphne asked, truly puzzled. Surely Lady Celeste hadn't told the sort of person who would gossip about it.

At that, he smiled. "I truly did learn of it when I was at the Home Office," he said. "Lady Celeste told a friend, who told a friend, who told one of my superiors. At the time I was far too busy working on . . . other things . . . to pay attention. But recently, I found I was in need of funds. And by happy coincidence, I learned that you'd inherited your very unusual portion of the Beauchamp House estate. So, I sought out both of the Sommersbys and we concocted a plan."

He looked almost apologetic as he continued. "I truly had no notion of involving you in this, my lady. Well, not for decoding the cipher in any event. Nigel was supposed to use his former friendship with you to garner an invitation into the house. Then he would search for the cipher, and when we found it, his father would decode it. We'd go retrieve the gold, and no one would be any the wiser."

"But that's not how it went at all," Daphne said, appalled at the whole notion of two men who'd been so close to her once using their connection to her as a means to get rich. They were no better than her father. Indeed, the Sommersbys were worse because at least Lord Forsyth made no secret of his intentions.

"Sadly, no," Foster said, moving to lean his shoulders against the wall, warming to his story. "Nigel, ever the hothead, decided to go to Beauchamp House the very evening after we met you by 'chance' on the road to town. He didn't tell me—likely because he knew I'd object—and using the knowledge I'd worked so hard to obtain from a former footman about the secret room, he slipped out and broke in. Fortunately, I suspected he'd try something rash like that, and I followed him."

"And killed him," she said, remembering with a shudder the sight of Nigel Sommersby dead of a stab wound on the floor of the secret room.

"The damned fool was planning to take the cipher without telling me," Foster said with a grimace. "Is there no loyalty anymore? He'd never have known that the cipher was even at Beauchamp House if I hadn't told him. He thought he was so clever, but in the end, that got him nothing but grief."

"But why didn't you simply take the cipher and disappear then?" Daphne asked, truly curious. It seemed foolish of him to remain behind, where he might be caught. "And why did you shoot at us?"

"Because running would make me look guilty," Foster said to her as if she were a simpleton. "And I shot at you because I could have no notion of whether you'd seen me leave through the window. I could hear your voices even as I shimmied down the tree outside. I haven't come this far only to be caught fleeing a murder scene. I was not made for such an ignominious end."

"If you think I'm the only one who can solve the cipher, then that wasn't the cleverest move on your part," Daphne couldn't help but point out.

At the criticism, Foster snarled. Clearly, he did not like being called foolish. "I thought I didn't need you," he said scowling. "Remember Sommersby had assured me that he was your better or equal when it came to codes and ciphers and the like. But, just as his son had done, he, too, betrayed me."

"What have you done to Richard Sommersby?" Daphne asked, fearful despite her disappointment in her mentor for allying himself with a man like Foster.

"After his little mishap with Lady Celeste's solicitor—really, it was too much of him to think the man would freely hand over all of his notes on the cipher—I saw to it that he was no longer able to impede my progress."

Daphne closed her eyes. "He's dead then?" Somehow she'd hoped that Mr. Sommersby, for all his faults, would at least escape this imbroglio with his life.

But to her surprise, Foster shook his head. "Don't get me wrong, the fellow deserves to die for the mistakes he's made on this operation. It's been one blunder after another for the man. And I can hang for one murder as well as two."

She suppressed a shudder.

"However," Foster said with a shrug, "there is the possibility that alone, you will be unable to unravel the cipher. So, I have kept Richard Sommersby on hand just in case you need his assistance in breaking the code."

Something relaxed within her chest. At least Mr. Sommersby was still alive, she thought. And really, he may very well have saved her from being taken earlier by Foster. She wondered if that had been at least part of his reason for touting his own skills at coding.

"Enough of this chatter," Foster said, stepping away from the wall, and lighting the lamp on the table. "It's time for you to begin."

Daphne looked down at the page, which contained the same set of jumbled letters as her own paper back in the library at Beauchamp House.

"I'll need a pencil," she said, looking up to find him giving her an assessing gaze. "Or barring that, a slate and a bit of chalk."

"I'm not comfortable untying your hands," he said

with a shake of his head. "You'll simply have to work it out in that beautiful head of yours."

"But I need to see the calculations on the page," she protested. He was right to resist untying her hands. Her first order of business if he had was to toss the lit lamp at him. "And I need to write out a key once I'm able to get one or two of the letters figured out. It's standard for such work."

He would not budge on the matter, however. "You're a resourceful lady. Figure it out."

And without a backward glance, he left her alone in the tiny room, with only the Cameron Cipher for company.

Chapter 20

When he returned to the library, Maitland was startled to find Daphne was gone. Thinking she'd gone to lie down, or to speak to one of the other ladies, he went first to her bedchamber—which was empty—then to the shared sitting room where the heiresses sometimes congregated.

"No," Ivy said, her eyes worried, "I thought you were with her."

With a curse, Maitland noticed that her page, with the coded message from the painting, and her calculations, had fallen to the floor. Picking it up, he scanned it for some clue, but there was no "help me" written in the margins.

Quickly, he stepped over to the shelf with the lever for the secret passage on it. But a check of the hidden room showed it to be unchanged from their visit earlier.

"Where is she?" Sophia asked as the three heiresses, followed by Serena and Quill, entered the room. "Who's taken her?"

It was a measure of just how odd the past few months had been, Maitland thought, that their first conclusion was that Daphne had been kidnapped.

Quickly he explained to them what Lord Forsyth had told him about Ian Foster.

"But I don't understand," Gemma said, her brows drawn. "I thought it was Mr. Richard Sommersby who was seen at the solicitor's office. And that he was the one who killed Nigel Sommersby."

"I don't know the whole of it," Maitland admitted, "but at the moment, that doesn't matter. We need to find Daphne. It's clear enough that the man is looking for someone to solve the cipher for him. And if he was willing to take her by force, then he's growing desperate."

"But we know nothing about the man," Kerr said, looking troubled. "We don't even know if he has ties to the area."

"I think that's not entirely true," Maitland said, moving to the French doors to look for signs that the former government agent had used this way to escape. "Remember, he worked with free traders. Perhaps he still has connections to them."

The small balcony overlooking the gardens looked no different than it had the last time he'd been out there. How the devil had the man gotten Daphne out of the house?

"I can ask Mr. Greaves if he knows of any particular places where the smugglers gather," Ivy said, moving to the door. "He knows everything that goes on in the neighborhood, good and bad. And perhaps he knows of some hideaway where they meet."

She left, and the others looked to Maitland for guidance. He wished he knew better what they should do to find Daphne. At the moment, he was just as much at a loss as they were. Still, there was one thing they could try.

"Since it's pretty clear that Foster didn't get Daphne out of here by lowering her out the window, I want to know how he got her out of Beauchamp House without being seen. I cannot imagine Daphne going quietly."

"Unless she was unconscious," Kerr said carefully, not wanting the notion to wound his cousin. "It might make it easier to get her out, I should imagine."

But Maitland had already considered the possibility and was well and truly terrified at the notion. But his terror wouldn't help find Daphne. "Let's go question the footmen. Perhaps they saw someone posing as a delivery man. Or someone who didn't belong."

"We'll speak to the maids," Sophia offered, already heading for the door leading into the hallway. "Let's meet back here in fifteen minutes to compare notes."

Nodding, Maitland followed them and felt his cousin step up to walk beside him as he headed toward the servants' hall. The ladies, meanwhile, went to the hall where the bedrooms were located, where the maids would be working at this time of day.

"We'll find her, Dalton," said Lord Kerr, using the duke's Christian name as he had done when they were boys. "If he needs her to solve the cipher, then at least we know he won't harm her."

But what would happen once she'd done what he wanted? Maitland wondered.

They found the footmen polishing silver in the dining room while the housekeeper looked on.

"If you're looking for Mr. Greaves," she said to them, "he's with Miss Ivy . . . I mean Lady Kerr in his parlor."

"In fact, Mrs. Bacon," said Maitland, "it's John and Andrew we'd like to talk to if that's all right. And you, if you have anything to add."

Looking surprised, the housekeeper nodded. Quickly, Maitland explained to them that Daphne was missing and had likely been taken against her will from the house.

"Oh, goodness," Mrs. Bacon said, aghast. "What is the world coming to? First Lady Celeste, and then that poor gentleman in the library." Daphne had never been a particular favorite with the servants—she was much too blunt for their liking—but the housekeeper's agitation seemed genuine enough.

"You must tell his grace at once if you know anything, lads," she said to the footmen. "Any little detail might help."

The two men were of similar height and build, and quite handsome—footmen were often chosen for their looks and similarity, and his aunt had been no different about that being a standard for hiring than any other society hostess.

"Did you see anything unusual?" Maitland asked them. "Someone who was somewhere they didn't belong. Or maybe a visitor you didn't know showed up?"

Andrew looked thoughtful. "That Mr. Foster was here this morning, your grace. But you saw him in the drawing room with Lady Daphne."

But John shook his head. "That was this afternoon," he corrected the other man. "I showed him up to the library myself. He asked to see Lady Daphne, and since he'd been here before I didn't see that it would be a problem. You were with Lord Forsyth at the time, your grace."

Maitland closed his eyes in frustration. He should have warned the servants to alert him to anything odd, or to any visitors asking for Daphne. "You saw him go up? What about when he left?"

The footman shook his head, "I'm sorry, your grace, but I didn't see him leave. Which was odd now I think of it. But I just assumed he was having a proper discussion with her ladyship."

"And you were in your place in the hall for how long?" Kerr asked.

"For an hour at least," John said, looking to Andrew and Mrs. Bacon to confirm it. "I stayed there until Mr. Greaves asked me to come polish silver with Andrew. And we've only been here for about a quarter hour now."

"What other way might Foster have used to get Daphne out of the house?" Maitland asked his cousin.

"If you please, your grace," said Mrs. Bacon, "but there's no way he could have gone out using the cellar door or the kitchen door without being seen by me or cook. Or any number of servants coming in and out of this area. Which means he must have used the doors off the gallery that lead out into the garden."

"If Daphne was unconscious," Kerr said thoughtfully, "how the devil did Foster manage to carry her all that way? He doesn't strike me as a particularly strong fellow. And no offense to her, but Daphne is rather tall."

Before he could respond, Ivy and Mr. Greaves stepped into the room.

"I believe we know where he may have taken her," Ivy said without preamble. With a nod to Greaves, she let him talk.

"There is a cottage off to itself, not terribly far from here," the butler said, his expression revealing how important he knew this information was. "It is known to the local authorities as being used from time to time by the local free traders. Lady Celeste never held with such goings on, so they never used the caves below Beauchamp House for their activities, but the owner of the Summerlea Estate a few miles away, is often away. And often turns a blind eye."

"Summerlea?" Maitland asked. "Isn't that Sir Thomas Devaney's place?"

"Yes, your grace," the butler said with a nod. "Sir Thomas's family has owned it for some years, but he has another home in Kent, I believe courtesy of his mother's family."

It was not uncommon for landowners all over England to only visit their estates once a year, or sometimes even less frequently. Maitland himself owned seven as part of the entitled properties of the dukedom. And it was simply not possible for him to spend a great deal of time at each of them. Considering what had been going on at the Summerlea, he made a vow to ensure that his own properties were not harboring criminals as soon as this business was finished and Daphne was safe.

"Let's go," he said to no one in particular as he turned to leave the dining room. But his cousin laid a hand on his arm.

"We cannot just go break down the door," he explained, though he did seem sympathetic. "We should inform Northman, and perhaps the local watch."

But Maitland was not willing to wait that long. "You can do both of those things. Indeed, I would appreciate if you would, but I won't wait another minute while Daphne is being held captive by a man who has killed one man and severely injured another."

"At least take one of the footmen with you," Kerr said, as Maitland strode away.

"They can both come," the duke called over his shoulder. "But only if they're prepared to fight."

And not waiting to see if they followed, he made his way to the stables to have his horse saddled. The footmen would just have to follow . . . on foot.

Her head aching, Daphne stared down at the coded message. She was grateful that Foster had left her alone to work on the code. Her head injury was making it difficult for her to concentrate with the same degree of rigor as she'd done in the library.

Still, she was able to recall some of the letters she'd already worked out when he took her.

So far, the message read: *o*a*—Ba**—S*mm** l*a—*s*a**

These she arrived at by adding 15 to the number designation for each letter of the alphabet, so if $a = 0$, then in the message, each letter would $a = 0 + 15$, which meant that the a in the puzzle translated to p. She'd tried a few other key numbers from Jacobite history before deciding on 15. She'd discarded 45 because she reasoned that Cameron hadn't wanted to make the solution that complicated. But 15, which was the year that the first rebellion happened, seemed less cumbersome. And, though she'd never admit to it, she had a gut instinct about 15.

She was working out the rest of the letters in the message when she heard the door to the chamber open.

Though she was tied to a chair facing the opposite direction from the door, she managed to turn just enough to see Mr. Richard Sommersby standing there.

"It's true then," she said, watching the man she'd once loved like a father. The man who'd taught her to harness the natural abilities her actual father had exploited for his own gain. "You did betray me. And your son."

Sommersby flinched a little at the accusation.

He looked exhausted. Dark circles shone beneath his once lively eyes. And in the years since she'd seen him last, his hair had turned completely white. When she'd known him, he'd been a handsome man of middle years. Now he looked as if he'd aged thirty years in the space of seven.

"It's not what you think, Lady Daphne," said Sommersby, moving farther into the room, crossing to stand on the other side of the table from her. "At least, I didn't start out with the intention of betraying you."

"Then how did it start out?" she asked. "Tell me why you got involved with the man who murdered your only son."

Sagging a little, Sommersby said, "I knew Foster through my son. I knew he was involved in some questionable activity, but when your father approached me about where he might find some smuggled brandy, I passed Foster's name along to him. In exchange, your father promised to let you finish your studies in peace.

Without his constant interruptions and attempts to have you win more money for him at cards."

Daphne hadn't known, though she did recall a sudden cessation of her father's attempts to persuade her away from her studies.

"I thought that was the end of our association," Sommersby continued. "Indeed it was for a while. But then Nigel told him about the Cameron Cipher. And Foster began to press me about it. By that point, Nigel had already left your father's house and Foster was becoming more and more insistent. He'd heard from one of his connections here on the coast that Lady Celeste Beauchamp had the cipher in her home. I didn't want to leave you, but he left me no alternative. If I hadn't, he'd have forced me to do things that went against my conscience. He was like a man possessed."

"Why didn't he simply steal the cipher himself?" Daphne asked, puzzled. "It's not as if he was bothered by breaking the law."

"I was a little acquainted with Lady Celeste from the Royal Society," Sommersby explained. "Indeed, I am the one who told her about you and your gifts. Foster wanted me to trade upon that acquaintance to ask her to show me the cipher. So that he wouldn't have to do it himself. It was like a game to him—he preferred pulling at my strings, as if I were some sort of puppet, to doing his own dirty work."

"What hold did he have over you?" Daphne asked, almost afraid to hear the answer.

Sommersby looked away, unable to meet her eyes. "Nigel had got himself into a bit of trouble. You were not the first young lady he'd . . ."

"Attempted to take by force?" Daphne asked bitterly. "You brought him into my home? Left me alone with him when you knew his proclivities?" If Sommersby's other betrayals had stung, this one pierced her heart.

He swallowed, looking down, dejected. "He was my only child. I'd already lost his mother, and I couldn't risk losing him, too. I did my best to keep him away from you. Indeed, I told him that if he touched you, I'd never speak to him again. And I meant it."

"But he couldn't help himself?" Daphne asked.

"He didn't care," Sommersby corrected softly. "He lied to me and said he'd never harm you. But then when my back was turned, he . . . did what he did. I sent him away the very next day. He went to Foster, who either guessed what had happened or to whom he told all. Either way, Foster conceived of a way to force me to do his bidding."

"So you agreed to help him find the cipher." Daphne's voice was flat. She'd never have guessed how weak her mentor had been. There was a time when she'd thought he was the most intelligent man in the world. And that he loved her as if she were his own daughter. She'd been wrong on both counts.

"I did," he agreed. "But I convinced him for a time that Lady Celeste didn't have it. We went instead to Paris, where Cameron had been trying to escape to. When we'd searched for a couple of years without success, however, Foster guessed at my subterfuge. And that's when he decided it was time to return to England and pay a visit to Little Seaford."

"How did he come to be working with Nigel?" Daphne asked.

"He'd been in Egypt, exploring treasure hunting opportunities there, but when Foster invited him back home to search for the Cameron gold, Nigel returned at once. We agreed to come to Little Seaford. And over my protests, Foster decided that Nigel approach you, since you and the other ladies had inherited Beauchamp House in the interim. You, he'd reasoned, were a much closer connection than Lady Celeste had been."

"But Nigel decided to search for it on his own," Daphne guessed. Nigel Sommersby had never been very patient. It didn't surprise her that he'd double-cross his own father.

Sommersby nodded. "And Foster followed him. Killed him. My only son."

His only son who had been a liar, a thief, and a rapist, Daphne thought bitterly.

Sommersby must have sensed some of what she was thinking because he looked up at her with remorse in his eyes. "I know I betrayed you, my dear. But I did try to keep Foster away from you. I told him I would be able to decode the message easily. Though I was aching at my own loss, I made every effort to solve the riddle for him. But it hadn't taken long for your skills with numbers and ciphers to fully eclipse mine. I stalled him for as long as I could. I even convinced him that Lady Celeste's solicitor might have some clue in his office."

"So you *did* attack Mr. Hargrave," Daphne said, shaking her head at the knowledge. Had she ever really known Mr. Sommersby? she wondered.

"No," Sommersby said vehemently. "It was Foster who did that. He took my spectacles and introduced himself as me—another bit of blackmail he could hold over me."

"But why try to hurt Hargrave? Surely if Foster threatened enough, he'd have given over whatever he had from Lady Celeste willingly."

"I don't know," Sommersby said, looking genuinely puzzled. "Perhaps Hargrave guessed that he wasn't who he said he was. Perhaps he sensed something was wrong. All I know is that Foster returned yesterday morning with a page of information on local springs and wells that he'd found in Hargraves's file on Lady Celeste. But without a solution for the cipher, it was useless."

"And so he decided to kidnap me," Daphne said. "Because you couldn't solve the cipher for him."

"I did try, Daphne," said Sommersby, a beseeching note in his voice. "But you know I was never as naturally gifted as you are with this kind of thing. And I thought perhaps if he brought you here, you could find a solution, and then he'd let you go."

"He will not let me go," Daphne said coldly. "Once he has the gold, he'll rid himself of us both. Because we have enough evidence to testify against him."

The sound of someone clucking their tongue came from the doorway. "My dear Lady Daphne, what a cynic you are. I can assure you I am wholly committed to your health and safety."

Foster walked leisurely over to the table where Daphne was still seated, tied up. He looked over her shoulder at the coded message. But since he hadn't untied her hands or let her use a pencil, the solution she had thus far was inside her head.

"Have you arrived at a solution in that brain of yours, Lady Daphne?" Foster asked in a darkly cheerful tone.

"If I have, I'll never tell you," she spat out. "You're a murderer and a manipulator. There's no way I'll ever tell you the solution."

Foster's expression grew cold. "If you don't tell me then I'll simply have to force your hand. Perhaps by harming the handsome Duke of Maitland. Perhaps I'll do something to harm all of your friends at Beauchamp House. Who is to say a fire won't break out there tonight while they're all snug in their beds. It will be dreadful if they cannot escape because the doors are nailed shut."

His words struck a bolt of fear through her. She didn't need to ask if he was serious. That was evident in the steady gaze of his eyes on her.

"Do not test me, Lady Daphne," he said softly. "Because I will win."

Blinking back the tears that had threatened at his words, Daphne took a deep breath. Perhaps if she told him what the cipher said, he'd go to find the gold and leave her here alone. She could perhaps convince Mr. Sommersby to untie her.

"Tick tock, Lady Daphne."

With a silent prayer that this would be all he asked of her, Daphne said, "All right. I will tell you. If you'll only promise not to harm my friends."

"I am a man of my word, Lady Daphne." He actually looked offended that she would think otherwise.

Deciding she'd find a way to escape somehow, she told him what she'd translated the cipher to mean.

Roman Bath Summerlea Estate

Chapter 21

It was already nearing dusk when Maitland tied his horse in the little wood not far from the smuggler's cottage. He didn't bother waiting for the footmen, who would only get in his way as he tried to effect Daphne's escape. Much easier to slip in alone, retrieve her, and slip back out.

On foot, he approached the cottage, which was sitting on a hill overlooking the sea. It would be quite close to some of the caves used by the smugglers to store contraband goods, he thought.

He had thought there would be some activity at the house, but he could detect no lights burning through the windows, and there was no sound coming from it either. Pray God they'd not harmed Daphne, he thought.

His heart in his throat, he walked softly to the kitchen door, and on trying it, realized it was not locked. Wishing he'd brought some kind of weapon, he opened the door but saw immediately that the room was empty. There was evidence that someone had been here earlier, however. Dirty dishes were on the table with the remains of a meal of bread and cheese. And he could smell the lingering odor of a fire in the hearth.

He listened for a moment, trying to detect any sort of hint that there was someone in the cottage, but it was silent. Perhaps a little too quiet for his peace of mind. Slowly he walked from room to room, every one empty of people. When he came to the bedchamber, the last room he'd had to search, he was both relieved to find it empty and concerned that he'd not yet found Daphne.

Crossing to the table in the corner, he saw his first clue that she'd been here. On the floor beside the chair that sat next to it, he saw a couple of discarded bits of rope. As if someone had been tied to the chair, then freed.

Daphne had been here. He knew it.

Then, as if she were sending him a message, he noticed something on the floor beside the chair. Kneeling, he saw it was the ruby ring she'd said belonged to her mother.

The ring she said she'd never taken off since the day her father gave it to her after her mother's death.

Plucking the ring off the floor, he stared at it for a moment as it lay in his palm. Then he closed his fist over it before shoving it into his pocket.

Voices below alerted him to the fact that the footmen had arrived.

As he hurried down the stairs, he saw Andrew clutching a piece of paper. "Your grace," the footman said, his excitement barely disguised as he brandished the page, "I believe I know where they've gone."

Curious despite his annoyance at their ham-handedness, Maitland strode over and took the page from him.

"Where did you find this?" he asked, his heart beating faster as he read the note, which was in an unfamiliar hand.

Roman Bath Summerlea Estate

"It was stuck out here beneath a stone on the path," Andrew said. "What does it mean?"

Not bothering to answer him, Maitland said, "I want you both to go back to Beauchamp House and get Lord Kerr. And bring any weapons that are available in the house. A shovel if there is no pistol or sword."

"Where are we to bring him, your grace?" asked John, the other footman.

"We're on the Summerlea Estate here," Maitland explained. "But the Roman Bath is only a mile or so from here. Kerr will remember it from when we were boys. And I know I do not need to remind you that time is of the essence."

He'd been foolish to strike out here on his own, he realized now. Because contrary to what he'd thought, Foster wasn't alone.

Sommersby had left the translation of the cipher for him, he was almost sure of it. But he didn't know whether he could count on Daphne's mentor to do more than that to help her. He'd already betrayed her more than once. If he was suffering a pang of conscience now, there was no guarantee it would last.

Praying that Kerr still recalled the location of the

Roman Bath, he hurried around the cottage, climbed onto his waiting horse, and galloped away.

"My apologies for making you walk all this way," Foster said from behind her, his knife prodding her back. "But we really cannot risk the noise and attention a cart would cause."

Daphne hadn't seen a single person on their trek across the Summerlea lands. But she guessed that their reasons for walking were less about noise and more about the fact that there was no road leading to the Roman Bath. Their way so far had been through woods and across fields.

She'd had no notion of what the cipher was talking about, but clearly Foster knew where he was taking her.

Them.

Sommersby still trudged along at her side, though she thought he was looking worse than he had when he'd spoken to her earlier. He was not a young man, and the stress of the past week was catching up to him, it would seem.

They walked in silence for a while through the dimness. Despite his claim of not wanting to draw attention, Foster held a lantern to light their way. It wasn't strictly necessary, but Daphne supposed she should be grateful for it. A sprained ankle was the last thing she needed when she was looking for every chance she had to run.

Finally, after it felt as if they'd been walking for hours, they approached a clearing. In the light of the lantern, she saw to the left were stairs leading into the smallest of the three arches. It was impossible to tell from this far away, but there seemed to be a small room beyond the arch. In the center, the largest of the three arches led into a moss-and-vine-covered grotto. There was nothing in the recessed areas, but it might have once contained some sort of display or statue. The third arch was in the side of a small stone tower built into the side of the hill.

But it was the rectangular pool leading out from the second arch that they were looking for, she realized. The light from the lantern reflected off the gently moving water of the bath, which she guessed was supplied from a natural spring.

"Here we are," said Foster with barely suppressed excitement. "The Roman Bath on the Summerlea Estate."

When Daphne held back, he shoved her forward until she stood at the edge of the pool.

"Watch your step," he said in mock concern. "I wouldn't want you to hurt yourself."

"Just get on with it," Sommersby said in a heated voice.

But if Foster was upset, he didn't show it. "I intend to, sir," he said easily. "Or rather, I intend to let Lady Daphne."

Her heart stuttered. "What do you mean?" But she'd already guessed.

"I intend for you to climb into the pool and get my gold, Lady Daphne," Foster said. "Let me help you off with your gown."

Because she was at the edge already, she couldn't run. And if he pushed her in, the weight of her skirts would undoubtedly pull her under if the pool was deeper than it looked.

"See here, Foster," Sommersby all but shouted, "there's no need to demean the lady like this."

Showing the first sign of temper, Foster said, "Shut up, old man. I don't even know why I brought you with us. You've already proved your usefulness. Now you are a liability."

"I have done everything you asked," Sommersby said, strain in his voice. "Let the girl go, and I will get your gold."

But Foster hadn't stopped unbuttoning the back of Daphne's gown. "We are both too large to search the bath thoroughly," he said as if he were speaking to a child. "Lady Daphne is the perfect size. And without her skirts to weigh her down, she'll easily be able to move within it."

The evening air was cool, and Daphne began to shiver as her back was exposed to it. She felt a wave of humiliation wash over her at the thought of standing before these men in only her shift. But the alternative was drowning. And she fully intended to survive this ordeal and go back to Maitland.

If he would have her after this fiasco.

Like an abigail helping her mistress undress for bed, Foster eased Daphne's gown down over her shoulders and helped her step out of it. Fortunately her stays tied in the front, so she was able to undo them herself and blocking her mind to the reality of her situation, she stood waiting for Foster to move away so that she could remove her slippers.

But he didn't move, only stood there behind her, no doubt memorizing every detail of her exposed body.

Finally, when she could endure no more, Daphne

decided to take matters into her own hands. Though she still wore her shoes and stockings, she stepped off the edge and into the rectangular pool.

He was still a quarter mile or so from the Roman bath when Maitland dismounted and tied his horse to a tree.

There was a need for stealth if he was going to catch Foster off guard.

It hadn't taken long for his eyes to adjust to the dark, and he managed to make it to the clearing without calling undue attention to himself. The closer he got, the lighter it became because Foster had a lantern that he held over the water.

Maitland didn't see Daphne, though, and her absence terrified him for a moment before he heard her voice calling out from the water. "There's a great deal of debris down there. It would take less time for me to search if you held the lamp closer to the water."

A splash told him that she was indeed in the water. He recalled from his visits there as a boy that the spring was warm, and with Daphne's height, it shouldn't be much higher than her waist.

"I can't get any closer without climbing in myself," Foster said in an aggrieved tone. "And I don't think you would like that, Lady Daphne."

There was a thread of menace in the man's tone that made the duke's blood curdle.

"No," Daphne responded hastily, as if she truly did fear what would happen if he joined her. "I will simply have to try harder. It's just that not knowing whether the gold is in some sort of box or purse makes it difficult to tell. But I will just be systematic about my search."

"Perhaps I should trade places with Lady Daphne," said Mr. Sommersby, who was seated against the stone wall of the grotto. It was difficult to tell from his position, but Maitland thought his hands were bound.

"Stay right where you are, old man," said Foster grimly. "You've already shown how useless you are. I don't wish you mucking this up as well."

"It would be easier if my hands were free," Daphne said. Maitland froze. He had to get her out of there sooner rather than later, dammit. It would be so easy for the rope around her wrists to get caught on something below the surface.

He was about to make his presence known when he heard Foster say, "Fine," in a petulant tone. "Give me your wrists."

Crouching beside the bath, he took out a knife, and as Maitland watched, cut the ties holding her hands together. "Now, no more excuses. Find my gold, or I won't be answerable for the consequences."

Daphne rubbed the skin at her wrists but then turned away from Foster and went below the surface.

The silence as they waited for her to come back up was one of the worst Maitland had ever experienced. Every part of him longed to burst out of the woods and attack Foster. But he couldn't do so while Daphne was under the water.

Finally, after what seemed like an eternity, she broke the surface, and the sound of her gulping for air made his gut twist.

"I . . . I . . . found something," she gasped out. Then extending her closed fist, she uncurled her fingers for Foster, who knelt so that he could see what she held.

Then, in a quick motion, Daphne struck while Foster was leaning over the bath, grasped him by the arm and pulled him over the edge and into the pool with a loud splash.

Maitland burst out of the woods and jumped into the pool beside them, boots and all, and pulled Foster off Daphne, whom the villain had been attempting to keep under the water.

He was much larger than Foster, but the other man was well muscled, and the water made it difficult to maintain a grip on him. Still, his anger lent him enough strength to swing his fist against Foster's jaw, and while he was still stunned, Maitland got him by the throat and pinned him against the carved-stone side of the pool.

A rage unlike anything he'd ever felt before filled him as he thought of the danger this man had put Daphne in. What if she'd drowned? What if he'd come to find her dead beside the Roman bath? Foster had already killed one man and wounded another, and he'd almost done the same to Daphne. He deserved to . . .

"Maitland! Duke!"

Somewhere in the periphery of his mind, he heard his name being called, and when he registered Daphne's grip on his back, he came back to himself and realized what he'd almost done.

"Dalton, stop!" she cried, and he loosened his grip on Foster's throat. The other man sputtered and choked.

Suddenly Kerr was there, pulling Foster from the water. "I've got him, Dalton," his cousin said. "Let go."

Nodding, Maitland let go and turned to see Daphne behind him.

"Come here." He pulled her to him and she flung her arms around his neck. "I thought I'd lost you."

"I knew you'd come for me," she whispered against his shoulder. "I knew it. But I had to try to escape him."

"Brave girl," he said, though he shuddered to think what would have happened if he hadn't arrived when he did. He'd had a hard time subduing the man—what chance would Daphne have had against him when he did. "Don't ever frighten me like that again. I love you too much to live without you."

She gasped at his admission, then, almost shyly, said, "I love you, too."

"Thank God," he whispered against her mouth as he took it in a firm kiss. "I was determined to plead my case, but you can be quite stubborn. And I had no certainty that I'd win the argument."

"I can be quite reasonable when the occasion calls for it," Daphne said with a small frown that was belied by the smile in her eyes. "In this case, I would be unreasonable to resist you."

He kissed her again. Until the sound of a throat being cleared interrupted them.

"I don't suppose you two would like to climb out of the pool now?" asked Lord Kerr from where he stood beside the footmen, who held a bound Foster between them.

Daphne stiffened in Dalton's arms. "I'm only wearing my shift," she said in a whisper. "And my slippers are on the bottom of the pool."

"Can you give us a moment?" Maitland asked his cousin, who wordlessly removed his greatcoat and placed it on a bit of dry ground.

Then, Kerr, the footmen, their prisoner, and a much-subdued Sommersby stepped away to give them some privacy.

"What about the gold?" Daphne asked, her brow furrowed as Maitland moved to hoist himself out of the water.

"The gold will just have to wait," he said from where he had twisted himself up to sit with his feet dangling into the pool. "Come here and I'll help you out."

But a mulish look came over Daphne's lovely countenance. "Dalton, I was almost killed because of this gold. If it is in this pool, I want to find it now. Before anyone else is hurt because of it."

Then, before he could argue, she disappeared beneath the surface and with a sigh, he slipped back in, wishing he'd removed his boots so that he could feel the bottom with his feet.

But he didn't have to wait long for her to surface with a shout of triumph. "It's there!" she cried. "A chest, in this corner. It's too heavy for me to lift, though."

Maitland nodded, and moving over to where she'd indicated, he dove under the water and felt around on the bottom for the chest. Just when he thought he'd run out of breath, he found it, and grasping it with both hands, he pulled, dislodging half a century's worth of dirt and leaves and other debris.

Surfacing, he lifted the chest onto the stones beside the pool. "There. Now will you let me take you home?"

Nodding, Daphne let him lift her to the edge and immediately began to shiver in the cool evening air.

Dalton wrapped her in Kerr's coat, then picked up the chest and led her to his horse.

Chapter 22

The morning of Daphne's wedding had dawned sunny and with no hint of the rain that had plagued them ever since they'd found the Cameron gold.

They'd had to postpone the nuptials for a few days because, despite the warm temperature of the Roman bath's water and Daphne's insistence that she was fit as a flea, Maitland insisted that she have time to recover from her ordeal. Also, Squire Northman took his sweet time interviewing them all about the events leading up to the capture of Foster. So even if Maitland had been more reasonable, the wedding would have had to be squeezed in between meetings with the magistrate.

"Are you nervous?" Sophia asked as the four Beauchamp heiresses stood waiting for the carriage to convey them to the church. "I would be quite nervous."

Daphne, who had chosen one of her favorite gowns— a white muslin shot through with jonquil—her favorite India shawl, and a rose-trimmed chip straw bonnet tied with matching jonquil ribbon, was pulling a pair of kid gloves over her trembling hands. "A little," she admitted. "But only because I do not wish to do or say the wrong thing. If it was a mathematics drill, however . . ."

"You would trounce the competition," Ivy said with a grin. "But you needn't worry. Maitland is head over ears for you. And no one else there matters."

"I suspect Maitland's mama would disagree," Gemma said as she tied her own bonnet beneath her chin. "She seems to have some very strong ideas about her own importance."

"No more than my father," Daphne said as they stepped outside onto the portico. "I was rather surprised that they seemed to get along with one another."

They walked down the few stairs and allowed one of the grooms to hand them into the open brougham.

Soon they were rolling down the lane toward the church where Maitland, Lord Kerr, and the few invited guests were waiting for them.

They were turning onto the road leading to the church, when Daphne spoke up. "I know I can be somewhat cold at times, but I wished to let you know, on today when my life will change irrevocably, I am grateful for all of you. And that Lady Celeste somehow knew that we would become friends."

"You're making me cry and the wedding hasn't even begun yet," Ivy protested from beside her. Though she took Daphne's hand in hers and squeezed it.

"I must admit that I wasn't sure of you at first, Daphne dear," said Sophia, dabbing at her own eyes, "but I cannot imagine Beauchamp House without you now."

"Has Maitland agreed to live there for the rest of the

year?" Gemma asked, looking worried about the possibility that he would not.

It was difficult to imagine that any of them would have missed her if she'd left earlier in their tenure at Beauchamp House, Daphne thought wryly. Had the situation been reversed, she would not have missed any of them. But somehow over the course of their first four months together they'd forged a bond. And now she couldn't understand how she would ever get on without them.

Aloud she said, "Yes, thank heavens. I was prepared to use every wile at my disposal to convince him, but fortunately it seems that he doesn't need convincing."

"Because, as I said before, he's smitten," Ivy said wryly. "Just as you are with him."

She didn't protest the assessment because it was quite true. Once upon a time, she'd never have imagined a man existed whom she would willingly give her hand to in marriage. From her perspective, the institution itself was like a pair of loaded dice with all the advantage going to the husband.

But, then, she'd never imagined there could be a man she trusted as she did Maitland. But he did exist, and she was lucky enough to be about to marry him.

The carriage pulled to a stop, and they saw Lord Forsyth and Squire Northman waiting outside the door, which had been festooned with roses from the gardens at Beauchamp House.

Ivy, Sophia, and Gemma all kissed Daphne's cheek, and, with a flutter in her stomach, she followed them into the dim outer chamber of the church. Then she watched as they stepped down the aisle, one by one.

"Are you ready, daughter?" asked Lord Forsyth, with

a suspicious dampness around his eyes. Daphne had never seen her father in the throes of any emotion but anger, but it seemed that he did feel something for her after all. And since it was her wedding day, and the last one she'd ever spend under his control, she kissed him on the cheek.

"Yes, Papa," she said slipping her arm through his as they stepped to the double doors leading into the nave.

And the rest was like a dream. She walked beside her father down the aisle to the sanctuary where Maitland stood waiting for her with that light in his eyes that he seemed to reserve only for her.

And then the vicar began the ceremony. Daphne repeated her vows in a clear voice, with only the slightest hint of a tremor, and Maitland's eyes were intense as he slid the ruby that had been in his family for generations over the fourth finger of her left hand.

It was over with far more speed than she could have imagined, and it wasn't until they were back at Beauchamp House celebrating the wedding breakfast in the ballroom that she had a moment to breathe.

She was sipping a cup of punch behind a pillar, when she felt someone watching her. Turning, she saw that Mr. Sommersby was behind her.

"I didn't mean to startle you, my dear," her former tutor said with genuine remorse. "I only wanted to wish you happiness. And to apologize for my role in the business with Foster."

It was painful to think about how much she'd been let down by his role in Foster's schemes. She had once thought Richard Sommersby the most honorable and intelligent man she could ever know. But that, like so many of her beliefs then, had been no more than an illusion concocted by a lonely girl who desperately needed someone to believe in.

The toll his time under Foster's thumb had taken on him showed plainly on Sommersby's face, which bore the signs of worry and fatigue even now, days after Foster had been apprehended. She didn't wish her mentor to suffer any more on her behalf. It was as much her fault for putting him on a pedestal as it was his for not living up to her elevated expectations.

"There is nothing to forgive, Mr. Sommersby," she said, taking his hand in hers. "Truly. Foster was an evil man who used us both for his own purposes. And you lost your son because of him. I cannot hold you responsible for his actions."

At the mention of Nigel Sommersby, the tutor looked even more dejected.

"I am sorry," she said hastily. "I should not have brought him up. It's too soon."

"No," he protested. "It's not that, not grief over his death at any rate."

She frowned. "Then what?"

"I wish I had done more to keep him from hurting you, my dear. I should have done more."

But this was not the time for talking about Nigel Sommersby and his sins.

"I will say this once more, Mr. Sommersby," she said firmly, needing to make sure that he understood her well. "I do not hold you responsible for anyone else's crimes. Not Foster's and not Nigel's. Now, please, I want you to enjoy yourself. This is a day for celebration."

She might have imagined it, but it seemed to Daphne

as if some burden lifted from the old man, and he seemed to brighten.

With one last wish for her happiness, he left, and Daphne stood for a moment looking after him.

"Here you are," said Maitland, who slipped up beside her and slid a hand around her waist. "I thought you'd run away from me already."

"Of course I haven't," she said, turning to step into the circle of his arms. They were shielded here from curious onlookers, and she took advantage by lifting her face for his kiss. "I would be a fool to run away from a man like you."

"And one thing you are not," he said, leaning his forehead against hers, "is a fool."

"I might be particularly gifted at mathematics," she said playfully. "Perhaps you've heard?"

Maitland's brows rose in mock surprise. "No. Tell me more about this mathematics you speak of."

"I would," Daphne said with a wave of love for this silly, brave, adorable man, "but we have the rest of our lives for that."

"Do we indeed?" he asked, grinning at her.

"Besides," she said, slipping her arms around his neck, "I've found something I'm better at than ciphering."

"What's that?" His eyes met hers, and the devotion in them made her breath catch.

"Loving you," she whispered as she took his mouth.

Maitland didn't speak, but she strongly suspected he agreed with her.

THE END

Don't miss the next Studies in Scandal novel
from Manda Collins

Wallflower Most Wanted

Coming soon from St. Martin's Paperbacks